W9-BSL-263

DEATH OF AN OLD FLAME

By Malcolm McClintick

DEATH OF AN OLD FLAME
THE KEY
MARY'S GRAVE

DEATH OF AN • OLD FLAME

MALCOLM McCLINTICK

A Crime Club Book

Doubleday

NEW YORK LONDON TORONTO SYDNEY AUCKLAND

A Crime Club Book
Published by Doubleday, a division of
Bantam Doubleday Dell Publishing Group, Inc.
666 Fifth Avenue, New York, New York 10103

Crime Club, Doubleday and the portrayal of a man with a gun are trade-
marks of Doubleday, a division of Bantam Doubleday Dell Publishing
Group, Inc.

Library of Congress Cataloging-in-Publication Data

McClintick, Malcolm.
Death of an old flame / Malcolm McClintick.-- 1st ed.
    p.   cm.
I. Title.
PS3563.C3415D4 1988
813'.54--dc19   88-2043
                                                                          CIP

ISBN 0-385-24606-4
Copyright © 1988 by Malcolm McClintick
All Rights Reserved
Printed in the United States of America
October 1988
First Edition

*To old flames, wherever they are; and
to what once was, and might have been.*

DEATH OF AN OLD FLAME •

ONE

Paul Ott was a small little man. He was of less than average height for a male, and his narrow face was made thinner by pinched features, close-set eyes that tended to squint, a small grim mouth, and hair trimmed nearly to his scalp, as if he'd recently enlisted in the military. He was a small little man, and he sat now, on Friday the eighteenth of December, in his small paneled den, thinking about blackmail and murder.

Ott was thinking about blackmail because he was actively engaged in it, and about murder because lately he'd begun to consider the possibility that his victim might decide to get rid of him. He sat at his desk, at a little after 8 A.M., and weighed the one against the other, trying to figure his chances.

Carla, Ott's wife, had already left for work so he had the house to himself. He wasn't due at his own office until nine; there was plenty of time. He could sit here over his cup of coffee and his cigarette, in the quiet seclusion of this room, and calculate. Plot. He did it coldly and objectively, without regard for anyone but himself. He knew that to be successful at something like this you couldn't allow yourself to worry about anybody else.

The factors tending to tilt the scales toward murder were, first, that it was always a chance in any blackmail scheme. Any human being had a limit; try to push someone beyond it, and they might suddenly react like a cornered rat and come out biting. Second, blackmail was a particularly cruel trap for the victim. It wasn't something that happened one time and then was over and done with; rather, it continued, like slow torture, unremittingly, with no end in sight. A person caught in a trap like that might easily see murder as the only possible way out. Third, blackmail tended to enrage even normally placid individuals, especially when the blackmailer was already an obnoxious or unlikable person to begin with—and Ott had been told all his life how obnoxious and unlikable he was.

So, he decided, the victim in this case had every reason to become enraged, to hate him, to come out biting, to see murder as the only alternative.

On the other hand, the victim in this case was especially weak. Not a rat, but a mouse. Some creatures by their very nature would never fight, even if cornered; instead, they'd cower in fear, trembling, sweating, whimpering. They were perfect victims. Ott thought of a boy in his fourth-grade class in school, little Butch, who had been like that. Each day at recess two or three of the other boys would lead little Butch out beyond the edge of the playground to a spot behind a tall hedge, force him down on the ground, and twist his arms and hit him, making him yell. Little Butch never fought back, never told the teachers, never kicked or hit, never even much resisted being taken across the playground and dragged behind the hedge; he merely went, red-faced, teary-eyed, accepting the inevitable.

Ott remembered. He had been one of the other boys.

This victim was like Butch, he thought, sipping his coffee and drawing on his cigarette. This victim was a mouse.

Therefore, Ott ruled out murder.

Casually, he ground out his cigarette and reached for the phone. He dialed a number, prepared either to hang up or to make some excuse if the wrong person answered—but it was the right person.

"Hello?"

The meek passive voice of a mouse.

"Hello," Ott said. "I'm calling to ask about the next payment."

"In a couple of days . . ."

"Yeah, I know. And I'm going to have to make it more. You can afford it, and I've got some new expenses."

There was a choking sound, then the words, "I'm paying as much as I can afford. Good lord, man, you're bleeding me dry the way it is."

Ott thought he heard a note of desperation there, but a mouse would always sound desperate. It was the state of their existence.

"That's bullshit," he said. "You're nowhere near dry yet. Would you rather go to prison? I can arrange it, you know."

"Look, you don't understand. Please—"

"No, *you* don't understand. Fifty more a week, or I go straight to the police." He paused, then added slyly, cruelly, "After all, I know where the money comes from, don't forget that."

"Can't we discuss it?"

"Fifty more, or jail. Those are your options. Goodbye." Ott replaced the receiver.

He leaned back in his chair. Blackmail and murder, he thought. Well, no murder here. He'll never murder anyone. Butch never hit back.

About two hours later, Sergeant George A. Kelso of the Clairmont City Police Department walked along the slush-covered sidewalk on Third Street, a couple of blocks from the Municipal Building, heading for the Pancake House for a coffee break. He was deep in thought. A particularly bothersome series of burglaries was plaguing the Detective Section—somebody was breaking into homes in the better sections of town, at night, when the only person in the house was a young attractive wife whose husband for whatever reason happened to be away. This somebody would force the woman at gunpoint to undress, he would tie her up either sitting in a chair or standing at a bedpost, then he would proceed to stroll around the house putting various expensive items into a laundry bag—jewelry, silver, antique carvings, in some cases money. Then, in each case, he would return to the bedroom and take several photographs of the nude victim, using a 35mm SLR, untie her hands, and leave.

By the time the woman could unfasten the cords around her feet it was too late, the burglar had gone. The police would be called and arrive to find no fingerprints, no clues.

There had been five such episodes within a four-week period, the most recent two nights ago.

George Kelso thought about this as he walked toward the Pancake House and listened to Christmas music blaring out from every storefront, dodging the shoppers who passed him or pushed by him, his eyes on the two inches of slush on the ground. The sun was out, it was over freezing, the streets were a mess from the recent snow. His shoes were wet and his feet were cold; moreover, he'd managed to lose the pair of gloves Susan Overstreet had given him last month for his birthday.

Susan Overstreet. That was another thing weighing on him. She lived with her Aunt Eleanor, her aunt was going to Cleveland or some such place for a week beginning today, and Susan had come right out and asked Kelso to leave his apartment and spend the week with her, at her house. In her bed. He was supposed to meet her for lunch today, and he would be expected to give her an answer. He shuddered. Life was always so damned complicated. She didn't understand that he valued his privacy, that it had nothing at all to do with loving or not loving her, that even if they eventually were to get married, for the present time he would feel uncomfortable simply moving in with her. Even for a week.

He supposed he'd have to say yes.

Then he'd have to make some kind of arrangement for his cat, who would have to be fed and watered in the interim. He'd have to pack stuff. He wouldn't be there if anyone telephoned. Maybe he should buy one of those answering machines.

Two people almost walked straight into him, probably because he hadn't been watching where he was going. Looking up, starting to step to the right to avoid them, he saw a small thin man in a heavy coat, with small squinting eyes and hair clipped close to his head, and a tall good-looking girl in oversized sunglasses, in jeans and a padded blue jacket, with thick reddish brown hair down to her shoulders. Something about her seemed familiar, and for a moment Kelso hesitated.

The two people stopped.

The girl was smiling, almost a smirk. She spoke to him.

"George?"

Kelso stared. It couldn't be, could it? After ten years?

"George Kelso?"

She reached up and removed her sunglasses, and he looked into beautiful greenish gray eyes. He felt numb. His scalp tingled and his knees were weak.

"Carla?"

She nodded, smiling.

Ten years, Kelso thought, and saw:

A beautiful tall long-legged girl standing in front of a tree in the woods surrounding some of the university buildings, smiling at him, putting her arms around his neck and kissing him tenderly at first and then passionately.

A girl standing in the rain with no hat and no umbrella, sobbing, the tears running down her cheeks indistinguishable from the rain-drops, her sopping hair over her forehead, her clothes soaked, telling Kelso that he would never get rid of her, that he would never lose her, that he would have her for the rest of their lives no matter what.

A girl on a park bench on campus, her head close to Kelso's as they held hands and planned the kind of wedding they'd have, the kind of house they'd buy, how many children they would have, how many dogs and cats, what it would be like at Christmas. He had always wanted a tree with all blue lights. "You'll have it, George. We'll have a blue tree." And she'd kissed him.

A girl standing in the lobby of her dorm, her eyes wet with tears, her jaw stubbornly set, her eyebrows fierce, telling him that it was over, there was nothing he could do about it, nothing he could say to change anything, it was simply over and that was that. And she'd walked away. Forever.

He hadn't seen her again for ten years. Until this very moment. But he could still picture that last scene in every horrible detail: the unwrapped birthday present in his hand, the smell of some guy's pipe nearby, the soft laughter and whispers of a couple who were making out in an alcove only a few feet away, the hollow echo of Carla's flats as she strode away from him on the hardwood boards of the lobby floor, the lingering scent of her perfume, the sway of her hips, even the blue shirt with little green vertical stripes she'd worn and the way her auburn hair tossed as she walked.

The gunshot sound of a door closing with a certain finality somewhere farther along the corridor, out of his view.

Kelso remembered that he'd carried the birthday present—a bottle of Chanel No. 5—outside into the late evening, where it had been cold and raining. Bareheaded, with no umbrella, he'd trudged here and there around the campus, walking aimlessly, for an hour or so, trying to let it sink in, trying to comprehend the terrible reality of it. At some point he'd tossed the wrapped package into a trash can. At some point he had sat on a bench in the cold rain and cried.

At the end of the semester he'd joined the police force in a distant city—this city—away from the college town and its campus and its memories. He'd met and dated Susan Overstreet. He'd become a sergeant, and a plainclothes detective.

And now . . . this.

"George?"

Shoving the memories from his mind, he cleared his throat and forced himself to look directly at her.

"Hi, Carla," he said.

"You *do* remember me, don't you?"

"Sure."

"I'd like you to meet my husband, Paul Ott. Paul, this is George Kelso, a, uh, friend of mine from school."

Ott looked sullen, peering at Kelso with narrow squinting eyes the color of bourbon. He reminded Kelso of a young second lieutenant he'd had the misfortune of knowing during his stint in the army, before college, a newly commissioned officer who'd thought that the best way to lead was to shout insults and breed resentment.

"How are ya?" Ott muttered, extending a thin hand.

"Okay." Kelso shook; Ott's hand was as dry and hard as a stick. "So you're Carla's husband?"

"Yeah."

He looked at Carla again; she was still smirking. People shoved past them on the sidewalk. From somewhere came the clang of a Salvation Army bell, and "Jingle Bells." A car horn blared and someone shouted, "You're another!"

"George? Would you like to come over for dinner tonight?"

"What?"

"Just the three of us. You and me and Paul. Nothing fancy—don't dress up or anything."

Reminding him, suddenly, of his crumpled corduroy pants, unironed oxford-cloth shirt, absence of a tie, hair that probably needed combing and that was receding over his high forehead. His shoes were scuffed and crepe-soled and wet. He was thirty-eight and felt even older; he was carrying several excess pounds around his waist. The comparison was inevitable. This little guy with the pinched face and almost shaved head looked well dressed and successful, with his good-quality heavy coat open at the collar to show off a silk tie and crisp white shirt, razor-sharp creases in his trousers, dress shoes glaringly polished even in this weather.

Carla, he thought, had always admired quality.

"Seven o'clock tonight?" she was asking, her eyes as big and round and innocent as if nothing at all had happened ten years ago, as if she weren't now married, as if she and Kelso were simply arranging yet another date after class.

Christ, he thought, do I have to put up with this?

"Yes," he said. "Seven o'clock. What's the address?"

"Lincoln Avenue—1704."

He took out a small notebook and pen and wrote it down.

"I can't believe it," she said. "Have you been living here all this time?"

"Yeah."

"And we've just now run into each other. Isn't that fantastic?"

"Yeah," Kelso said, unable to force even a slight smile. "It's fantastic."

"See you at seven, George," she told him, as she took Ott by the arm and moved off along the slush-filled sidewalk.

Kelso hurried forward, shoving freezing hands into his pockets, head down, glowering at the pavement as his crepe-soled shoes stamped hard and splattered slush up onto the legs of his corduroy pants and got his socks wet. He was furious with himself for having accepted the dinner invitation; now, like an idiot, he was stuck with it, he'd have to show up, sit around with the two of them on display while Carla played the game of showing him off—parading him for her husband. See, Paul, here's the guy I dated ten years ago. George was crazy about me, he's the one I told you about, the one who bought me dozens of sentimental cards and stuffed animals all the time, the one who proposed to me at least twice a week, the one who made a fool of himself over me.

Turning the corner, Kelso entered the Pancake House and sat down heavily in a booth. When the waitress came he ordered coffee with cream and three pancakes, then lit his pipe and sat staring at the empty seat opposite, wondering what to do, thinking about Susan Overstreet and thinking about Carla.

Kelso knocked at the door to 1704 Lincoln Avenue that night at seven o'clock and it was opened almost immediately by Carla Ott. She smiled. Her greenish gray eyes were bright, she was wearing a tan corduroy skirt that came just to her knees and a beige blouse. There was gold at her ears, neck, and wrists. She looked like a million dollars. It made him feel underdressed in his tan corduroy jeans, oxford shirt, and sweater.

"George! I was afraid you wouldn't come."

"Well, I'm here."

"Come inside. Dinner's about ready. It's good to see you."

He followed her into a spotless hallway, grimacing as his wet shoes squished on the thick carpet. She hung up his coat in a small closet. She turned and stood quietly for a moment, looking directly into his eyes. The dimness of the hall was dreamlike; he felt transported back in time to her college dorm, where on just such evenings as this he'd met her in the darkly paneled lobby and kissed her before walking her across campus to a movie and then pizza. Her expression now was strange, he thought he saw desire in her eyes—but it had been ten years and her husband was somewhere in the house. Maybe he could no longer trust his instincts.

Then she smiled quickly and said, "Old times, huh?"

"Yeah. I guess so."

She turned and led him back to a dining room, where Paul Ott, in dress pants and a white shirt, sat at one end of a long table spread with a heavy beige cloth. The table had been set and platters of food were already there. Carla went to the other end of the table, indicated that Kelso was to sit between them, and said cheerfully,

"Well, time to eat, I guess."

It was awkward. They both seemed to stare at him while he ate. At one point Ott broke the terrible silence.

"So, whaddya do, anyway?"

Kelso cleared his throat. "I'm a detective on the city police force."

Ott stared. Kelso shifted uncomfortably in his chair, which was wooden and straight-backed and hard.

"A cop?" Ott asked, frowning. "You're a cop?"

"Well, yes . . ."

"That sounds really interesting, George," Carla said. "Paul and I don't know any policemen. Not socially."

Ott muttered something Kelso didn't catch, and sat pouting like a small child. Kelso felt miserable. He was getting a headache; it had started in his forehead and already he could feel it expanding downward into his eyes, one of those tension things that would pulsate and throb and ultimately make it difficult to see. It would affect his stomach, too, and there would go his appetite. He ate quickly and thought, Ott, I hate you.

"Did you like the green beans, George?" Carla asked.

He nodded. "They were good." They hadn't been, actually.

When at last the meal ended, they adjourned to the living room, where a gigantic Christmas tree reached all the way to the ceiling, forcing the angel's halo to one side. Over the fireplace, greeting cards lined a long wooden mantel, which was hung with two enormous red stockings bearing His and Hers in green felt letters.

The lights on the tree were all blue. Kelso's headache worsened. It was the blue tree he and Carla had talked about. It was *their* tree. She seemed to be smirking at him. She's testing you, he told himself. But what the hell kind of a test was it, and what were the answers?

He couldn't even understand the questions.

"Have a seat, George," Carla told him, pointing to a large armchair that matched a long sofa onto which she and Ott sank.

"So you're with the police," she said.

"Yes." He was beyond smiling back. His face felt numb; he may as well have been shot up with novocaine. The pounding in his eyes made the blue tree lights appear to shimmer. The only other illumination came from the fire licking at two logs on the grate. Under other circumstances it would have been intensely romantic. He couldn't think straight.

Carla kicked off her flats, drew up her knees so that her short corduroy skirt rode partway up her stockinged thighs, and put one arm around Ott's shoulders, her other hand resting on one of his knees. Her eyes glinted with the flicker of the fire and the blue of the tree lights.

The hell with it, Kelso thought. I'm leaving. I don't have to stay here and take this.

"Paul's in computers," Carla said brightly, patting his knee. "He's a software manager."

"Good for him," Kelso said, then immediately felt guilty. He stood up and wiped at his forehead. "Sorry."

Carla took her arm from Ott's shoulders, got up, and gazed at Kelso with wide solemn eyes. She spoke quietly.

"Don't you feel well, George? Maybe you should leave."

"I think I should," he managed.

Ott stood up too, looking disgusted. "No dessert?" he asked, frowning hard. It sounded sarcastic.

"I've got to be going." Kelso's head and eyes pounded, his stomach churned. He stepped toward the hall door.

A telephone rang.

"Would you get that, Paul?" Carla asked.

Glaring, Ott went through a small door to the right of the fireplace, closed it hard, and the ringing stopped. Carla followed Kelso out into the darkness of the hall and opened the closet door.

He was standing directly behind her. Suddenly she turned and, before he could move, put her hands tightly on his upper arms, and gazed at him with a strange half-smile. She kissed him.

They were practically the same height. She didn't have to tilt her head; her lips were firm and direct on his. He was too surprised to respond. Then she pressed her body against him, he felt her thighs and hips and breasts meeting the entire length of him, he stood flat-footed with his own hands dangling uselessly at his sides.

She opened her mouth and forced her tongue past his lips. It was a long wet kiss. Involuntarily, he felt himself relaxing, starting to respond. She smelled of good perfume, and with a jolt he realized it was the same thing she'd always worn, and the same stuff Susan wore—Chanel No. 5.

He raised his arms to hold her, remembering their two years together, remembering when a kiss like this would've been a mere prelude, forgetting where they were, just wanting her—and then, as if a switch had been thrown, she stiffened and pulled away from him, let go of his arms, and stepped quickly backward.

He stood helplessly as she got his parka from the closet; he put it on. He was baffled, there was nothing rational to think, he didn't know if she was still in love with him or merely a slut. Furious, he moved to the front door and opened it.

"George?"

"What."

"I'm sorry. I hope you aren't mad."

"Why should I be?" He spoke gruffly, wincing with the throbbing in his eyes and the burning in his guts.

"You *are* mad." She shook her head sadly. "I really am sorry. I don't have time to explain. Can I call you sometime? Will you have lunch with me?"

"I'm at the police department," he replied. "It's in the book." Then, like an idiot, he shrugged, pulled out his notepad and pen, and scribbled the detective section number on a sheet, tore it out and handed it to her. "Here."

"I'll call you," she said.

He went out into the cold and pounded his way through the slush to his VW. He climbed in without looking to see if Carla was still at the front door or not, cranked the engine, revved it a few times, and backed out of the driveway. He shifted gears violently and roared away into the black freezing night, shaking like a dead leaf in a gale.

TWO

Arnold Huff poked a fork into the stack of pancakes on the plate before him and tried to create an appetite by an effort of will, but he was unsuccessful. He had failed at many of his life's endeavors and now he was failing even at such a simple task as forcing himself to eat breakfast. Sighing heavily, he leaned back in the padded booth and peered morosely at the other customers in the restaurant. It was ten o'clock on a Saturday morning, the nineteenth of December, and the place was packed. Almost everyone else seemed in high spirits, Christmas music spilled softly from hidden speakers, people laughed.

On the other side of the booth, Huff's wife, Anne, seemed to be enjoying her eggs over medium with sausage patties and white toast. Her expression was bland.

The Huffs had been married for seven years, but he had only recently come to realize that there were things he was afraid to mention to his wife. He was a large man, not especially tall, but heavyset, big-boned, and plump from head to toe. He had thick, jet black hair, very dark eyes, and black horn-rimmed glasses that tended to slip down onto his nose, so that he was constantly pushing them up again.

Anne was attractive but not really pretty, with short dark hair, dark eyes under rather heavy lids, and small features. Compared to Huff, she was petite, only about five three and thin. And yet there was a vitality about her that Huff knew he lacked. It was her energy that had attracted him to her; he wondered what she'd seen in him. The promise of money, with his good job at the bank?

"Why aren't you eating, Arnold?" she asked. It wasn't nagging exactly; she just wanted to know.

"I'm not hungry."

"You haven't been lately. What's the matter?"

Huff put down his fork and took a sip of coffee. "You know what the matter is."

"If it's what we talked about last night . . ."

"Of course it is."

She smiled faintly. "Then, if that's all, there's nothing for you to be so upset about."

"Christ. That's easy for you to say. I'm ruined, is all, and there's nothing for me to be upset about?"

"You're not ruined, Arnold." She sounded a little disgusted.

"No? Then what would *you* call it?"

"I'd call it giving up." Sometimes in the middle of what Huff perceived to be an incredibly emotional situation, Anne would suddenly become extremely cold. She was doing it now, sitting calmly with one hand in her lap, the other holding her fork poised over her eggs and sausage, shoulders slightly hunched in the way that meant her legs were crossed under the table, gazing at him with those cold emotionless eyes. "You always give up, Arnold. It's like the man in that movie we saw on TV the other day, the one where his wife told him he always went limp in a crisis."

Huff grimaced. "I thought that was a comedy. I think that was a joke, and she was referring to his ability to perform in bed."

"No she wasn't. At any rate we're talking about you, not a movie."

"You're the one who brought it up."

"Nevertheless," she said, "you do go limp in a crisis, Arnold. You always have. You exaggerate everything, you only see the bad side, you—"

"Jesus, Anne, there *is* no other side to this. There *is* only the bad side."

"You don't have any backbone, Arnold," she told him quietly. "If I were you . . ." She took a bite of sausage and chewed carefully, as though they were discussing the weather.

"If you were me you'd do *what?*" he demanded loudly, so that several people turned to glance his way.

Anne Huff finished chewing, taking her time, and washed it down with a long slow drink of coffee. She patted her lips with a napkin, put the napkin back in her lap, and gazed cooly at her husband.

"If I were you, I'd do something about it."

Huff shook his head. It was hopeless. She had no idea what he was up against. Do something. Sure.

But what?

He wondered if they would send him to jail.

Russell Bushnell sat in an armchair in the bedroom, puffing at a pipe, legs crossed, watching his wife get dressed. It was Saturday morning, a little after ten, less than a week before Christmas. Outside the thinly curtained windows the sun seemed to be shining, but with any luck it would cloud over and snow again. There was nothing Bushnell disliked more than a Christmas without lots of snow. Well, there were a few things he disliked more. He looked at Liz, his wife, and remembered when he used to find it arousing to watch her putting her clothes on. Or taking them off. These days, things were different. He bit down hard on the stem of his pipe.

Bushnell was fifty-six, would turn fifty-seven in January. He didn't feel especially old, but neither did he feel young anymore. He liked to say he felt mature. Life wasn't too bad just now—things in the law firm were going well, he had been dabbling more and more in politics and there was quite a bit of support—money support—for him to enter the race for the Senate next fall. His daughter's marriage was the only questionable thing currently. She was considering a divorce, possibly because Paul didn't seem interested in a family. Maybe the little bastard was impotent or something. Bushnell knew it couldn't be Carla; she, unlike her mother, appeared to be interested in sex, judging from things she said.

Elizabeth Bushnell had aged gracefully. At fifty, she could have been mistaken for a woman ten years younger. Tall, slender, her face had kept a kind of vitality about it, a smoothness, with the help of creams and lotions, and she'd pampered her figure, exercising and watching her diet. It was all vanity, though; she seemed to care less about sharing anything with Bushnell in bed.

He watched her. She was smoking a cigarette which lay in an ashtray and from time to time she would pause to draw on it, freezing in the act of pulling on her hose, fastening her brassiere strap, zipping up her skirt. It might have been a striptease in reverse. And the curious part of it was that she kept glancing Bushnell's way, at intervals, with a curious expression, almost as if to make certain that he was still watching.

If she was somehow or other trying to tease him, then it was his own fault. No one was forcing him to sit here and observe.

She was angry about something this morning; her black brows were fierce over her dark eyes. She muttered faint words.

"What?" Bushnell asked. "I didn't catch that."

"I said, that damned Fredricks."

Bushnell tried to place the name. It was vaguely familiar, from somewhere out of the remote past, but it meant nothing to him now.

"Who's Fredricks?"

Liz puffed at her cigarette, standing with one hand on her hip, stockinged feet wide apart, wearing a dark skirt and a beige bra but not yet a blouse. She glared.

"You remember, Russell. That guy Carla dated for a while, just at the end of her college. Henry Fredricks. Dull and quiet and emotional. Not very mature."

"Oh. Him." Bushnell remembered now. A nice young man, level-headed, intelligent, attentive. Bushnell had always regretted it that Carla had broken up with him to date, and then marry, Paul Ott. "Yes, I remember Fredricks. He was a hell of a lot more mature than Ott. Had a lot on the ball. He was going to law school, as I recall. Too bad. Could've used a son-in-law in the firm."

"Henry Fredricks was a little creep," Liz said, putting down her cigarette again and turning toward the closet to look for a blouse. "He was only interested in one thing from Carla. Don't you remember the way he always looked at her? Remember when we walked in early one night and found them half-naked on the sofa?"

"Seemed sort of natural to me."

"Of course it would, to *you.*"

"So what're you so upset about, Liz? That was eight or nine years ago, wasn't it?"

She chose a blouse and turned to face him while she put it on and began buttoning it up the front, completing her little show.

"He's come back."

Bushnell chuckled, got up, and went over to the fireplace to tap out his pipe. "My God, you make it sound like the return of the dead or something. He's come back? What the hell does *that* mean?"

"I mean back here, to Clairmont City. Fredricks wrote a letter to Carla last week, and then he called her up, and now he's here in town."

"Really?" Bushnell watched her fasten the final button. "Carla tell you all that?"

"Yes."

"And that's it? That's what's upsetting you?"

"As you damn well know, Carla and Paul've been having problems. The last thing they need is for one of Carla's old boyfriends to come slithering back to bother her. I've a good mind to find him and tell him to get out of town."

"I think that was something the sheriff did, Liz. Not the local schoolmarm."

"It's not funny, Russell. I can't help it. I despised that bastard and I still do." She took a final puff on her cigarette, ground it out angrily, and gave him a grim look. "Almost as much as you despise Paul Ott."

Bushnell shrugged, pocketed his pipe, and left the room without any reply.

Paul Ott sat hunched over the desk in his den, trying to think. He felt depressed and irritated, he wanted to lash out at someone but there was no one but Carla, and he couldn't easily lash out at her. Things had gotten bad enough, and then this goddamned cop had come barging in, actually invited by Carla, this ex-flame of hers. He hated the whole situation but could think of nothing to do about it.

It had been ten years ago but there was obviously still something between them; after the cop had left last night, Carla had been in one of her sulking moods, and when they'd gone to bed she'd simply rolled over and slept. Things had gone about as far as they could, and he wasn't going to put up with it anymore.

Screw it. He didn't need Carla. Not for that. He picked up the phone, listened a moment to make certain Carla wasn't listening in on the extension, then dialed a number. It rang twice and was answered.

"Yes?"

"Liz? It's Paul."

Nothing but silence.

"I said, it's Paul—"

"I can't talk to you now!" She hung up.

Ott slammed down the receiver and put his head in his hands. She couldn't talk to him now. What did *that* mean? Russell was there, or something else? Was she getting tired of him, was that it, and rather than coming out and telling him she'd just refuse to talk to him from now on?

The door to the den opened, and he heard Carla's voice.

"Paul? What're you doing in there?"

"What difference does it make?" he snapped, without looking up. He pressed his hands into his eyes. "Can't you just let me alone?"

"I'm sorry. I just wondered what you wanted to do about lunch. It's almost eleven-thirty."

"I don't want to do anything about lunch, Carla. I'm not hungry. Can't you eat lunch without me?"

After a silence, she replied quietly, "Certainly, Paul." And closed the door.

But almost immediately it opened again, and Carla's voice came once more, softly, almost tentatively.

"Paul?"

He looked up and jerked around in his swivel chair. "*What*, for God's sake?"

"Tonight's that office party I'm supposed to go to. I'm sorry. I just wanted to be sure you were aware of it."

"I'm aware of it. I'm aware of it."

"Okay. Well, I'll see you later then."

"Fine." He put his head back in his hands. The door closed. He heard nothing else; it was difficult for sounds to penetrate Ott's den. After some time he pulled open his top right-hand desk drawer and lifted out a bluesteel revolver which he set down on the green blotter.

He stared at the weapon for a while, thumbing the lever that released the cartridge cylinder, checking to see that all six bullets were in their chambers, then closing the cylinder again. Finally he returned the gun to its drawer and sat very still, not moving, trying to think of nothing at all.

In room 726 of the Downtowner Hotel, on the southwest corner of Third Street and South Central Avenue in Clairmont City's main business district, Henry Fredricks paced nervously back and forth, smoking a cigarette and sipping Coke from a can he'd bought from the machine down the hall by the ice machine. He was just under six feet tall, about thirty, with light brown hair, a short brown mustache, and amber eyes. He was wearing dress pants, a white shirt open at the collar with no tie, black socks, and loafers.

Out the window of his room seven floors above the street, he could see the spire of a church a block or two away.

There was a brown briefcase on the bed, and on the bedside table next to the lamp was a framed photograph of a young girl smiling directly into the camera, a girl with long auburn hair and striking greenish gray eyes. The picture was full-face, from the shoulders up, and in the lower right-hand corner it had been inscribed in clear blue handwriting, "Hank, All my love forever, Carla."

Fredricks paced the room, pausing from time to time to flick cigarette ashes into the tray or to gaze for a moment at the photograph of Carla. When he'd finished the cigarette, he sat down on the bed, opened the briefcase, and looked through its contents.

It was filled with letters postmarked ten years before or so, and other memorabilia: a few restaurant napkins, some with handwriting on them; some Christmas and birthday cards; a tiny plastic figure of Santa Claus; an envelope of old snapshots.

Under all of this lay a small .22 caliber pistol.

Fredricks slammed the lid of the briefcase, picked up the telephone receiver, pressed nine for an outside line, and punched Carla's number. He waited, holding the receiver tightly against his ear. Finally someone answered and he heard her voice.

"Hello?"

"Carla? This is Hank."

"Hank." There was a long pause before she said, "I was just on my way out."

"I'd like to talk to you, Carla. Please?"

"I would prefer not to talk, Hank. Thank you."

"I'm in 726," he said quickly, almost shouting. "Room 726, the Downtowner Hotel. You can call me—"

"Goodbye, Hank." A click, followed by the dial tone.

Fredricks slammed down the receiver and got to his feet. "Goddammit." He glowered at the picture of Carla smiling, then lit another cigarette and began pacing again, muttering and shaking his head.

THREE

At fifteen minutes till seven that evening Paul Ott sat in his den gazing moodily at the TV set. He was in slightly better spirits, but didn't actually want Carla to know it. Let her go off to some damned party, what did he care? As soon as she was out the door, he'd try calling Liz again. There had to be some reason why the woman had refused to talk to him earlier in the day.

Things had gotten to the point where he'd about decided to do something. He could no longer tolerate the situation as it now stood. This constant battling with Carla, playing two roles, it was too much of a strain.

She poked her head through the den door.

"Paul? I'm leaving now."

He swiveled around to glare at her, and noticed that she was smartly dressed and had on all her jewelry—earrings, necklace, bracelet, fancy watch.

"What kind of party is this, Carla? You trying to impress somebody?"

"It's just the office Christmas party. I've already told you about it."

"Yeah, and I still don't understand why spouses aren't invited."

She sighed and replied patiently, "I've explained that, too. It would double the number of guests, and they couldn't afford it."

"That's bullshit."

"Nevertheless . . ." When he didn't say anything, she went on, "I probably won't be too late. Will you be all right?"

"Oh sure." He might as well play on her sympathy a little. "I'll be fine. You never got to the store, did you? Still, don't worry about me. I'll choke down some peanut butter or something; maybe there's still some bread in the house. I'll just sit here and stare at the tube."

"Why don't you watch one of those movies you've got on video-tape, the ones you're always complaining I won't watch with you."

"Just go to your damned party," he snapped, suddenly tired of the whole thing. "And leave me alone."

"Goodnight, Paul," she said quietly, and was gone.

Ott glowered at the TV screen. Maybe he would watch a movie after all. But first things first. He waited a few minutes, then reached for the telephone on his desk and dialed a number. It was answered on the third ring.

"Hello?" It was Elizabeth Bushnell's voice.

"Hello, Liz? This is Paul. Don't hang up."

"Why should I hang up?"

"Hell, you practically did earlier when I called."

"I apologize." She sounded pleasant. "I was in a hurry."

"Listen, Liz—"

"Russell's still here," she said in a quiet voice, as though she wanted to avoid being overheard. "Can you hear me?"

"Barely."

"He's going out later on. Maybe in an hour or so. I'll call you back, all right?"

"I guess so. Listen, I—"

She interrrupted him again, this time speaking loudly and brightly. "Thanks, Stella. Right, I'll call you next week. Bye-bye." And hung up.

"Shit," Ott muttered, and slammed down the receiver. Still, she'd promised to call him back. He glanced at his watch. An hour or so. That would put it somewhere between eight and nine. Leaning back in his chair, he began scanning the row of videotapes on a stand nearby, then changed channels on the television to see if there was a ballgame on. An hour or two. Well, he thought, he supposed he could stand to wait an hour or two.

Vaguely, he wondered what Bushnell would do if he ever found out, then shuddered and dismissed the thought entirely.

Carla didn't especially relish the idea of office parties, but she did always enjoy the company of Tony Deal. In the law firm of Baxter, Eisenberg, Ubik, and Baxter, Deal was at the bottom of the heap. Baxter and his son and the other two were the senior partners, then there were several junior partners, and finally a number of associates, of which Deal had been the most recent acquisition. So he sat in a tiny stuffy office all day, alone, doing the tedious chores no one else wanted—looking up cases and statutes, drafting motions or pleadings to the extent that there was to be some departure from the standard forms, writing something called interrogatories, or taking papers down to the court clerk's office to be filed. The hours were long, the job was boring, and the pay was mediocre.

On the other hand, Deal's law school record was excellent, the Baxter firm was one of the best in the city, if not the state, and there was every reason to believe that he had a chance to move up to junior partner in a few years, maybe even eventually to senior partner.

Carla told him that often, at any rate.

It wasn't what Tony Deal wanted. He told her he felt like a racehorse being forced to trot. The firm, with its traditions and routines and politics, was suffocating him. He wanted to strike out on his own, open his own office, be his own man.

Meanwhile, she knew he enjoyed showing up at parties with her. It was a severely traditional firm; the only two female attorneys were capable but nothing much to look at. Carla, only a secretary, always made male heads turn when she walked into a room. Tony Deal was tall, handsome, and well built; Carla felt that they complemented each other.

"You know Carla Ott," Deal said now, introducing her to a short balding man whose suit seemed tight across his middle. "From the secretarial pool."

"Oh yes."

"Carla, this is William Ludke, one of the associate partners."

Carla smiled and extended a hand. She had to glance down at Ludke's eyes; even without her high heels she'd have towered over him. She was conscious of the fact that she was stooping slightly; irritated at herself, she straightened up and stood tall and straight.

"I'm glad to meet you, Mr. Ludke. It's an honor."

The round little man's pudgy hand was sweaty; he squeezed her hand too hard and his squinty little eyes dropped quickly from her face to her breasts, then rebounded to her eyes again, unabashedly.

"Glad to meet you, Miss Ott."

"It's Mrs. Ott," she said quickly. "But you can call me Carla."

"Ah. Married are you?" Ludke leered at Deal.

"Her husband couldn't make it tonight," Deal said casually. "Carla asked if I'd mind escorting her."

"Pleasure having you with the firm," Ludke told her, ogled her breasts again, grinned, and waddled away toward the bar.

"Bastard," Deal muttered. "You've been working for them for over a year now, and he didn't even know you were there till tonight."

"He probably regards secretaries as machines during working hours," Carla said.

"The way he was undressing you with his eyes?"

She smirked at him. "Jealous?"

"Not as long as it's just with his eyes." He glanced at his watch. "It's almost seven-thirty. Are you feeling well?"

"No."

"Maybe you'd better go lie down for a while."

"Maybe the bathroom first," she said. "Get along without me for a while, okay?" She put a hand over her stomach and wandered off. Partway across the room she paused to tap someone on the shoulder.

"Excuse me . . ."

Old Baxter turned to look at her. The senior partner and founder of the firm. Tall, white-haired, with watery blue eyes, a white mustache, a red nose. He was scowling, but as his gaze fell on Carla the scowl disappeared and he grinned.

"Hello, my dear. Where's that husband of yours?"

"Paul wasn't feeling well tonight," she said. "As a matter of fact, neither am I. Can you tell me where the ladies' room is?"

He put a thin reddish hand on her arm and squeezed. "Can I do anything for you?"

"Just directions to the rest room will do." She smiled.

"Go out that door, down the hall to your right. Second door."

"Thanks, Mr. Baxter."

"Not at all. Are you sure I can't do anything?"

"No, really. I'll be fine. It's just a little stomach thing." She hurried away. Baxter had had too much class to look down at her figure, the way Ludke had done, but she was certain the old man was watching her walk toward the hall. One thing about me, she thought, men don't forget seeing me. Most of the time.

She made several visits to the rest room. On one of these trips, at a few minutes before eight, she found a telephone in an empty room and used it, watching the door to make sure no one came in and overheard her.

When someone answered on the other end, she said, "Hank . . . ?"

FOUR

Russell Bushnell looked at his watch and saw that it was almost nine o'clock. With a sigh, he tapped his pipe ashes out, stood up, and stretched. It was cold outside, and a front moving in was supposed to produce clouds and snow, and he'd much rather stay here in his warm comfortable house—but he'd promised Vandenberg and to him a promise was a promise. Besides, it was easy to get lazy when you were fifty-six. He didn't want to get lazy; he had a lot of things still left to do with his life, including the possibility of a run for the Senate. It wouldn't do to get old and lazy now.

Leaving the living room, he went out into the hall and found his coat and hat on the hall tree.

"Liz?"

From somewhere back in the house she called out a reply.

"Russ? That you?"

She appeared at the far end of the hall and approached. For a wistful moment he thought how good she looked, in black slacks, black pullover sweater that emphasized her heavy bust and narrow waist, black hair and eyes. He wondered what it might've been like if she'd been a little more interested—and not for the first time wondered why he'd stayed with her, why he'd put up with it for so long. A sense of duty? A failure of courage? Guilt?

"Where're you going?" she asked, a lit cigarette between two long thin fingers of one hand, her other hand fisted at her waist.

"Out." He did it just to see what she'd say. A little game.

"Out where?"

"I thought I told you—I promised Larry Vandenberg I'd meet him tonight."

Her eyes burned like black coals and for a moment he thought she was going to challenge him; but then she merely shrugged, took a puff on the cigarette, hissed out a thin stream of smoke, and frowned.

"Have a good time." Her voice was low, a little hoarse.

"I shouldn't be too long. It's just about insurance."

"I'm aware of the fact that he's our insurance agent, Russell. So what the hell're you doing talking insurance on a Saturday night? Doesn't the man have office hours anymore?"

"I'm going to buy him a drink," Bushnell said. "He's also a friend of mine."

"Then what're you acting so mysterious about?"

"Mysterious?" Bushnell stared, trying to read her thoughts. He pulled on his gloves and situated his hat on his head. "I'm not acting mysterious about anything. What's gotten into you?"

"Does this have anything to do with that Fredricks guy?"

"Of course not. It's insurance, and a drink. Are you still mad about Fredricks?"

Abruptly she turned and went back down the hall, pausing at the end to say over her shoulder, "Have a good time."

He couldn't tell whether she was being sarcastic or not.

"Thanks," he said, and went out. It was starting to snow.

Fredricks, he thought, getting into his car and using the wipers briefly. What the hell was the matter with Liz? Fredricks. He backed into the street and drove slowly away from the house. Personally, if Carla wanted to get rid of Paul Ott and marry Fredricks, that was fine with Bushnell. He'd even be willing to hurry the process along, if it were within his power.

Power, he thought.

Power was something he had a bit of. Maybe he could do something. He would think about it.

He drove on, deeply in thought.

As soon as Bushnell had been gone for five minutes, Elizabeth picked up a phone and dialed Ott's house. She let it ring nine times, then depressed the button, got another dial tone, and tried again, this time waiting for twelve rings before finally slamming down the receiver.

"Goddammit," she muttered, and grabbed her coat and gloves. Her car was in the garage. She backed it out quickly, lit a cigarette with the dash lighter, slammed the gear stick into drive, and roared away, heedless of the snow and potentially slick streets, headlights probing the night.

"You damned little creep, Paul Ott," she muttered. "You stupid little creep."

At twenty past nine that evening John Engel sat in his heavy leather armchair, sipping orange juice and gazing at his TV set. One of the networks was showing a movie about mobsters. Engel enjoyed mobsters. He was a retired building inspector, and had always fancied that he and FBI men had a lot in common. He sipped his orange juice and wondered what Doris was doing over by the window again.

"It's that Bushnell woman," Doris said, holding the curtains to one side and peering out. "That's her Lincoln, just went roaring up into the Otts' driveway."

"Ain't none of our business, Mother," John told her, frowning. "Why don't you just leave them people alone."

"A person's got a perfect right to know what goes on in her own neighborhood, Jack. Specially with all the crime nowadays. My land!" She kept her face to the window. "You read about that there burglar what strips them women buck naked, ties 'em up, and takes their picture after he steals all their valuables?"

"Ain't no burglar in his right mind want to take any naked pictures of you, Mother. And the Bushnell woman ain't any burglar." John Engel paused for a minute to visualize a burglar's reaction on entering their house and discovering that his female victim was not some pretty young thing, but a skinny old lady. Engel felt a little wistful; he could remember a time, it didn't seem that long ago, when Doris hadn't been so skinny, so wrinkled. But times changed, people got old, he himself was now fat and bald whereas before he'd been, well, plump maybe, and definitely not bald.

"She's going into the house," Doris announced, sounding to Engel like a sportscaster doing a race or something.

"She's Carla Ott's mother," Engel said, returning most of his attention to the movie, where a beautiful blond lady in very few clothes was being menaced by one of the mobsters. "Why shouldn't she go into the house? Hell, the Bushnells probably paid for half that damn house at least."

"Paul Ott's got a perfectly respectable job," Doris said, still not taking her eyes from the scene outside. "He's in computers."

"His wife's a secretary. When they bought that house Ott'd only just gotten his job. No way they could've afforded it without help from the Bushnells."

"I didn't see anybody let'er in," Doris observed.

"Thought you said she went in."

"She did. But I didn't see anybody *let* her in."

"Maybe she's got a key," Engel suggested. "She owns half the damn house, it'd only make sense for'er to have her own key."

Doris was quiet for several minutes. Engel sipped orange juice and watched the TV screen, where a cop had saved the blond lady from the mobster and was now attempting to make love to her. Engel hoped his wife didn't turn around; no reason for her to see this part. All there was on TV these days was sex. Couldn't have a decent cop show anymore without sex. Too bad it was the network. If it was on cable they probably would've showed her more than just from the neck down when it was obvious she was taking off her clothes. Engel watched with disapproving interest.

"She's coming out again," Doris announced. "Awful hurry. Getting in her Lincoln. There she goes."

Engel heard the car's motor.

"So what you think, Mother? You satisfied now? I mean, Elizabeth Bushnell went to visit her daughter and left again, that sounds pretty damn bad to me. Maybe you ought to call up the cops and report it."

"Ain't no call for your sarcasm, Jack." She turned away from the window finally and moved back to her rocking chair. "That just as well might've been some burglar. I'm doing those people a favor by keeping an eye on their house. Hope they do the same whenever we're away." She paused. "Come to think of it, I believe I saw Carla leave earlier this evening. Liz must've been going to visit Paul."

"Her son-in-law?" Engel chuckled. "Hell, she don't even like him."

"Maybe," Doris Engel said, "that's why she only stayed ten minutes."

John Engel made no reply. He was once more totally immersed in his mobster movie. He didn't really care what the Otts or the Bushnells did. He watched the blond lady and the cop and daydreamed about being a G-man.

At 10 P.M. Carla Ott left the office party and walked out to her car with Tony Deal. She'd parked down the street from the house, so they were out of view of anyone there. It was snowing, putting down a fresh white layer atop the dirty slush that by now had begun to freeze. Opening her car door, she lowered herself into the driver's seat and looked up with a smile as Deal bent to poke his head inside. He kissed her.

"I probably won't call," she said.

He nodded. "I know."

"But I'll let you know how everything goes."

"I hope your stomach feels better."

"Very funny." She let him kiss her again, then pushed him gently away. "I've got to go. Somebody might see us."

Deal straightened up. There was snow in his dark hair. "I'll talk to you later then. Be careful driving."

"I will."

He looked as if he were about to add something, then nodded, squared his shoulders, turned, and walked away, back toward the house. Carla closed the door, started the engine, and drove away. The snow swirled in her headlights.

When she reached the house she stood on the front porch and fumbled in her bag for keys, then stopped. The front door was slightly ajar. She looked at it for a moment, then pushed it open with the toe of her shoe. There was no light on in the hall.

She entered the house, closed the door, and reached for the light switch. It was very quiet. As she had done countless times, she stood in the hall and called out,

"Paul?"

There was no answer.

He must be in his den, she thought, taking off her coat and gloves and putting them in the closet. She walked along to the rear of the house. The door to the den was closed.

"Paul?"

Still nothing. She felt just the faintest stir of apprehension, but nothing really bordering on fear. She knocked at the door and heard nothing. She opened the door and went in.

The den light was on. Her husband sat with his head down on his desk, both arms hanging straight down at his sides. He was facing away from her. For a long time she stood frozen, staring at him, looking at the wound in the side of his head, looking at the blood, looking at the revolver—his revolver—lying on the floor just beneath his dangling right hand.

Finally she left the room. She walked woodenly and automatically, like a robot, to the kitchen, and picked up the phone. In her purse was a slip of paper on which a number had been written. She unfolded the paper, lifted the receiver, and dialed. Someone answered, and she was a little surprised at how calm her voice sounded when she spoke.

"Could I speak to Sergeant Kelso please? There's been a murder."

FIVE

At ten-fifteen on that Saturday night, the nineteenth of December, George Kelso decided that he'd put off making the decision for as long as he possibly could. Already it was fifteen minutes past the time he'd promised Susan Overstreet a phone call, and if he didn't call her in the next few minutes she'd probably call him and demand to know what was going on. He'd fed the cat, packed a bag, smoked his pipe, checked the weather forecast, and watered his one and only plant. He'd adjusted the heat, turned off the TV set, and checked all the windows and doors. There was nothing left.

He kept thinking about Carla.

At ten-sixteen he reached for the telephone receiver and the phone rang. He froze, glaring at it. Too late. Sighing and shaking his head, he picked it up.

"Yes?"

"This is Shirley, George. At headquarters?"

Kelso grimaced. Among other things he was on standby this weekend.

"Hi, Shirley."

"Sorry to bother you, but there's been a homicide."

"How nice," he muttered.

"Don't sound so depressed. At least you're not stuck here all night at the dispatch desk."

"Okay. Give me the address."

"It's 1704 Lincoln Avenue. Uniforms are on the way. Can you pick up Smith?"

"Yeah. I'll pick him up." He started to write down the address, then realized he didn't have to. His stomach jumped. "Shirley? Do you know the victim's name?"

"Nope. Male Caucasian is all I know."

"I'm on my way," he said, and replaced the receiver.

He got a dial tone, punched Susan's number. When she answered he said, "Susan? It's me. I'm sorry, dispatch just called. I have to go see about a homicide."

"What about tonight, George?"

He hesitated. There was no more time. The decision was demanded now.

"I'll be there sometime or other tonight, if you feel like waiting for me."

"You have to ask?"

"Okay. I'll call you in a while."

"I'll be here." She sounded annoyed.

"I love you," he told her, and felt his face go hot. He realized he'd never spoken those words to her on the phone before, and rarely even in person. Was it guilt, because of Carla?

After a long pause she said quietly, "I love you too, George."

"G'bye."

"Bye."

He hung up and glanced around helplessly. His packed bag sat on the floor by the front door. With a shrug, he put on his parka, picked up the bag, and went out.

Kelso picked up Detective Karl Smith at his near-downtown apartment and then drove north toward the address, which was the residence of Carla and Paul Ott. It was snowing lightly and blowing a little, but the streets weren't too bad. Some salt trucks were out.

"Know where you're going?" Smith asked, lighting a Kent and cracking the window.

"Of course I know. Dispatch gave me the address."

"You seem to have it memorized. Or did they give you a map as well?"

Kelso stopped for a traffic light and glanced over at his partner. Karl Smith was tall, over six feet, and quite thin, with a pale narrow face, short blond hair, cold blue eyes, always well dressed. He could be irritatingly perceptive.

"I was there last night," Kelso said gruffly.

"What?"

"I ran into her yesterday on the street." He described what had happened at dinner the evening before, but left out the part about the kiss. "It was terrible. I was embarrassed the whole time. Not only that, but she kept looking at me, smirking at me, and Ott didn't even try being pleasant, just glared and pouted."

Smith chuckled. "Maybe she's still in love with you, and she's bumped off her husband so you can marry her."

"Very funny."

"Watch out for that truck."

"I'm not blind," Kelso said irritably. "I can see trucks."

"Why don't you trade this thing in, Kelso? The heat doesn't work properly, it's too small, and half the time it's in some garage being fixed."

"The heat's working. Can't you feel it? Maybe you should close your window."

"You know, you may have a serious problem here." Smith's voice changed. He was no longer joking.

"Yeah?"

"Yeah. I know you pretty well, Kelso. From what you said just now, I get the impression you might still feel something for this girl."

"So what?"

"Has it occurred to you that this is a murder investigation we're about to begin, and that you might have a serious conflict of interest? Suppose it turns out she did it? Hell, you know the statistics on domestic murders as well as I do. You know what a high percentage of 'em turn out to be the spouse."

Snow seemed to fall toward the little yellow Beetle's windshield and headlights rather than straight down, as Kelso drove east on Washington Avenue, then turned left and headed north on Lincoln Avenue. They were only a couple of blocks away. He reached out nervously and turned on the radio. They were playing "God Rest Ye Merry, Gentlemen," a big booming brass version of it, very upbeat and jazzy, with lots of bass and drums. He realized it was from an album Susan Overstreet had and that she had played for him a few nights ago in her living room, with only the Christmas tree lights and the fireplace to provide illumination, as they lay stretched out on the floor in front of the fire, side by side. The image blurred uncomfortably with the night before, Carla Ott's living room, her blue tree, her fireplace. The two views overlapped, the way an old 3D movie looked without the cardboard glasses. Angrily, he shifted into second as they approached the house.

"I don't have a conflict of interest," he said. "I'm a cop. A professional detective. I'll do my job no matter what."

"Famous last words," Smith said quietly.

"Go to hell," Kelso said, and pulled up into Carla's driveway. Then, before switching off the engine, he added, "Would you mind not mentioning this to Leill?"

Smith looked at him. "I thought we were friends."

"We are."

"And I'm your partner, right?"

"Right."

"Then, either way, you shouldn't have to ask."

"Okay."

"Well, didn't you say something about spending the week over at Susan's place?"

"Uh huh."

"This should be rather interesting," Smith said, and got out of the car.

Kelso killed the engine, got out, and followed Smith up to the Otts' front door. The usual assortment of personnel had already arrived—marked cruisers parked on the street, the big white lab van, Dr. Paul's car. Smith knocked, and the door was opened by a uniformed cop named Zebrowski, a tall heavyset guy with thick black eyebrows that met over his nose.

Kelso and Smith went in and stood in the hall. It was here that Carla had kissed him only a few hours ago; it gave Kelso a strange feeling. No conflict of interest, he told himself; my mind's open, if she did it she did it. He shuddered.

"What've we got?" he asked.

Zebrowski referred to a notebook. "Victim's name is Paul Ott. He's back in the den. His wife, Carla Ott, came home about quarter after ten tonight and found her front door ajar. She went in and found her husband dead at the desk in his den. Shot once in the stomach and once in the head. She's in the kitchen with Weiss and the doctor."

"How is she?" Kelso asked.

Zebrowski shrugged. "Upset, but not too upset. She cried a little. I'd say she's in control of herself enough to be questioned, if that's what you mean."

"That's what he meant, of course," Smith remarked, smirking slightly.

Kelso glared. "You say she came in and found him. Was she out when it happened?"

"According to her, she left the house around seven, and he was alive. She didn't come back here until after ten. According to the doc, he's been dead between two and three hours."

"Hmm," Smith said.

"I suppose we can check her alibi," Kelso said. He unzipped his parka and started to remove his gloves, then remembered that he wasn't wearing any, he'd lost them. The ones Susan had given him for his birthday. His hands were cold; he shoved them into his pants pockets. "Are the lab people still with the body?"

Zebrowski nodded. "By the way, Sergeant, it might be suicide. The head shot's close range, and there was a gun on the floor right at his fingertips. A .357 Magnum with one round fired."

"I thought you said he'd been shot in the stomach also."

"That's right." Zebrowski's forehead wrinkled in thought. "Maybe it wasn't suicide."

"Maybe," Smith suggested, "he was a bad shot, and the first time he missed."

"Very funny," Kelso muttered.

"There's hot coffee in the kitchen, if you want some," Zebrowski said, putting away his notebook.

Kelso said, "Okay," and wandered over to the door to the living room. He stood gazing into the room for a while. It looked the same as it had the night before, the tall blue-lit tree scraping the ceiling with its angel, the cards lining the mantel, the giant red His and Hers stockings hanging alongside the fireplace. There would be no presents in the one marked His, Kelso thought. Not this Christmas. And nothing for him under the tree. He wondered what she would do with his gifts. Return them for a refund? Burn them? Donate them to charity? He wondered how she was taking it. The night before, she'd curled up next to him on the sofa with her arm around him and her hand on his knee. Had that been her way of telling him that she loved her husband? Then what had the kiss in the hall meant?

He turned angrily and said to Smith, "Come on, let's go to the kitchen."

"I could use some coffee," Smith said.

They went down the hall. In the kitchen Carla Ott sat at a small square table spread with a green cloth. In the center of the table was a fat red Santa Claus candle that had never been lit. Someone had tacked a string from one end of the wooden cabinets to the other and suspended red and green letters from it, spelling Merry Christmas. There was a lot of plastic holly and plastic mistletoe here and there. All merry and bright, Kelso thought.

She was wearing a skirted suit, the kind of thing young professional businesswomen wore these days, a neat gray thing with a light yellow blouse and a red, yellow, and gray tie in a big floppy bow at her neck. On her left jacket lapel was a small expensive-looking pin in the shape of a green wreath with a tiny red bow. She was wearing gold earrings, a gold watch on her left wrist, a gold bracelet on her right wrist, and gold engagement and wedding rings on her left ring finger.

She looked tired. Her legs were crossed, she sat slumped forward over the table, leaning on her left elbow, slowly stirring coffee with her right hand. A burning cigarette lay in a glass ashtray near her cup. There were faint dark shadows under her eyes, and when she looked up as Kelso and Smith entered the room, she didn't smile.

Even so, Kelso thought, she still looked beautiful. She looked slightly wistful, like a little girl who's just lost her favorite doll. He had the urge to put his arms around her and tell her it would be all right, and he remembered a time ten years ago when he'd done just that, when she'd been upset about something.

But that was then, and this was now.

A uniformed officer named Weiss stood in one corner of the kitchen, sipping something from a ceramic mug and looking bored. Near Weiss the hands of a large wall clock pointed to eleven o'clock. The kitchen windows were black. Despite the overhead light, it seemed gloomy and dismal in the room, and it felt cold.

"Hello, George," Carla said. Her voice was small and strained. She looked a little dazed, as though she'd just awakened from a dream and was trying to separate it from reality.

"Hello, Carla." I'm a professional, he thought. I'm not going to let this get in the way of my investigation. "I'm sorry about your husband."

"Thank you."

"I'm going to have to ask you some questions."

She nodded. "I know."

He just stood there, feeling big and useless. Next to him, Karl Smith made a kind of strangled noise and went over to peer out the window over the sink. Officer Weiss rocked back and forth on the toes and heels of his shoes, which squeaked slightly as if new.

"Would you and your friend like anything? Some coffee?"

"Yes, please."

She got up, poured coffee from a pot into two mugs, set them on the green tablecloth near a matching ceramic sugar bowl and cream pitcher, and sat down again. It seemed to have taken an effort.

"Thanks." Kelso sat next to her and Smith took the seat opposite her. Kelso stirred in a couple of teaspoons of sugar and some cream. Weiss's shoes squeaked. "I understand you went out earlier tonight, and he was here—is that right?"

"Yes. There was an office party, a Christmas party. Did I tell you

I'm a legal secretary? I don't remember. It's Baxter, Eisenberg, Ubik, and Baxter. Anyway, they didn't want husbands or wives, just the office, so I went with a friend of mine, one of the lawyers. A guy named Tony Deal." She paused, and something flickered briefly in her gray-green eyes. "You know him?"

"No."

"Oh. Well, anyway, I met him there, and he was sort of my escort for the evening."

"A friend of yours?" Smith asked from the window, not turning around.

"That's right." She glanced quickly at Smith, then back at Kelso. "Just a friend. So anyway, I left here around seven."

"And your husband was here?" Kelso asked.

"Paul was here, in the den."

"What was he doing?"

"Doing? Oh, I don't know. Watching television I think. He was at his desk."

"What was his mood?"

"Not great. I think he was upset about the party—you know, about not being invited. But he's been in a foul mood lately anyway. I mean, had been."

Kelso thought he saw tears in her eyes, but only for a moment. Last night Ott hadn't been in a very good mood. At the time, Kelso had thought it was because Carla had invited her old boyfriend to dinner, but maybe it had been something else.

"I'm sorry to ask this, but were you and he having any problems?"

She shrugged. "Well, in a way. I mean, things hadn't been especially great recently, but it wasn't anything really serious."

"Do you have children?"

"No."

"How long have you been married?"

"It would be, uh, nine years next month."

"I'm sorry," he said again.

"You don't have to be."

Smith coughed, and came over to the table.

"Go on with your story," Kelso said. "Paul was in his den watching TV, he was in a bad mood, and you left to go to this party."

"That's right. There's not much to tell. I stayed till about ten, then I left and drove straight back here. It was only about a ten or fifteen minute drive; it was Mr. Baxter's house, the senior partner."

"I see."

"And when I got back, I noticed that the front door wasn't closed all the way—you know, it was hanging slightly open, slightly ajar, maybe an inch or two. I remember wondering if I'd forgotten to close it, or if maybe Paul had gone out for some reason and left it open."

"At that point"—Smith said, sitting down again—he kept getting up to go to the window and returning to his chair—and fixing her with his cold blue eyes—"it didn't occur to you that somebody might've broken in?"

She blinked at him. "No. That didn't occur to me."

"I'm sorry," Kelso said. "I forgot. Carla, this is my partner, Detective Smith."

"How do you do?" she said.

"Okay."

"What happened next?" Kelso asked.

"I went in and called out, called his name, but he didn't answer. I went to the den to see if he was still there, since that's where I'd left him, and he was sitting at his desk, with his head resting on it, and his arms straight down."

"How far into the den did you go?"

"Far enough to see that he'd been shot."

"You saw the wound, the location of it?"

"In his head, if that's what you mean." She sounded slightly angry.

"I'm sorry. Yes, that's what I meant. And then what'd you do?"

"I went back out, I came in here, to the kitchen, and called that number you gave me. And they said it was the Detective Section but you weren't there, and when I told them what it was, they hooked me up to the dispatcher. And then I waited, and some policemen came, and . . ." She shrugged and lit another cigarette.

Kelso sighed. "Carla, I'm going to have to ask you if you know of anybody who might've wanted your husband dead, anybody who might've hated him or wanted him out of the way for any reason."

Something definitely flickered in her greenish gray eyes this time. Her eyelids fluttered, she frowned very slightly as she pulled on her cigarette and breathed out smoke, and she glanced down at her coffee cup. There seemed to be some sort of conflict going on in her mind. Just when Kelso was about to say something to prod her gently, she looked up at him again with wide eyes and spoke in the same high, tired voice.

"I hate to say this, George, but the person who comes to mind right away, and please don't read anything into this, but the person who probably despised him is my mother. But she wouldn't have killed him, she couldn't kill anybody."

"But she despised him," Kelso said.

"Yes. I hate to admit it, but she did."

"Why?"

"I've never been really sure. Do you remember that she more or less liked you? When we were dating? I mean, she didn't hate you, which for her was something. And I don't suppose you know this, but after . . . after we broke up, there was another guy before I met Paul, a guy named Henry, and my mother despised him, too. And then Henry and I broke up and I met Paul, and she hated Paul. Maybe she just didn't feel that Paul was good enough for me."

Smith said, "That's usually the way fathers feel."

"Well," Carla said, almost smiling, "Dad didn't like Paul very much either, but he didn't exactly despise him." Then she paused, blinked, and added thoughtfully, "Well, on the other hand, maybe Dad did despise Paul. What the hell, it probably doesn't matter; my parents aren't murderers, after all."

"There're a lot of murderers with children," Smith said.

Carla frowned at him. "What's *that* mean?"

"Their children probably thought the same thing, until one of their parents got arrested and charged with killing somebody."

Smith had stood up again and was behind his chair, watching Carla with calm icy blue eyes.

"Ignore him," Kelso said gently. "Carla, did your mother ever actually tell you how she felt about your husband?"

"Yes. Several times she actually used that word. Despised. She'd say something like, 'Carla, I don't know how you could've married that man. I despise him.' Things like that."

"Tell us about your marriage," Smith said, peering down at her. "You said you'd been having problems. Was it any particular thing, like sex for example?"

Carla's eyes went hard, and Kelso thought she was going to refuse to answer, or yell something. But she replied, slowly and in a lower than normal voice, "If you really want to know, it wasn't sex as such. It's just that I . . . I'd decided a few months ago to have a family, to have children, and we talked about it. I mean, we'd had nine years to ourselves, Paul's career was going well, I'm not getting any younger, I thought it was time to start a family. He said fine, but then he just didn't seem interested when it came right down to it."

"How uninterested was he?" Smith asked.

"Damned uninterested. We'd pick a certain night, for example, and suddenly he'd be really tired, or he'd have this splitting headache, or he'd have to go out to see some business associate, or all hell would break loose at his office, and he'd have to go in and try to fix some stupid computer problem. It was always on a night when we'd decided to try . . . you know . . ."

Kelso wondered why she had to pick certain nights, why it couldn't have been simply spontaneous, but she wasn't his wife and he wasn't a woman. Maybe he'd ask Susan about it. The thought reminded him of where he was supposed to go tonight if he ever got out of here— reminded him that tonight he wouldn't be sleeping in his own bed. He gazed at Carla and wondered what it would be like to stay here with her; then he forced the thought from his mind.

"Did you ever talk to him about it?" he asked.

"Sure." She shrugged. "He always had some excuse, or he'd get mad and accuse me of pressuring him."

"Maybe," Kelso said softly, "he'd changed his mind about a family, and couldn't bring himself to admit it."

"Or maybe," Carla said, without any hesitation, "he was fooling around."

"Fooling around, huh?" Smith paced back and forth behind his chair, watching Carla. "Who with?"

"I don't know. I really don't."

"Don't you see," Kelso told her, "if he was having an affair, whoever it was with might have killed him."

She seemed strangely unmoved. "I suppose so. Anyway, that's always been our problem, from day one."

"An affair?"

"No, not an affair. Communication. Paul would never open up and talk to me, tell me things that were bothering him. He couldn't talk to me."

Then why the hell did you marry him, Kelso wondered.

And said, "Yes?"

Suddenly she became quite animated, anger flashed in her eyes, she made her left hand into a little fist and struck the green tablecloth with it, her long auburn hair bounced. "Our friends don't have that problem. The Huffs, for example, don't have it. Arnold Huff would never dare keep anything away from Anne, he just wouldn't dare!"

"Wait a minute," Kelso said. "Arnold and Anne? Who?"

Heavy footsteps sounded in the hall, approaching rapidly. A tall attractive middle-aged woman with black hair, dressed all in black under a long coat, stomped into the kitchen in black high-heeled boots and stood glaring around. Behind her, Officer Zebrowski hurried in.

"Sorry," Zebrowski said. "I told her she couldn't come back here, but she—"

"Shut up," the woman snapped. "What the hell's going on here, anyway? What *is* all this?"

Carla Ott looked up, wide-eyed, and said, "Mother!"

SIX

Kelso pushed back his chair and got to his feet, as he had been taught to do when a lady entered the room, and looked at her. Ten years before while dating Carla he hadn't seen much of her mother, but there had been the distinct impression that she hadn't cared much for him. He'd had more hair in front in those days, and less weight around his middle, so there was a chance she wouldn't recognize him. But as her gaze fell on him her eyes narrowed.

"You're George Kelso." It sounded like some sort of accusation.

"Yes I am," he admitted.

"What're *you* doing here?"

"Police, ma'am. Sergeant Kelso." He emphasized the rank very slightly. "My partner, Detective Smith. Officer Weiss. And you're Mrs. Bushnell . . ."

"Elizabeth Bushnell." She looked at Carla. "What's going on here? Why are the police here?"

Carla's demeanor had changed totally. Whereas before her mother's arrival she'd seemed rather poised, rather calm, despite the evident tension and fatigue, now she appeared upset. Jumping up from her chair, she stepped over to Elizabeth, threw her arms around the woman's neck, and said, "Oh God, Mother . . . it's Paul."

Kelso couldn't see Carla's face. Elizabeth was frowning, standing awkwardly, not returning her daughter's embrace, her black angry eyes on Kelso.

"What about Paul?"

"He's dead, Mother."

"What?"

"Somebody killed him."

Slowly but firmly, Elizabeth Bushnell gripped Carla's arms, pulled them away, and pushed her to one side. They stood next to each other, mother and daughter, both tall and slender, but Carla had her father's auburn hair and fair complexion, not the black hair and eyes of her mother. Behind them, Officer Zebrowski stood at the door to the hall, looking grim; he'd let her get inside, now apparently he intended to see to it that she didn't get out again. Smith leaned against the kitchen sink, very casually, a faint smirk on his lips, his icy blue eyes riding up beneath his eyelids. He looked slightly ghoulish.

"Who killed him?" Elizabeth Bushnell demanded. Her voice was low and hard, much lower than Carla's.

"We don't know yet, ma'am," Kelso said, and sat down again. Carla sat, too, and lit a cigarette with trembling fingers. Kelso wondered if she was suddenly nervous because she'd just been telling them how her mother had hated Paul Ott. She might be thinking that Kelso suspected her mother. "We'll have to ask you a few questions."

"Why?"

"It's our job," Smith said. "We always have to ask questions when somebody gets murdered."

Kelso heard the sarcasm in Smith's tone, and wondered if Mrs. Bushnell had heard it too.

"What questions?" Her frown stayed directed at Kelso.

"Would you mind telling us where you were this evening? Starting, say, with around 6 P.M. or so?"

"You actually have the nerve to ask me for an alibi?"

"Any reason we shouldn't?" Smith asked.

She looked over at him. "Apparently you don't understand who I am. So I'll tell you. My husband is Russell Bushnell. He's a very well-respected attorney in this city, and in the entire state. He's been an Indiana state senator, and a deputy state's attorney general, and an aide to the governor. And he's seriously considering running for the United States Senate next fall." She tilted up her chin and squared her shoulders. "Now do you have any questions for me?"

"Yeah," Smith said. "Where were you tonight?"

"My husband will hear about this."

"He sure will," Smith told her calmly. "We'll have to question him, too."

"Meanwhile," Kelso said, "would you mind telling us where you were?"

"They're only doing their job, Mother," Carla said, and puffed at her cigarette. She seemed to have calmed down again; her hands no longer trembled.

Elizabeth Bushnell reached out and grabbed the chair Smith had used off and on, pulled it toward her, sat down on it, crossed one leg over the other very smartly, and folded her arms over her chest, holding her head up high. Her eyes flashed like shiny black coals.

When she spoke, her voice was still hard and low, but no longer loud. She spoke with grim assurance.

"From the time you mentioned, about six, I was at home with my husband, Russell. Around nine o'clock he left, but I stayed. At some point, I don't know the hour, I tried calling here to speak to my daughter, but there was no answer. It was probably about ten, maybe a little after. Fifteen or twenty minutes ago, I decided to go out for some cigarettes, since there didn't seem to be any in the house, and I thought I might as well stop by and see if Carla was home yet. And I saw the police cars and came in to see what the matter was."

"So," Smith said, "until nine o'clock your alibi's your husband, and after nine o'clock you don't have an alibi."

"I don't need any damned alibi," she snapped. Smith had succeeded in baiting her. "Are you going to stand here in front of these witnesses and accuse me of murdering my own son-in-law?"

"Nobody's accusing you," Kelso said politely. "Honest, ma'am, it's just routine. Everybody connected to a homicide is asked for an alibi. So we can eliminate all possible . . ." He shrugged.

"Suspects," Smith completed for him.

"You people obviously find this quite amusing," Mrs. Bushnell said. She nodded. "Well, I'll remember everything that's been said here. Everything."

"Did you hate Paul Ott?" Smith asked.

Kelso had to force himself not to smile.

She eyed the blond detective for a moment before replying, speculatively, as if deciding whether to slice him up in thin strips or just cut him in cubes.

"I despised Paul Ott. Does that make you happy, Detective Smith? I suppose Carla's already told you that. He was a little creep, a vain little man, ineffectual, pouty, immature, and obnoxious. Carla could've done much much better." She turned her head slightly and her eyes flickered at Kelso. "Even you, George, wouldn't have been as bad as Paul Ott."

"Thank you," he said politely.

"I don't suppose you despised him enough to kill him?" Smith asked. He seemed almost bored now.

"I despised him enough to kill him a thousand times, young man. But I'm not a killer. I didn't kill him, and, besides, I've already told you I was at home with my husband."

"What if we told you Ott was killed after nine o'clock?" Smith asked.

She raised her dark eyebrows. "Was he?"

"We don't know yet."

"Then ask me again, when you know."

"You'll have to forgive my mother," Carla said, and yawned. "She's tired. We're both tired. And she's not used to being questioned by anyone."

"Don't make excuses for me, dear."

"I'm not making excuses, Mother. I'm just explaining."

"Explaining? Well, in that case . . . have you explained to them yet about Henry Fredricks?"

Kelso and Smith exchanged glances. Smith's expression meant he didn't know what the woman was talking about. Neither did Kelso. Who was Fredricks? The "Henry" Carla had mentioned earlier?

"Mother, you don't have to—"

"Hush, my dear. We can't lie to the police, can we?"

Carla looked upset again. Her face had gone pink. Kelso knew the look—she was very angry about something. In his dating days with her, he'd have instantly backed off.

But not now.

"Who's Henry Fredricks?" he asked, taking out his notebook and pen.

Elizabeth smiled and said, "Just a boy she used to date."

"Mother—"

"Oh that's right," the woman said. "George doesn't know about Henry, does he? George, let me tell you about Henry. You see, you're not the only guy Carla dumped. Right after she got rid of you, she decided to lower her standards by taking up with a drab little animal named Henry Fredricks. Hank—isn't that what you used to call him, dear? Hank. Yes. Well anyway, Hank took your place, George. I mean, I don't know if she actually slept with him, but they were hot and heavy for about a year. Then she dumped him, or he dumped her, or it was mutual—these things run together in my mind—and along came Paul Ott, another notch lower on the evolutionary chain."

This is really some mother-daughter relationship, Kelso thought. Carla had never said much about her mother, mostly she'd talked about how wonderful her father was. Now he could see why.

"Where is this Fredricks guy now?" Kelso asked.

"Well, that's the interesting thing. I'm sure my daughter hasn't told you this, either—"

"*Mother!*"

"—but Fredricks has suddenly reappeared like a long lost snake.

Apparently he wrote to her, and then tried to call her, and he's here in town. They may've even seen each other by now. Did you tell the nice policemen all that, dear?"

Carla lit another cigarette and hissed out smoke.

"Mrs. Bushnell," Kelso said, "would you mind waiting in the living room for a few minutes?"

Surprisingly, she simply stood up and stepped to the door.

"I don't mind. But I can't wait very long, I have to get home."

"It'll be just a minute," Kelso assured her.

"It'd better be." She brushed past Officer Zebrowski and stalked off down the hall. Zebrowski followed.

As soon as she was gone, Carla looked up at Kelso with big wide eyes, the innocent little girl look he knew so well, and spoke in a thin shy voice.

"George? Do you want to know about Henry?"

"I think it's best."

"It sounds so terrible the way Mother told it. He's just somebody who came along, so to speak, after you and I broke up. I dated him for a while. He was really serious about me, but it was pretty one-sided, you know? When I wouldn't marry him, he went away. Left town, I mean. I didn't even know where he was living till I got a letter from him about a week ago."

"Where's he living?"

"Kokomo."

"Kokomo?" Smith looked perplexed. "Jesus, I didn't know anybody lived in Kokomo."

"He's kidding," Kelso said. "Go ahead."

"Well," Carla said, "he wrote to me, out of the clear blue sky. I didn't answer, I didn't know what to say. Then, a few days later, he called me. I guess it was from Kokomo, the line had that faraway sound to it, lots of static and stuff; anyway, he wanted to talk, but I told him I didn't want to and I just hung up. Then he called again, earlier today. I forget what time. Early this afternoon I think. And I told him I preferred not to talk. He said something about a hotel. The Downtowner, I think he said. And I hung up."

Kelso didn't say anything. He'd known Carla well. She was lying about something, or making something up, or, at least, omitting something. What was it she'd always said, when they were dating? Oh yeah, a quasi-lie. One of her little witticisms. Are you quasi-lying, Carla?

"Have you seen him since he got to town?" Smith asked.

She shook her head. "No. Of course not."

"I've got to ask this, Carla," Kelso said. "Do you know how Fredricks feels about your husband, or felt about him?"

Her eyes widened slightly. "How would I know that? I've hardly spoken to the guy."

"And he hasn't been over here at all?"

"Of course not."

"Is he a guy who gets mad?" Smith wanted to know. "Did he have a violent temper? Was he ever armed?"

"Henry isn't violent. Or he wasn't. And he never had a gun, if that's what you mean. He hated guns."

Something had occurred to Kelso. "What about your husband?"

She blinked. "What about him?"

"Did he have a gun?"

Very gravely, she replied, "Yes. Of course he had. Wasn't that his gun, lying there on the floor?"

"I haven't talked to the people working in there yet," Kelso told her. "We'll assume it could be his but it'll have to be checked. Do you know what kind of gun he had?"

"I'm sorry. I don't know much about guns. Wait—Paul told me once. Some sort of number. Three fifty-eight?"

"How about three fifty-seven?" Smith asked wryly. "Could that've been it?"

"Oh. Yes, I think it was. Three fifty-seven."

"A .357 Magnum," Kelso said. "And do you know where he kept it, and whether it was loaded or not?"

"It was in a drawer in his desk, in the den." Her voice was very small and thin. Her eyes were wide. "Upper right-hand drawer. And, yes, he kept it loaded."

Zebrowski poked his head into the kitchen.

"Sergeant Kelso? That Mrs. Bushnell in the living room, she's about to have cats, she wants to leave. And they're through with the den; you and Smith can go in there now if you want."

"Thanks," Kelso told him. "Tell Mrs. Bushnell we'll be right with her." He smiled politely at Carla, wondering how much she really knew. It occurred to him that she could be protecting her mother. "I'm sorry, Carla. I'll, uh, talk to you later."

"I hope so." She glanced quickly at Smith, then at Kelso again. "Alone? Lunch or something?"

"We'll see," he said.

He and Smith went down the hall to the living room, but before they got there, Dr. Paul, the young pathologist from the coroner's office, stepped into the hall from a side door and approached them.

"Hello, George, Karl."

"How's it going?"

"I've got some information I think you'll want to hear."

"No we won't," Smith said.

Paul smiled. "It's this. Ott was shot once in the head, right side just above the ear, with a large caliber weapon. It's consistent with the .357 they found on the floor. There's a big exit wound. The shot was point-blank. Also, he was shot once in the stomach, at very close range, but not point-blank."

"We know all that," Smith said.

"We didn't know what the range of the stomach shot was," Kelso said. "Do you think he was shot in the stomach first?"

"It's worse than that," Dr. Paul stated. His dark eyes were grave. "The stomach wound is very small caliber. Not the same weapon at all as the head wound. And the investigators found an ejected cartridge from a .22 caliber automatic."

"Oh Jesus Christ," Smith muttered.

Kelso sighed heavily. "Are you saying he was shot with two different guns?"

"I'm just telling you what we found. Well, you'll get the usual report. By the way, I'd put the death at between eight and ten right now, give or take an hour either way. See you later."

"Two guns," Kelso said. Suddenly he felt very depressed.

"Two guns," Smith muttered. "Two murderers?"

They went on down the hall and into the living room, where Elizabeth Bushnell stood scowling impatiently in front of the blue Christmas tree.

SEVEN

"Well?" she said. "Do I have to stay here all night? It's almost midnight."

"Just a couple of other questions, Mrs. Bushnell," Kelso said. "How well did you know this Henry Fredricks?"

"Well enough to know I'm glad Carla didn't marry him."

"Was he ever violent? Do you know if he owned a gun?"

"He was the opposite of violent. I wouldn't know about a gun, but I'd be very surprised if he had one. He was a mouse."

"Earlier," Smith said, smiling, "you said he was a snake."

"He wasn't violent."

"Mrs. Bushnell," Kelso said, "do you own a weapon of any kind?"

"Absolutely not."

Kelso felt suddenly tired. He sighed. "I think that's all for now. Unless Karl . . ."

"Who're the Huffs?" Smith asked. "Anne and Arnold Huff."

"Friends of Carla and Paul's," she replied. "Why?"

Smith shrugged. "Carla mentioned them. I was just curious."

"Talk to Carla," Mrs. Bushnell said. "I don't know them personally." She sniffed.

They must not be in her social stratum, Kelso thought. "Well, thanks, Mrs. Bushnell."

"That's it? You kept me waiting around for that?" She stalked past them into the hall and pulled her long coat around her. It was fur and looked expensive, but Kelso wasn't very familiar with furs and wasn't sure what it was. Mink, maybe.

"Goodbye," he said, from the hall doorway.

She jerked open the front door, muttered something about her husband, and was gone. The door slammed.

"Nice lady," Smith said. "Maybe I'll ask her out."

"Her husband's a politician," Kelso said.

"Then I'll ask him out." Smith yawned. "Nice room. Nice tree. Nice fireplace. God I'm tired. Are we going to go look at the body any time tonight?"

"Let's see if they're through in there."

The crime scene investigators were just leaving. A man named Bremer, as tall and blond as Smith but pink and slightly plump, approached them.

"You guys'll have fun with this one."

"Why?" Kelso asked. But he knew the answer.

"Two gunshot wounds in this guy. Two different guns. One's a .22, probably, since we found an ejected .22 cartridge. Other one's a .357. Come on in here, we're all finished up, I'll show you exactly what I'm talking about."

They followed Bremer into the den. Kelso stood just inside the doorway, looking around, taking it all in. The walls were paneled. An overhead light in the ceiling was on. The carpeting was dark, and it seemed gloomy. To the left was a large wooden desk and a wooden swivel chair. Ott sat in the chair, head down on the desk, arms straight down. Kelso took a few steps forward. Directly beneath Ott's right hand, a revolver lay on the floor.

"See that?" Bremer said cheerfully. "That's the revolver. A .357 Magnum, fully loaded, one round fired. There's a box of the same ammo in the upper-right desk drawer. Look at the position of the gun. If this guy shot himself in the head, right side, and fell forward with his head on the desk blotter like he is now, and his arm dropped down like it is, the gun could've fallen onto the floor exactly where it is now. Don't touch anything, by the way."

Smith gave him a hard look. "I always wander onto a crime scene and touch every damn thing I see."

"Right." Bremer nodded happily. "But the thing is, the fascinating thing is, this other wound. This .22 in his guts. Now." He rubbed his plump pink palms together briskly. "Let's say somebody came in here and pumped a .22 into his stomach. You guys know what that feels like? Any idea?"

Smith grimaced. Kelso frowned and shook his head. He preferred not to contemplate it.

"A lot of pain," he murmured.

"A lot of pain." Bremer looked smug, like a math professor making an esoteric point about derivatives. "And here he is, in his den, in a lot of pain, and he's got this loaded .357 in his desk drawer. So what's he do? The pain gets excruciating, it gets unbearable. He wants to die and get it over with, but he doesn't die, he just hurts, he—"

"Okay, okay," Smith snapped, in a rare display of temper. "We get the goddamned point."

"He takes out the .357," Kelso said, "and kills himself."

"Ah." Bremer did the thing with his hands again. "Precisely. Just precisely. He kills himself."

"Here's an interesting point," Kelso remarked, going over to the far wall and facing them. "Somebody came in here and put a .22 bullet in Ott's stomach. That's attempted murder. Then Ott shoots himself with his own gun, killing himself instantly. That's suicide."

"So?" Smith asked.

"So there's no murder."

Bremer and Smith looked at him for a moment. Smith nodded slowly. Bremer looked slightly crestfallen.

"I hadn't thought of that," Bremer said. "I was thinking of this as something on the order of a double murder. You know—a twice-killed man. And now . . ."

"Now it's just an attempt and a suicide," Smith muttered.

They all stared at the body for a while. Then Kelso said,

"Well, I suppose we still have a would-be murderer to look for." He shoved his hands into the pockets of his corduroy pants and wondered if Carla had access to a .22 automatic. But she had an alibi, she'd been at a party from 7 P.M. until after 10 P.M., and that was the time interval for the shooting. She'd been with some guy named Tony Deal, and presumably many other people had seen her there. Everything could easily be confirmed. He was conscious of a strong desire to have her alibi corroborated.

"It's after midnight," Smith remarked. "We going to stand around here all night?"

"Yes," Bremer said. "We really should go ahead and get the body out, and the gun. Don't touch anything. The gun hasn't been examined yet. For fingerprints, I mean."

"We're not schoolchildren," Smith said. "Did they find anything else?"

"Just this." Bremer walked over to a stand on which stood a TV set and, on a lower shelf, a videotape recorder. Kelso noticed that some sort of indicator light was flashing. "This is a VCR," Bremer said.

Smith coughed. "The man's an absolute genius."

"And this is a Sony color TV. Notice that it's currently tuned to the weather radar channel."

"Ott was watching the weather when he was shot?" Kelso asked.

"Maybe he was taping the weather," Smith said.

Bremer smiled. "There's a videotape in the machine, and its power is on, but nothing's playing. See that flashing light? We did an experiment."

"They did an experiment," Smith remarked.

Bremer rubbed his hands together. Once again he was happy. "An experiment. Now, notice this light. This machine happens to be a JCPenney VCR, one of their higher-priced models I believe. It has many nice features."

Smith nodded. "It's a nice machine. So what?"

"This lighted display area is called the indicator panel. The flashing symbol looks like a tiny double spool of tape, and in fact is called a cassette-in indicator."

"How do you know that?" Kelso asked.

"We found the owner's operation and care manual on a shelf. Anyway, that indicator can be in one of three states. It can be off, meaning no tape cassette is in the unit. Or it can be on but not flashing, meaning there's a tape in the unit but it hasn't finished playing yet. Or—" He gave them a big smile. "Or, it can be flashing, meaning the tape played through to the very end and automatically rewound to the beginning again."

"So," Smith said, "there's a tape in there, and it played through to the end and got rewound."

"Wait," Kelso said. "I get the point now. The murder occurred—"

"Attempted murder," Bremer corrected.

"Attempted murder occurred while a tape was playing."

"Ah." Bremer rubbed his hands even more rapidly than before. "Exactly, Sergeant Kelso. Just exactly. While a tape was playing."

"What about recording?" Kelso asked.

"Yes." Bremer nodded. "Very good point. Yes, if something was being recorded, at the end of the tape automatic rewinding would also occur, and the indicator light would still be flashing, just as it is now."

"So he could've been either watching or recording," Kelso said. "Exactly."

"What's on the tape?" Smith wanted to know.

"An old movie. Something called *Topper Returns*. It's got commercials mixed in with it, and station identifications. It's been taped."

"And," Smith said, "what the hell does this have to do with anything?"

Kelso took his hands out of his pockets. "I see what it has to do with. If Ott was taping *Topper Returns* when he was shot, then all we have to do is look in a TV schedule, see when the movie was on, and we've got a definite time interval for the murder."

"Attempted murder," Smith muttered.

And Bremer, beaming and rubbing his pink palms together, said, "Exactly. Just exactly."

They left the house and went out into the snow. It was twelve-thirty in the morning, Sunday, December twentieth. There was no wind, the snow fell straight down in cold hard flakes, very dry. The body, Kelso thought as he climbed into the VW, would be taken to the county morgue and fingerprinted. This could be a tedious process, he knew. Most of the time a corpse's fingers had become shriveled, making normal fingerprinting impossible. A technician would inject fluid into the fingers to puff them up and make them soft again, so that they could be printed. Meanwhile, the .357 Magnum would be removed in an evidence box to the crime lab, where it would be checked for latent prints using a new technique that involved placing it inside an airtight container and filling the container with a chemical. The chemical was the basic ingredient found in so-called superglue. Any latent prints would be brought out in this way, without disturbing other particles on the weapon.

At that point, the police would have two sets of prints to compare— those of the dead man, and those found on the gun. An inference would then be possible as to whether Ott had actually held the gun. Additionally, of course, Ott's hand would be checked for gunshot residue.

He started up the VW, backed into Lincoln Avenue, and drove toward the city. Everything looked like Christmas. He turned on the radio and heard "I'll Be Home for Christmas."

"Shut that damn thing off, will you?" Smith snapped.

"Sorry. What's eating you?"

"I'm just not in the mood for it." After a pause, he said, "I don't like it."

"Neither do I. There are much better versions of that song."

"Not the song. The case. The whole situation."

"You don't think somebody shot Ott with a .22 and then he put himself out of his misery with his .357?"

"Absolutely not."

"As a matter of fact," Kelso said, "neither do I."

"Let's see if your reason's the same as mine," Smith said.

"Okay. My reason is this. Ott was sitting at his desk. He was at least in the room when he was shot with the .22. Somebody must've entered his den. If I was in my den and somebody came in and pulled out a .22, I'd have my drawer open and the .357 out before you could say Santa Claus. I'd have at least fired it at the person with the .22. I wouldn't have sat there waiting to be shot. At the *very* least, once I'd been shot, I'd have gotten out my .357 and gone after whoever it was, and taken a few shots at them. The .357 had been fired once. It doesn't make sense."

"No," Smith said. "It doesn't."

"So my theory is, somebody shot Ott with a .22, and then somebody else shot him with his own .357. Somebody who knew where he kept it."

"Or somebody used a .22 on him and then used his .357 on him, just to confuse us."

"Carla was at a party," Kelso said.

"It's going to be interesting to find out when that movie was shown tonight. What was it called?"

"Topper Returns," Kelso said.

"Yeah."

They drove on through the dark snowy streets.

EIGHT

By the time Kelso had dropped Smith off and driven all the way back
to the northwest side and into the curving street with its dark and
brooding houses, it was almost 1 A.M. He pulled the VW into the
drive, went up the walk to the door, and pressed the bell button.
There were lights on in the house; even the Christmas tree lights
were glowing in the front window.

Susan Overstreet opened the door and, smiling, ushered him inside. Without even a "hello" she threw her arms around him, hugged
him tightly and kissed him, then stood back.

"I was about ready to call. I didn't think you were coming after all."

"I said I would."

"Don't be gruff. Sometimes you chicken out."

"No I don't."

She looked good. She was maybe three inches shorter than Kelso,
slender, with thick short blond hair, wide brown eyes, and a good
figure. Just now she was wearing faded jeans, a dark red sweater over
a blouse, and running shoes. She had on tiny gold earrings and
smelled strongly of Chanel No. 5, the same stuff Carla had been
wearing. Involuntarily, he compared her to Carla, then forced the
thought from his mind.

"You look bushed," she said. "Want some coffee?"

"I've had too much coffee." He removed his parka and followed
her into the living room. "I forgot my bag. It's in the car."

"Get it later. Sit down. Do you want some milk? I've got a sack of
doughnuts in the kitchen."

He sank onto a sofa. There was a fire in the fireplace. Susan shared
the house with her Aunt Eleanor, and he could always tell when the
old lady was away because she couldn't tolerate temperatures under
eighty degrees. Now, the room was pleasantly warm, not hot. He was
tired and, for some reason, nervous.

"I'm not that hungry. But the milk sounds okay."

"You stay there. I'll get it."

"Susan? What kind of doughnuts?"

"Chocolate-covered cake."

"Hmm. Maybe just one . . ."

She smiled. "I'll bring the sack."

When she came back he drank some milk and they had a couple of doughnuts. Then she sat beside him and he told her about the case while she massaged his neck and shoulders.

"So here's this guy Ott with a .22 in his stomach and a .357 in his head. Well, not in his head, it went out the other side. And the .357's there on the floor under his hand, but there's no .22 in the room. So we don't know what the hell's going on."

"Who is he?" Susan asked. "I mean, does he have a wife or somebody living there with him? Have you arrested anybody?"

"We don't even have a real suspect at this point. His wife was at a Christmas party with lots of people all during the time of the murder, or the attempted murder, whatever it was. Her mother popped in briefly, she's got basically an alibi, at least until nine o'clock. We don't know enough about them yet. When we find out about them, maybe we'll find a motive. With the front door ajar like that, it might've even been a robbery attempt."

"Doesn't sound like attempted robbery to me," Susan said. "Why would a robber go into a house and shoot a guy and not take anything? You said the TV and the VCR were still there?"

"Yeah. It probably wasn't a robbery. Besides, the front door was open, but it hadn't been forced. I think Ott let the person in, and when they left they simply didn't close the door all the way."

Susan stopped rubbing his neck and looked at him with her wide brown eyes. "George?"

"Yeah?"

"Are you not telling me something about this case?"

He felt his face going hot and was glad the only light in the room was from the fire and the tree. "What's that mean?"

"I mean, I just get the feeling you're holding something back. I mean, I know you, George. You act like you're not telling me everything."

"I'm telling you everything," he lied, feeling himself go tense as he thought about Carla. "That's all there is. One dead body, two bullet wounds, two different calibers of probable weapons, no definite suspects. Well, there's the tape in the VCR." Videotape to the rescue, he thought, and told her about the tape of *Topper Returns* that had played or been taped to the end and then automatically rewound to the beginning again.

"We can check that right now," Susan said, getting up and going over to a low table by the TV. She picked up a television magazine. "Okay, here're the listings for Saturday. What was it called? *Topper Returns?* Hmm. George, I hate to tell you this, but nobody showed that movie last night, or at any time yesterday."

"Are you sure?"

"Sure I'm sure. Wait, let me check the movie index for the month. Here we go. Topper, Topper . . . George, that movie hasn't been on all month. Either on the networks or the local channels or any of the cable stations. It's just not on."

Kelso sighed. "Well, if that's true, then Ott wasn't taping it. It must've been an old tape. So we can't use that to tell anything about the time of the shootings." He shrugged. "Well, Dr. Paul will narrow it down for us, and we've still got approximate times. We know it was after seven when Carla left the house, and before ten or ten-fifteen when she got back and found the body."

Susan put down the guide and came back over to the couch. She stood looking down at Kelso with her hands at her hips.

"That's it, isn't it, George?"

"What's it?"

"You get this funny sound in your voice when you talk about this Carla person. And you've got a funny look in your eyes. What aren't you telling me about her?"

"Nothing."

"She's beautiful, is that it? She's tall and blond and better looking than me, and she turned you on. Go on, admit it, I won't mind."

"She's short and fat and looks like that weird cousin of yours, the one with the double chins."

"Go get your bag. It's time for bed."

Reluctantly, Kelso went out to the VW and got his suitcase. It had stopped snowing, leaving about an inch on the ground. A few big puffy white clouds moved across the black sky, showing crisp bright stars in between. It was cold. Shivering, he went back inside. Susan was turning out the lights.

He used the guest bath to undress, brush his teeth, wash his face, and put on his pajamas, which were cotton with blue and white vertical stripes. He slipped his bare feet into a pair of leather slippers and padded out into the hall and into Susan's bedroom.

She was standing near the bed, smirking at him, wearing some kind of shortie thing in sheer red see-through material and nothing underneath. Just for a brief moment he committed the unforgivable sin of wondering how Carla would look in something like that, then willed her from his thoughts and concentrated on Susan.

"Do you like it?" she asked. "I got it just for you."

"It's very nice. Uh, we *are* going to sleep, aren't we?"

She moved toward him. "Eventually, George. Eventually."

Eventually, Kelso went to sleep, and when he opened his eyes again the room was flooded with brilliant sunshine.

NINE

Kelso took her to one of those Sunday brunch places, where for a flat price of $8.95 you could fill your plate as many times as you liked from a buffet that included Belgian waffles, pancakes, eggs prepared in various ways, sausage and bacon, chicken, ham, and—since it was almost Christmas—turkey. There were also sweet rolls, some kind of lemon cake, and supposedly fresh fruit that didn't look especially fresh to Kelso. They sat in a red booth in a quiet corner, surrounded by paintings, photographs, and old movie posters, with a brass lamp on the table between them, eating mostly bacon and eggs and sweet rolls with coffee and orange juice.

"So what're we doing today, George?"

"I don't know what you're doing, but I've got to work on the case."

"But it's Sunday."

"Very astute observation, but a homicide investigation doesn't grind to a halt just because it's Sunday. Not when I'm on call all weekend."

"Oh." She pouted a little, then brightened. "Well, you'll be coming back tonight, right?"

"I have to. My bag's still at your house."

"Don't be an ass, George."

"Me?"

"So are you going to talk to that Carla woman again?"

He nodded, pouring more coffee. "Yeah. As a matter of fact, we were sort of tiptoeing around with her last night, with her husband freshly dead so to speak. But we're going to have to ask her a few tough questions. Such as whether she owns a .22 automatic pistol, or knows anybody who does. We're going to have to find this Tony Deal she says she was at the Christmas party with and have him and his law partners corroborate her story. There's some couple called the Huffs, social friends of the Otts, who I suppose we'll have to question, just in case. And then it gets tough."

"Tough how?"

"Carla's parents. Her mother bothers me, I don't know why. She was with her husband until nine, then he left and she was alone. I'd like to ask both of them a few questions. And, of course, there's Carla's old boyfriend, this guy Fredricks. Karl Smith was supposed to check the hotel and make sure Fredricks is still there and stays there till we can question him."

Susan looked thoughtful. "You want to know what I think, George?"

"Sure. I don't have any choice, do I?"

"I'll ignore that. I think it was Fredricks. It just fits. Nine years, is that what you told me, nine years ago Carla jilted him, and he's never gotten over it. So he comes to town and looks her up, but she more or less tells him to go to hell. Fredricks is obsessed with getting her back. How to do it? Get rid of her husband. He watches her house, sees her leave to go to that office party, goes right up and knocks on the front door, with a .22 pistol in his pocket. Paul Ott opens the door and Fredricks barges in, takes Ott to the den at gunpoint and shoots him."

"With the .22?" Kelso asked.

"With the .22."

"So how do you explain the shot in Ott's head with his .357?"

"One of two things. Either Fredricks found the gun and did it himself to create confusion, or after the one shot with the .22 Fredricks panicked and ran away, and Ott shot himself."

Kelso sighed and took out his pipe. "I'm sorry, but I don't really buy either theory."

"Well, I still say it was Fredricks. One way or the other."

"I guess we'll see."

"George?"

"What?"

"Did you enjoy last night?"

He struck a match to his pipe, puffed a couple of times, then replied with a straight face, "Well, the mattress is a little soft, but once I got to sleep—"

She kicked him under the table.

He took her home, kissed her goodbye, promised to return for supper, then drove downtown to Karl Smith's apartment, arriving there at 1:30 P.M. Smith had just gotten up and was lounging around in his living room in a pair of denim jeans faded almost white, a pair of beat-up tennis sneakers, and a sweatshirt that said "Property of the United States Army" across the front. Smith had been a captain in the infantry prior to joining the police force. His short blond hair was slightly mussed, and he was smoking a Kent and sipping black coffee from a huge ceramic mug.

The living room was nothing fancy, but clean and neat. There was a tasteful sofa and matching armchair, an oval woven rug on the hardwood floor, a couple of nice lamps, a good quality stereo system with a turntable and a tape deck. Directly over the stereo stand the December *Playboy* Playmate of the Month had been taped to the wall.

"I thought you didn't like nude women," Kelso remarked, eyeing the foldout.

"I love nude women," Smith said.

"I mean, in magazines."

"She's not in a magazine. She's on my wall. You want some coffee?"

Kelso shook his head. "No thanks, I just had a big brunch with Susan."

"When're you going to marry that broad, Kelso?"

"I'm a confirmed bachelor."

"You tell her that?"

"Of course not."

Smith sighed and put out his cigarette. "I've got to get dressed."

"Why?"

"And then I'll be ready to go. By the way, I found that guy Henry Fredricks. He's in Room 726 of the Downtowner Hotel, and I told him to stay there till we could talk to him. I told him it'd be this afternoon. He wasn't too happy about it."

"Did you tell him about Ott?"

"Don't be silly. I'll be back in a minute. If you want coffee or juice they're in the kitchen." He stood, drank down the rest of his coffee, stretched, yawned, ran long thin fingers through his yellowish hair, and left the room.

Kelso wandered over to the windows and peered out through the curtains. It was starting to cloud up again. More snow was predicted. Definitely a white Christmas this year. He grimaced. He wasn't in the mood for Christmas, which was only five days away now. He felt that he had to do something about Carla, but couldn't decide what. Already he was feeling guilty about not telling Susan about her, and he also wondered what Carla would think about Susan. It was too complicated, and since he had to pursue the murder investigation there was no way he could simply ignore it or avoid it.

Smith entered the room again a few minutes later, his hair neatly combed, wearing a dark well-cut suit, white shirt, silk tie, and highly polished shoes.

"Is that a new suit?"

"Redwood & Ross. So are the shirt and tie."

Kelso whistled. "Did you rob a bank?"

"I save my money, Kelso, and then I spend it on top-quality products that look good and last." He leered. "Unlike some detectives I could name."

Kelso was wearing an aging corduroy suit he'd bought on sale at Sears, crepe-soled walking shoes, and an oxford shirt with no tie.

"I dress for comfort," he said, a little defensively.

Smith nodded. "Obviously. Are you ready to go?"

"I've *been* ready."

"If you don't mind," Smith said, "we'll take my LTD this time. If I have to work Sunday, I'm damned if I'll spend all afternoon cramped up inside that stupid Beetle of yours, with no heat."

"It has heat."

"Penguins think there's heat at the north pole. But I'm not a penguin, I'm a warm-blooded mammal."

"Penguins live at the south pole."

"And in your Volkswagen," Smith said.

They took the LTD and drove several blocks to the Downtowner. It was a tall old brick building on the southwest corner of Third Street and South Central Avenue. Recently renovated, it offered basic comfort without a lot of high-priced frills. The corridors were thickly carpeted and quiet, and you got the impression that a good night's sleep was quite possible here. They stood outside the door to Room 726 and knocked.

"I like good hotels," Kelso murmured. "I could spend two weeks in a good hotel, and it'd be a nice vacation."

Smith glanced at him. "You're weird."

The door opened and a man looked out at them, probably just under six feet tall, early thirties, with light brown hair, a short brown mustache, and amber eyes. He was in dark slacks, a white shirt with no tie, and black loafers. He looked wary, tired, and slightly confused.

"Yes?" he asked, in a rather high voice.

"Sorry to bother you, sir," Kelso said. "Are you Henry Fredricks?"

The amber eyes darted from Kelso to Smith. "Yes . . ."

"Police officers, Mr. Fredricks." Kelso took out his police identification folder and held it up. "I'm Sergeant Kelso, this is Detective Smith. Could we come in and talk to you for a few minutes?"

"Well I . . . I guess so . . ." Fredricks backed away, letting them in. The room was rather nice, with a queen-sized bed, two armchairs, a large table, a dresser, two windows. There was the smell of cigarette smoke, and a burning cigarette in an ashtray on the bedside stand sent smoke spiraling toward the ceiling. A sliding closet door stood open, revealing a suit coat and an overcoat on hangers and a large suitcase on the floor. At the foot of the bed lay a leather valise, closed.

Smith strolled over to one of the windows, peered out through the drapes, then turned and gazed calmly at Fredricks, his expression bland, his blue eyes cold. Kelso rested an elbow on the top of the dresser. Fredricks seemed nervous; he went to the bed, started to sit down, seemed to think better of it, and wound up standing with his back to the wall at the head of the bed, his hands thrust into his trouser pockets and his shoulders slightly hunched.

"So," he said, "what can I do for you gentlemen?"

"We're investigating a homicide," Kelso said politely. "We'd just like to ask you a few questions."

Fredricks stared. "A homicide? Whose homicide?"

"Mr. Fredricks, do you know a woman named Carla Ott?"

"Oh my God. Is Carla dead?"

"Not Carla. Her husband. A man named Paul Ott. He was shot to death last night." Kelso watched the man's face closely for any reaction, but Fredricks looked honestly stunned.

"Her husband?"

"Mr. Fredricks," Kelso said, "we've spoken to Carla, and we understand you dated her a few years ago, and you've come here from Kokomo just to see her. Is that right?"

Fredricks slowly shook his head. Frowning, he took his hands out of his pockets, wet his lips, then put his hands in his pockets again. "That's right. I came here . . . to see her."

Smith didn't say a word. Sometimes when Kelso and Smith worked with a witness or a suspect, Smith did most of the talking; this was especially true when the suspect tried to act tough or was evasive or otherwise uncooperative, since Smith's height and size and stern demeanor could be intimidating. But with other suspects, people who were frightened or shy or already intimidated, Kelso did most of the talking, in his usual polite calm way.

"Mr. Fredricks," Kelso said softly, "when did you actually get here from Kokomo?"

"Well, I left there Friday morning, I guess, and got here early in the afternoon and checked into this hotel."

"Would you mind telling us exactly what prompted you to drive down here to see Carla?"

Fredricks took a deep breath, let it out, fumbled in his pockets for another cigarette, and lit it with a disposable lighter. "This is going to sound sort of strange, I guess. See, about nine years ago, Carla and I dated for a while."

Kelso felt a brief sharp pang of jealousy. He said nothing.

"We went together for almost a year and a half. I was, you know, really crazy about her, and I guess I thought she was crazy about me." He shrugged. "But one day out of the clear blue sky she told me it was over. No reason why, just over." He snapped his fingers. "Like that. Well, I cried and begged and pleaded, but it didn't do any good. I graduated from law school that year and moved to Kokomo and I've lived there since then, practicing law."

"Are you married?"

"I was. We got divorced last year. After two years. It just didn't work out."

"I'm sorry," Kelso said. "So what made you come here?"

"Yes. Well, after my divorce I started thinking about Carla, and, well, you know, I guess I was thinking how it might've been if I'd married her instead, and the more I thought about it, the more I wanted to see her, just see her and talk to her, find out how she was doing."

"Maybe," Smith said, "try to get her back again?"

"Maybe." Fredricks darted a quick glance at Smith, then looked at Kelso again. "I don't know. I just wanted to see her."

"How'd you know she was here?" Kelso asked.

"Well, this is where she was living when she was in college. I still had her home address—I mean, her parents', address. She was Carla Bushnell then. But I didn't think she'd still be living with them. It turns out that the university publishes an alumni directory. So I bought a copy, and there she was—Carla Bushnell Ott, with her address. I wrote her a letter, but she never answered it."

"Excuse me," Kelso said, getting out his pad and pen and starting to take notes. "When did you write to her?"

"Let's see, that would've been about a week, maybe a week and a half ago."

"Just one letter?"

"Yes, that's right. And she never answered. So I called her up."

"From Kokomo?"

Fredricks nodded. "I got her number from Clairmont City information. Well, when I called her up and she answered, when I told her it

was me she just hung up. So finally I decided to drive down here and
try to see her."

"And when was that, Mr. Fredricks?"

"Let's see." He frowned, touched a finger to his mustache, then
replied, "Friday morning. I thought I said that . . ."

Kelso nodded. "Yes you did. Sorry. You checked into this room,
and then did you call her again?"

"Yes. From here. And she hung up on me as soon as I said my
name."

"What did you do after that?"

"I was depressed, and I was going to leave, but I decided to try
again once more time. So the next day, Saturday—that was yesterday,
right?—yes, yesterday, I telephoned her, I don't know, maybe around
one in the afternoon, I don't recall exactly. I told her who it was, and
she just said she preferred not to talk. And before she could hang up
on me again I more or less shouted my hotel room at her, Room 726
here at the Downtowner, and then there was just the dial tone."

"Do you think she heard you?" Kelso asked.

"Well, she must've, because she called me here."

For a moment there was silence in the room as Kelso considered
this. He looked over at Smith, whose face was blank. After he had
gone over the various implications of Fredricks' statement, he said,
"She called you here. And when was that, Mr. Fredricks?"

"Last night. A little before eight."

"You took the call here in this room?"

"Yes, right here."

"And what did Carla say?"

"She apologized for, you know, hanging up on me and all, and she
asked me if I'd like to come over to her house for a while and talk
about everything."

Smith muttered something under his breath; now he looked disgusted. Kelso was no mind reader, but he knew approximately what
his partner was thinking now: that he and Kelso had probably found
their murderer, or would-be murderer.

The atmosphere in the hotel room changed. Kelso was now on his
guard.

"She was calling you from her house?" he asked.

"Well, as far as I know. I mean, she asked if I could come over."

"And this was just before eight, last night."

"Yes. I was looking in the paper to see what was on TV at eight, and

I checked my watch. It was about ten till, and then the phone rang and it was her."

"What'd you tell her, Mr. Fredricks?"

He shrugged, put out his cigarette, clasped his hands together nervously, and replied, "I told her it sounded great, I'd be right over. She gave me instructions on how to get there."

"When did you actually go?"

"As soon as I hung up. I got there around eight-fifteen."

"And she was there?"

Fredricks gave Kelso a funny look. "Of course she was there."

Smith smirked. Kelso felt depressed. "All right. Tell us everything that happened from the time you got there, to the best of your recollection."

"Well. I was pretty nervous. She let me in and stood around in the hall talking to me for a minute or two. Just small talk, the weather, how I looked, Christmas, nothing important. Then suddenly she put her arms around me . . . this is kind of embarrassing."

"Just tell us," Smith said.

Kelso was gritting his teeth, remembering when Carla had kissed him in the hall on Friday night, and visualizing her kissing Fredricks in the hall last night. He fought down his temper. It was no damned concern of his, whatever they'd had, had ended ten years ago; she could kiss anybody she pleased. But he didn't understand it.

"Well," Fredricks said, clasping and unclasping his hands, "she kissed me several times, and then she told me how sorry she was about everything." He spoke rapidly, as though trying to get it all out as quickly as possible. "She said she was thinking of divorcing her husband—"

"What?" Smith stared.

Kelso said, "Divorcing Ott?"

"That's what she said. Anyway, she said she'd never really gotten over me, and she wanted a chance to prove how she still felt about me. So . . . this is the embarrassing part . . ."

"Just spit it out," Smith snapped.

Kelso said kindly, "Take your time, Mr. Fredricks."

"She asked me to go to bed with her," Fredricks blurted.

This is really the last straw, Kelso thought. The last damned straw. He felt his face going instantly hot.

"And?" Smith asked. "Did you sleep with her? It's not going to shock *us.*"

"She took me upstairs to her bedroom," Fredricks said, looking worried.

Kelso had noticed something. The closed valise lay at the foot of the queen-sized bed, and from time to time Fredricks glanced down at it, then quickly away. He seemed not to want to be caught looking at it. Kelso wondered what was in the valise.

"Go on," Smith urged irritably.

"I went to her bedroom with her. She told me to get undressed, and, well, this is the weird part. I asked her about her problems with her husband, why she wanted to divorce him, and she told me that for a year or so she'd wanted to have kids, start a family, she was really desperate to get pregnant. And suddenly I had this terrible feeling that I was being used. You know—to get her pregnant. In other words, that it wasn't me she was interested in at all, she just wanted to use me to get pregnant."

"So what'd you do?" Kelso asked.

Again Fredricks' eyes darted to the valise and away. "I stepped into the bathroom to undress; I was embarrassed to do it in front of her. And that's when I changed my mind. Please, just let me tell it. I stood there, and all kinds of little noises were in my head. I remember everything sounded abnormally loud, like in a dream or something, or some kind of Bergman film, with tap water dripping like a gong being struck, and the sound of a car backfiring down in the street, and the heat running, and my heart banging away. I'm sorry to sound so melodramatic; I just want you to understand why I was like I was. I had my shirt off, the dripping water was driving me crazy, I couldn't think, I kept seeing her lying in bed, naked, waiting for me, knowing she wasn't on the pill or anything, knowing all she wanted was my sperm, putting on a show of liking it like some prostitute, and I couldn't do it." He stopped talking, looked at the valise.

"Go ahead," Kelso said softly.

"I buttoned my shirt up and put my shoes back on and went out, into the bedroom."

"Was she still there?"

"She was sitting on the bed in her bra and panties."

"I see." Kelso clenched his teeth.

"I apologized, I told her I was too nervous, made some excuse or other, and, well, she just blew up."

Smith blinked. "Blew up? Got mad?"

"She was as mad as I've ever seen her. She got up from the bed and shoved my briefcase at me, and started putting on her skirt and blouse, she was yelling at me the whole time."

"What'd she yell?" Smith asked.

"She called me names, said I wasn't a man, I was a wimp, she used some obscenities. She, uh, questioned my sexual ability. Mainly she ordered me out of her house and told me she never wanted to see me again. She called me a son of a bitch, several times."

Kelso nodded. "And did you leave?"

"Of course. What else could I do?" He shrugged. "I came back here, had a couple of drinks down in the lounge, and went to bed."

"And you haven't heard from her since, or seen her?"

"No."

"Mr. Fredricks, what were your feelings about Carla's husband?"

"My feelings? I don't know, I guess I resented him. Resented the fact that he was married to her. Him instead of me."

Kelso looked at his notebook, then at Fredricks. "You said when you came out of the bathroom she got up and shoved your briefcase at you. Are you referring to this one?" Kelso pointed at the leather valise on the foot of the bed.

Fredricks became distinctly uneasy. "Well, yes . . ."

"You took that with you, to Carla's house?"

"Yes."

"Why?"

"It's sort of strange . . ."

"Just tell us," Smith said.

"While I was in law school and dating Carla, she wrote to me whenever we were away, like on vacations, Christmas, semester breaks, that kind of thing. I kept every one of her letters. Also some of the napkins, like from coffee shops and places we'd eat and write little things to each other, and matchbook covers, some cards she gave me for birthdays and Christmas or whatever. Everything's in there. And her picture."

"So why'd you take that stuff to her house?" Smith asked.

Fredricks shrugged. "I thought we'd talk about old times. I planned to show her that stuff, to prove that I'd kept all of it, you know, to show her I'd never stopped caring about her."

Kelso said, "Do you mind if we see it?"

A different look formed on Fredricks' face. It was like watching a special effect in a movie, a science fiction movie in which some weird alien takes over a human. The facial features changed, as though in the grip of some unseen force. Fear distorted the man's face. As if to see if it was still there, he touched a finger to his mustache. His hands were shaking.

Finally he let out a long sigh and said, "I've got a gun in there."

Smith straightened up instantly and unbuttoned his suit coat, for ease of access to the .357 in his shoulder holster. Kelso was alert, but not worried. They had him outnumbered, and he looked too scared to try anything. He wasn't even close to the briefcase.

"What kind of gun?" Kelso asked. It's a .22, he thought.

So he wasn't particularly surprised when Fredricks replied, in a slightly quavering voice, "It's a .22 caliber automatic."

TEN

Kelso stepped over to the foot of the bed, snapped the latches on the briefcase, and opened the lid. He saw bunches of old letters held together by rubber bands; some restaurant napkins with things written on them in pencil or ballpoint pen; greeting cards; some wrapping paper and a mashed bow; a framed portrait of Carla with "Hank, All my love forever, Carla," written across the bottom; and a small gift box on which was written in faded pencil, "cuff links, present from Carla, Fall Fling."

Kelso looked up at Fredricks. "You wear cuff links?"

"It was a formal dance."

"Oh."

Gently, he lifted up the letters and other items. There, lying loose at the bottom of the case, lay a pistol that would be technically referred to as a semiautomatic, or an autoloader, but that in everyday handgun parlance was simply called an automatic. It was a bluesteel .22 caliber, about a four-inch barrel, with wooden grips. The named stamped on the barrel said Charter Arms Pathfinder.

Kelso stood with his right hand at his side, his left hand holding up the lid of the briefcase, and gazed steadily at Fredricks.

The decision to effect an arrest, he was thinking, or at least to take someone into custody, was both a legal and a practical matter. Lawyers could debate probable cause for hours after the fact, but the detective in the field had precious little time to make the decision, and the facts were often ambiguous. Kelso was very close to making the decision, but he would put it off a little longer. There was no real hurry yet. On the other hand, it was about time to advise Fredricks of his rights.

"Mr. Fredricks, before we go any further with this I think I should inform you of your constitutional rights—"

"Please." Fredricks held up a palm. "I'm a practicing attorney. I know my rights." He seemed very upset.

"Still—"

"I'll waive them. I understand them. Consider them read, okay?"

"As long as you understand that you've been advised."

"Consider me advised," Fredricks said.

"This is your gun?"

"Yes."

"You had it in your briefcase, this briefcase, when you went to Carla Ott's home last night sometime after 8 P.M.?"

"Yes. But—"

"You have a license to carry a gun, Mr. Fredricks?"

"That's a legal gun," Fredricks said, rather hotly. "It's registered, and I've got a permit to carry it. Look, I practice mostly criminal law, my office is in what you'd call a rather back-street section of Kokomo, I've had threats on my life from clients of mine who've gone to jail, sometimes threats from their families. I've carried this gun with me, legally, since shortly after I began practicing law."

It occurred to Kelso that Carla had said several things about Fredricks. One, that he hadn't resented her husband. Two, that he hadn't been at her house. Three, that he wasn't violent, he'd never been armed, he hated guns.

He supposed it remained to be seen whether Fredricks was violent, but apparently he'd been to Carla's house, he'd resented her husband, and he obviously had a gun.

"Why'd you take the gun with you to Carla's house, Mr. Fredricks?" Kelso asked casually.

"I didn't. I mean, I took it, but not intentionally. See, when I packed before I left Kokomo, the gun wound up in the briefcase. It's simply where I packed it. Okay? So when Carla called last night and asked me to come over, and I decided to go and take her letters and things with me, I simply grabbed up the briefcase and took it. I didn't stop to think that the gun was in there or that it wasn't or anything at all. I just went."

"While you were at her house last night, did you at any time have the briefcase open? Did you show her any of this?"

"Absolutely not." Fredricks paced forward toward the foot of the bed, blinked uncertainly, then returned to the head of the bed and stood once more with his back to the wall. He lit another cigarette and puffed hard at it. "I never had that case open the whole time. In fact, if I may anticipate your next question, I haven't fired that gun since early November at an indoor range in Kokomo. And I cleaned it after that, and loaded it with a full clip, and that's exactly the condition you'll find it in when you examine it. And I assume you'll examine it."

"You assume right," Smith remarked.

"Mr. Fredricks," Kelso said, "will you let us take the gun to the lab and have it looked at?"

"Sure."

"You'll have to sign a form."

"I'm perfectly aware of that."

"Smith, have you got an evidence box in your car?"

Smith glared. "No, I never carry police equipment in my car. Jesus." He strode across the room to the door. "Of course I do. I'll bring it up. And a form."

"Thanks."

Smith went out. Fredricks puffed smoke and said, "I just don't understand what you hope to find, is all."

"I don't *hope* to find anything, Mr. Fredricks. But this is a homicide investigation. Paul Ott was shot with a .22. You admit you were there last night, within the time frame of the shooting. The only way to eliminate you, or not, is to check the weapon at the lab. We've got the bullet for comparison."

Fredricks smiled suddenly. "You're in for a disappointment, Sergeant Kelso. I'll tell you exactly what you're going to find. My gun hasn't been fired. My prints are on it. The bullet in Carla's husband didn't come from my gun."

"Well, if that's what we find, then you'll be in the clear, and we can get on with the investigation."

Neither spoke for a while. Kelso felt confused by Fredricks' attitude. He didn't act like a man who'd tried to commit murder and who now was on the brink of getting arrested and charged. But sometimes murderers could be cool under fire. Earlier, though, Fredricks had seemed frightened and quite nervous. Nothing made any sense.

The door opened and Smith came in with a gun box and an evidence form. Kelso slipped a piece of string through the trigger guard of the automatic and held it up to his nose. He sniffed at the barrel, then lowered the weapon into the box. He watched Smith close the box and seal it with tape, and both he and Smith initialed the attached form. Smith filled in the blanks as to time, location, weapon, suspect. Fredricks signed the form indicating he'd surrendered his gun to the police.

"Any more questions?" Fredricks asked, almost defiantly.

"Just one," Smith said. "Did you kill Ott?"

"Absolutely not."

"I don't suppose you know who did?"

"I haven't any idea."

Kelso looked at Smith. In Smith's cold blue eyes was an expression Kelso had seen before. It was a very sarcastic expression, very cynical. Smith thought Fredricks was lying.

"Mr. Fredricks," Kelso said, "I'd like to go over this one time with you, and then I'd like you to come down to police headquarters some time or other and make and sign a formal statement."

"Why not?"

"Fine." Kelso glanced at his notes. "Correct me if I've got any of this wrong. You drove here from Kokomo on Friday the eighteenth and checked into this room. You telephoned Carla but she hung up on you. You telephoned her again on Saturday the nineteenth and she hung up on you again, but that time you managed to give her your room number here at the hotel. On Saturday night at ten minutes till eight she called you here in your room and invited you over to her house, and you went. You took your briefcase with you, and in the briefcase was your loaded .22 automatic, which is registered and licensed to you. When you got there, Carla kissed you, told you she was considering divorcing her husband Paul Ott, told you she was desperate to become pregnant and Paul was being uncooperative, and asked you to go to bed with her. You went upstairs and started to undress in a bathroom, but changed your mind and got dressed and left the bathroom. Carla was on the bed in bra and panties. She shoved your briefcase at you, shouted insults at you, and ordered you to leave. You left." Kelso looked up at Fredricks. "Is that about it?"

"Yes. That's about it." Fredricks seemed less sure of himself again. "Can you tell me . . . are you arresting me?"

"No. Not now. But we'd like that statement, tomorrow morning'll be okay, and we'd like you to stay in Clairmont City unless you advise us differently. If that's not a problem."

Fredricks shrugged. "I more or less cleared my calendar for the week. My Christmas vacation, so to speak."

"Yes." Kelso nodded.

"I've got one question," Smith said. His voice was hard. "When you came out of that bathroom and found her sitting on the bed in her underwear, was she wearing panty hose?"

Fredricks stared. Kelso suppressed a chuckle.

"Just a bra and panties," Fredricks said, looking embarrassed.

"Right." Smith yawned with a hand over his mouth, strolled to the door carrying the evidence box containing the .22, and opened the door. "Let's go, Kelso. It's almost two-thirty. I could use some coffee."

"Thanks for your help, Mr. Fredricks," Kelso said.

"What time tomorrow morning, and where?"

"Anytime after eight is okay." Kelso pointed to the windows. "That street out there is Third Street, it runs east and west. You're facing north. Go a block north to Fourth Street, and the Municipal Building's two blocks west."

"A big ugly gray thing like a bomb shelter," Smith said. "You can't miss it."

"I'll be there," Fredricks said, rather glumly.

"Ask for the Detective Section," Kelso said. "Somebody'll escort you up. Well, goodbye."

He and Smith stepped out into the thickly carpeted corridor and pulled the door closed. As they walked along toward the elevators, Kelso asked, "What was all that about panty hose?"

"Pure eroticism, without redeeming social value."

"I'm serious."

Smith leered. "So am I." He frowned. "If you must know, I was wondering if Carla was really serious about going to bed with the guy. If she still had on her panty hose, then maybe she wasn't all that serious. But if she had'em off, then maybe she was." He pressed the down button. "It probably doesn't matter, because probably Fredricks is lying out his ass. It seems pretty clear to me that he went over there for the express purpose of blowing away Paul Ott. There's just one thing I don't get."

The elevator arrived and they got in. A fat lady with a tiny white poodle in her arms glowered at them and reeked of nauseating perfume. Neither detective spoke until they had reached the ground floor, at which point the doors opened and Smith said, as the lady was getting off, "I hate poodles."

She paused without turning around, the back of her neck got red, then she hurried away. Smith chuckled.

Kelso shook his head. "Why do you do things like that?"

"Just for fun."

"What is it you don't get?"

"Oh, yeah. What I don't get is why you didn't arrest the son of a bitch."

"I guess I'm not totally convinced yet. All the facts aren't in. We've got to talk to Carla's alibi witnesses, and her friends the Huffs, and her parents. I'll admit Fredricks looks good for it in some ways, at least for the .22 shot in Ott's belly. But I don't see him using Ott's

.357, and there's an awful lot about this that still doesn't make any sense at all."

"Well," Smith said, "I'll agree with you there."

They went out into the street. On Sunday afternoons Clairmont City was dead. The only thing open was an occasional drugstore, hotels, here and there a coffee shop. Very few cars moved along the slushy streets. A few lackadaisical flakes of snow spiraled slowly downward from a drab gray-white sky. It felt very cold.

They put the evidence box in the trunk and climbed inside the LTD.

"Time for a coffee break," Smith said. "It's freezing out here. What do you think—Hunter's?"

"Too far away. Why don't we just try the cafeteria."

"You got it." Smith turned up the heat as he drove. "Say, Kelso, are you taking this okay?"

"Why wouldn't I be?"

"All this about Carla trying to get Fredricks into the sack and everything. I mean, if you've still got any feelings left for her . . ."

"I'd rather not talk about it," Kelso said.

"Sorry. But if it's going to affect your ability to deal with the case—"

"It's not affecting my ability to deal with the case, okay?"

"You don't have to get defensive about it," Smith said. "By the way, I did notice what you did back there in the hotel room."

"Meaning what?"

"You sniffed Fredricks' gun."

"Oh. That."

"Smell like anything in particular?"

"As a matter of fact," Kelso said, "it smelled like guns usually smell after they've been fired but not cleaned."

Smith glanced around at him, then back at the street. "You're kidding."

"Sure. I'm kidding. I made it up." Kelso sighed. "No, I'm not kidding. It's been fired. Obviously it's impossible to say when, just from smelling it, but it's definitely been fired since the last time it was cleaned."

"Which makes Fredricks a liar," Smith said. "Well, what'd I tell you? Jesus, we should've arrested him. You want to go back and take him in?"

"He'll wait. Let's get the lab results on his gun first."

"You're impossible. If it's been fired, and he admits he took it over there, then he did it. And if he didn't fire it, then who did? Santa Claus?"

"Maybe."

Smith muttered something and pulled into the cafeteria parking lot. It was nearly 3 P.M. on Sunday, December twentieth. Just before they got out of the LTD, Kelso said, "Do you remember what Fredricks said he did in Carla's bathroom?"

"Sure I remember."

"I was just wondering. And oh, by the way, we'll have to take Fredricks' .22 over to the crime lab sometime this afternoon. Okay?"

"You're nuts, Kelso. They don't work on Sunday."

"I'll bet they work this Sunday."

They got out and went inside the cafeteria.

ELEVEN

Wyatt's Cafeteria was one of Kelso's favorite food spots, a large comfortable establishment with early American decor, lots of wood paneling, imitation antique furnishing, a fireplace with a real fire, huge chandeliers, dark red tablecloths and matching napkins. Along one wall, tall velvet-draped windows looked out onto Fifth Street, where snow fell gently onto the almost deserted pavement. Christmas songs came over the Muzak system.

Smith, a vegetarian of sorts, ate a vegetable plate while Kelso indulged himself with roast turkey and dressing, mashed potatoes, lima beans, and coconut cream pie.

"Don't you even give it up for Christmas?" Kelso asked.

"Give what up?"

"All this vegetable nonsense. I mean, a little turkey never hurt anybody."

"I had a turkey sandwich once," Smith said. "It gave me indigestion." He swallowed some green peas. "So what do you want to do next?"

"Talk to Tony Deal. I want to make sure about Carla's alibi before we decide anything else. If she really wasn't at her house between seven and ten last night, then Fredricks is lying. And that really confuses me."

"Why?"

Kelso frowned. "If Carla really wasn't there, then why would he make up such a terrible lie, knowing we'd easily catch him at it? It's almost like he's asking to get caught."

Smith's portable radio buzzed and he picked it up. "Smith."

"Karl? This is dispatch. Are you with George?"

"Affirmative."

"Detective Sergeant Meyer's looking for you two. He's at the office. Can you call him right away?"

"I suppose," Smith said, and put the radio down. "It's Meyer. You want to go call the little creep, or you want me to do it?"

"He's your best friend."

"He's slime."

"Okay. I'll call him." Kelso slid out of the booth. "He's slime? Any other message you want me to give him?"

"Make one up," Smith said, and took a bite of creamed carrots.

Kelso found a pay phone and called the detective section number. Meyer answered.

"Kelso? I've been looking all over for you guys. Listen, Leill's put the crime lab in gear, they're all pissed off about having to work on a Sunday, but some kind of political pressure's coming down the pipe on this case, from way the hell up. The dead guy's wife is the daughter of some political hotshot, guy named Bushnell. So anyway, I've got some info for you and Smith."

"Shoot," Kelso said, taking out his notepad and pen.

"First, there's some kind of love angle in this case. They found some letters in Ott's den, implying an affair or at least sex. They're weird. Apparently this woman liked his body but not his mind."

"What woman?"

"Pay attention, damn it. What'd you say? The Bushnell woman, of course."

Kelso shook his head. Sometimes Meyer was virtually incomprehensible. "Are you trying to say that Ott was having an affair with Mrs. Bushnell? Carla's mother?"

"I'm not trying to say anything, Kelso. It's in the letters. They're from her to him, and they talk about sex with him. Now listen to me. Ott's wife agreed to be fingerprinted, so we could eliminate her prints from the ones we found around their house. Hers were all over the place, but not on that .357."

"Whose prints were on the .357?" Kelso asked.

"A set of prints belonging to Ott. And a fabric pattern. They say it's probably from a glove."

Kelso thought. "But Ott wasn't wearing gloves."

"Exactly. Sometimes your brilliance amazes me, Kelso. Now here's something else. They examined Ott's clothing, including the area around the .22 bullet hole. There was blood on the floor and blood and brains on the desk, and they dug the .357 slug out of the desk. Are you getting all this, Kelso? Am I going too fast for you?"

"Keep going," Kelso muttered.

"Based on all this, they think Ott was shot with the .22 while standing near his desk, then he sat down and was shot with the .357 while his head was actually resting on the desk blotter."

"That's interesting."

"It's not supposed to be interesting, it's supposed to be informative. Are you getting it all? Oh, yeah, and they found one of Ott's shirts in the dirty clothes hamper, and it had some kind of makeup on it, rouge or something, but it didn't match anything Carla's got in the house."

"Mrs. Bushnell?" Kelso asked.

"Or some secretary. Who the hell knows? So what're you two guys doing?"

Kelso told him about Fredricks and the .22.

"Have you got him in custody?"

"He's in his hotel room."

"What? Are you stupid? Arrest the son of a bitch."

"Look," Kelso said patiently, "number one, he's not going anywhere. Number two, we don't really know that he shot anyone yet, until we run the gun against the .22 from Ott's body. Number three, I'd like to check Carla's alibi."

"If you screw this up, Kelso, Leill's going to make you eat your badge, or sit on it, or both."

"I'm not going to screw it up," he told Meyer, and they said good-bye.

Back in the booth, Smith sipped a cup of hot tea and raised his thin pale eyebrows. "Well? What'd the little bastard want?"

"New developments. Ott had some love letters from Elizabeth Bushnell in his possession. He's got a woman's makeup on his shirt and it's not Carla's. There's a glove imprint on the .357. And the lab thinks he was shot with the .22 standing up, and then in the head with the .357 while sitting with his head on the desk."

Smith thought about this. Then he leaned back and sighed. "Well, I've got it all figured out."

"Tell me."

"I will. Here's what happened. Mrs. Bushnell and Ott are having an affair. Fredricks wants to get rid of Ott so he can have Carla to himself. Mrs. Bushnell goes to the Ott house to see Ott, but Fredricks gets there first and Carla lets him in. Fredricks lied about everything else after that. Carla left and went to the party at seven o'clock. Fredricks is in the house with Ott. Fredricks follows him to his den, takes out the .22, and shoots him. He's a bad shot, he gets him in the stomach, then he panics and runs out, leaving the front door slightly ajar. Okay so far?"

Kelso nodded noncommittally. "Keep going."

"Thanks. So Fredricks is gone. Now Mrs. Bushnell arrives. She doesn't need a key because the door's already open. She goes in, finds Ott in his den bleeding and in a lot of pain. She's already decided to get rid of him because the affair's about to come out in the open, and her husband is going to run for the Senate. She wants Ott dead so he can't blab about her affair with him. She probably knows he's got a gun. After all, she shared his bed, she probably shared his little secrets. So she's wearing gloves, she pulls out the desk drawer, picks up Ott's .357, and shoots him in the head as he lies there. Sits there, I mean. Head down on the blotter. She puts the gun on the floor at his fingertips to make it look like suicide, and leaves, not bothering to close the front door all the way. Carla gets back at ten something, finds the body, and calls the cops. Neat, huh?"

Kelso started in on his coconut cream pie. The music in the background was "I'll Be Home for Christmas," and the view out the tall windows was like a Christmas card. And he had to sit here trying to dissect a murder.

"Sort of neat," he said, wishing he could be sharing this atmosphere with Susan Overstreet. Or with Carla. A conflict there—he'd have to resolve it. He shoved it onto a back burner and concentrated on the problem of Ott.

"Whatta you mean, sort of?"

"For one thing, it still leaves the question of why Fredricks would make up the story about Carla being at the house and trying to seduce him. If he was there before seven and Carla left, why would he tell us he was there with her after eight, knowing we could check easily?"

Smith shrugged.

"For another thing, why would Carla lie to us about Fredricks? I mean, if he was there with her before she left for the party, why didn't she say so? She told us he'd never been there at all."

"Maybe she's trying to protect him," Smith suggested.

"Why?"

"Because, Kelso, she's still in love with him." He paused, giving Kelso a direct hard look. "And not with you."

"Gee, thanks."

"Don't mention it. I told you you'd have a conflict with this case."

"For another thing," Kelso said gruffly, "why would Mrs. Bushnell murder Ott to keep their affair secret, but not bother to find and take back her love letters to him?"

"Maybe she didn't know he still had'em."

"Well I'm sorry, but I don't buy it."

"Finish your pie and let's get out of here." Smith lit a Kent. "Tell you what, I'll go call this Tony Deal guy and see if he's home and can see us."

"Go ahead."

Smith left and came back quickly. "He's there. He was just going out, but he'll wait for us. Aren't you through with that pie yet?"

"Coconut cream pie has to be savored," Kelso said testily. "It's not like eating peas and carrots."

After a few more minutes they left Wyatt's, dropped off the .22 automatic at the crime lab, then drove across town.

Tony Deal didn't live in the kind of house Kelso expected a lawyer to have. It was a rather small Cape Cod, white with blue trim, an unassuming little thing on a tiny lot with a couple of forlorn trees in front. Deal let them in and they sat in the living room, which was furnished in early bachelor—a nondescript sofa, two armchairs that matched neither the sofa nor themselves, a ratty carpet. The drapes hung unevenly, the lamp shades were crooked, and the whole place was cluttered with newspapers, magazines, and books. Kelso sat in one of the chairs and noticed that everything in the room was dusty, and there were cobwebs in the corners and all along the baseboards. Everything smelled like the cigar Deal puffed, something long and black.

Tony Deal was thirty-something at the most and looked like the kind of man young girls would go for. He had very broad shoulders and a heavy chest, with lots of black hair visible at the open collar of his dress shirt. His trousers were tight, showing off muscular thighs. He had thick black hair, black eyes that were squinty and piercing, and an aggressive jaw. Kelso thought he resembled a cross between a professional football player and a movie star, maybe one of those guys who played macho cops on TV.

And there was something slick about him, too, something not quite reputable. Or maybe it was simply that Kelso knew he was a lawyer.

"So you guys are cops," Deal said. "Can I offer you anything? I've got some eggnog, I bought it at Kroger, it's not bad. I've got some Bacardi rum to put in it."

"We don't really drink much on the job," Smith told him.

"You could have it without the Bacardi. Or I've got some instant coffee, I could heat some water. And there's some canned Coke. Classic Coke."

"We just ate a big meal," Kelso said. "But thank you anyway."

"We'd like to ask you a few questions about the Ott murder," Smith said.

Tony Deal shrugged his broad shoulders and puffed at the foul-smelling cigar. His black eyes squinted. "The Ott murder. That's the damnedest thing, gentlemen. I knew the man, of course. Not personally, but his wife is a secretary in my law firm. I did tell you I'm an attorney."

"It got mentioned somehow," Smith murmured.

"Yeah. Well, Carla works with us, she's a damn good little girl, too, which is unusual for anybody as good looking as she is, if you know what I mean."

Kelso and Smith exchanged glances, but neither said anything. Kelso was wondering what Carla could find appealing about working for a bunch of cocky sexist lawyers, but maybe they weren't all like Tony Deal. He made his face bland.

"Anyway, I can't imagine who'd have wanted to kill her husband. There's probably not a lot I can tell you." He waved his cigar in the air. "But ask away, I'll do my best."

"That's nice of you," Smith said, with a certain amount of sarcasm which the lawyer appeared not to get. "What firm do you work for?"

"I'm an associate with Baxter, Eisenberg, Ubik, and Baxter. It's one of the better firms in the city, with a statewide reputation. We've handled all the big cases. You remember the Ace Manufacturing thing about a year ago, big labor dispute? That was one of ours. We wound up making a bundle on that. The settlement was in the millions. Our senior partner—"

"What were you doing last night, Mr. Deal?" Kelso asked politely.

There was just the flicker of annoyance in Deal's black gaze, then a shrug of the big shoulders and a wave of the black cigar.

"Yeah," he said, "the facts. I guess you guys just want the facts, right? Just like on "Dragnet." Where was I last night? That's simple. I was at the firm's annual Christmas bash. It was at old man, uh, Mr. Baxter's home, over on Ridgeway Drive. What a house that guy's got. This place"—Deal indicated the room with a wave of his cigar—"isn't much, of course, but I'm sort of the new kid on the block in our firm, sort of low man on the totem pole for the present time. But I'll move up fast. These guys compensate talent. I graduated number two in my class, and I'd have been on the damned law journal if I'd had the time."

"When were you at the party?" Kelso asked, keeping his voice calm with an effort. What a pompous ass, he was thinking.

"Let's see. I don't know, I guess I arrived at the Baxter place a little before seven last night, and I stayed till maybe ten-thirty, maybe a little later. Could've been closer to eleven. You lose track of time at those things. Baxter put on a spread, really threw the booze around, good quality stuff naturally. I think I had several zombies, and the food—"

"Did you leave at all, during that time?" Smith asked.

"Of course not. Why would I?"

"You tell us." Smith's blue eyes were cold, steady.

Kelso decided to back off for a while and let Smith ask the questions. The lawyer's attitude was irritating; if he persisted he'd lose his cool—as Susan liked to say—and allow his temper to show through, giving Deal the upper hand. But Smith was capable of handling a suspect like Deal without giving away anything.

"I already told you," Deal said. "I was there the entire time. Besides . . ." He paused to examine the ash of his cigar, then met Smith's gaze. "What difference does it make?"

"Simply, that you could've left the party, gone over to Ott's place, shot him, and returned to the party." Smith said it very evenly, without so much as a blink.

Deal seemed to be smirking; then, as if to stop the smirk from going any farther, he shoved the smelly black cigar directly into the center of his mouth, forming his lips around it in a tight O, and puffed slowly. When he took the cigar away again the smirk was gone.

"Well, that's an interesting theory, Smith."

"Detective Smith."

"What? Oh, of course. Detective Smith. Quite interesting, but damned unworkable. For one thing, I didn't have any reason to kill Ott. For another, I never left the party, and I've got all kinds of witnesses to that effect. And as a third thing, I wouldn't have killed Ott even if I'd had a reason to." He grinned suddenly, showing a lot of flashy white straight teeth. "Hell, I appreciate the problem you boys've got, with this murder case to solve, and Carla's old man being one of the local bigwigs. I know how these things work. Probably you've got a lot of heat coming down from someplace high up in the ranks, much more important guys than yourselves turning the screws, and down here on your level you've simply got to slug it out and make a showing. I wish I could help you out." He shrugged, showing his teeth again. "But I'm just a lawyer, and if I ever hated somebody I wouldn't murder the guy, I'd sue his ass."

"Did you have any reason to hate Ott?" Smith asked. "Or to sue him?"

"Of course not."

"Then why'd you say that?"

"Just to show you where I'm coming from, that I'm not a violent man."

"Was Carla at that party with you?"

"Well now," Deal said, "that's what we lawyers call an ambiguous question. Do you mean was she there at the same time I was, or do you mean was she there with me personally?"

"Why don't you answer it both ways." Smith's face was a grim mask.

"As far as I can tell you, she arrived a little after seven, and I spent most of the evening either with her personally or within easy view of her, and she left around ten. How's that?"

Smith very slowly and steadily looked around the clutter and cobwebs in the living room, then said, "You must not make a lot of money, Mr. Deal."

Kelso saw the lawyer's face go red. The narrow black eyes closed almost to slits, the aggressive jaw set hard, the lips stopped smiling and went sullen and tight. Smith had drawn blood.

"That's a hell of a thing to say. I don't know that it's any of your goddamned business how much I make. That's just a plain insult."

Smith smiled, and it wasn't a pleasant sight. "You said you were the low man on the totem pole in your law firm. I was making a simple statement of fact."

"I probably make a hell of a lot more than you guys."

"Maybe so," Smith said. "Maybe not. I was only observing." He glanced up at a corner, where a small spider hung in a web near the ceiling. It seemed to have something there with it, maybe a dead bug. "You plan to stay with the firm, Mr. Deal, or go out on your own after a while? Ever thought of hanging out your own shingle?"

"I don't know." Deal was still sullen. "I'll cross that bridge when I come to it."

Kelso thought the lawyer was full of original remarks. Smith was giving up for the time being; he unfolded his lank form from the armchair, strolled over to a window, and stood with his thin hands clasped loosely behind his back, apparently gazing out at the snow that was still falling. It was Kelso's turn again. Kelso decided to try a new tack.

"Were you and Carla good friends?" he asked politely.

Deal eyed him with a faint frown. "Meaning what?"

"Meaning, how well do you know her?"

"You put the question in the past tense," the lawyer said stubbornly. "Carla and I were friends, and we still are. I don't get the point." He paused. "I mean, she's a secretary at the firm, but we talk, we have the occasional lunch. Sure we're friends."

Maybe Smith was right, maybe Kelso had a conflict of interest in the case. He'd put the question in past tense because, he realized uncomfortably, he tended to think of her as somehow belonging to him again. Belonging to Kelso. Her husband was dead, she'd kissed him in the hallway. Angry, he shoved the thought from his mind. She'd kissed Fredricks, too, unless Fredricks was lying. He didn't own Carla. And it was all in the past; his present was Susan. I hate this, he thought.

"I was just wondering," he said, forcing a bland smile, an even tone, "whether Carla ever confided in you about her husband. For example, we understand she and Ott were having some marital problems."

"Oh that." A wave of the cigar again. "Yeah, I heard that. Who *isn't* having marriage problems these days, huh? Well, she may've mentioned something about it." He'd regained his brash demeanor. "As a matter of fact, and I only tell you this because you guys are cops and you're investigating Ott's murder, she told me just a week or two ago that she was pretty pissed at him because she really wanted to get pregnant, start a family, and Ott wasn't being especially cooperative." He chuckled. "Can you imagine being married to that little piece and not wanting to help her out in bed? She wouldn't have to ask *me* twice, I can tell you that." He grinned, then puffed hard at the cigar.

With an effort, Kelso asked, "Do you know if there were any other problems with their marriage? Besides the pregnancy thing? Do you have any idea, for example, whether either of them was involved with anyone else?"

Not even a flicker in the lawyer's black eyes. He'd become smug again, totally in control.

"I'd bet money that Carla wasn't. Like I said, we were friends, I know her pretty damn well. She's not the kind of woman who'd cheat. But Paul Ott . . ." He shrugged. "He's another story. I don't know anything one way or the other, but for my money he was a sneak. Just an impression I got. I saw'im at a party once, one of the law office things and Carla brought him along. Lots of other women were there, some of'em real nice pieces. Ott's eyes were getting a workout the whole evening; he stripped the clothes off of every girl under the age of thirty-five with that look of his. But who knows what he'd do besides look."

"Do you have any idea at all, Mr. Deal, who might've wanted to get rid of Carla's husband?"

"Nope." A satisfied smile.

"Do you know Anne and Arnold Huff?"

"I think Carla's mentioned their names once or twice, but I don't know'em. Never met'em."

"You ever meet Carla's parents?"

"The Bushnells? Sure. Who hasn't? If you're anybody at all in this town you've met the Bushnells. Of course, you guys probably don't live in that particular social register."

"You don't happen to know the Bushnells' opinion of Paul Ott, do you?"

"Wouldn't have a clue."

Kelso could stand it no longer. He got up from his chair and crossed the room, stepping over a pile of magazines and several newspapers and books, to the front door. "Well, thanks for your help, Mr. Deal."

"No problem, guys." Deal got up from the sofa, holding the now stubby cigar in one hand. "Anytime."

Smith turned from the window and moved to join Kelso, who opened the door, letting in a cold gust that rattled the newspapers and sent a brief shower of snow onto the carpet. As they were leaving, Smith turned.

"Hey, Deal."

"Yeah?"

"I hope you get out of your low-man position sometime, so you can make a little money."

Deal's face turned to stone again, but didn't go red. He glowered.

"G'bye," he muttered, and sucked at the cigar. As Kelso and Smith started out across the yard toward the curb, the door slammed like a gunshot behind them.

"What an asshole," Smith said.

"What was all that about his money?" Kelso asked, climbing inside the LTD. "You really struck a nerve, whatever it was."

"I don't have any idea." Smith started the car and drove off along the snowy street. "But it's my experience in a homicide case that when a guy gets as hot under the collar as Deal did over some particular subject, he's got something to hide."

"So you think Deal's hiding something?"

"Yep. I don't know if it's got anything to do with Ott, but he's hiding something. He sure as hell is." He drove for a while, then added, "What an asshole."

"I couldn't agree more." Kelso leaned back in the seat of the big car and watched snow-covered lawns glide past outside the windows. It was growing late in the afternoon, snow still fell, the windows of many of the homes glowed with Christmas-tree lights or decorative candles. A house on the right sported a huge red Santa on the front lawn, and another had Santa in a sleigh with two reindeer on the roof. He felt totally depressed, as though he were in a foreign country which didn't even celebrate Christmas, watching a holiday special on television via satellite. The lights and the decorations seemed alien and remote; he couldn't connect emotionally with them. He was numb. Something occurred to him: he wanted to be alone with Carla. He gritted his teeth.

"Where to?" Smith asked.

"Let's see if we can catch the Huffs in, or the Bushnells, then maybe have some supper."

"We just had lunch."

"I don't care." He flipped the pages of his notebook. "We're closer to the Huffs, let's try them first. Turn right at the next street."

"You realize," Smith said, "that, unless he's lying, Deal just corroborated Carla Ott's alibi. Which shoots Fredricks' story all to hell."

"I realize that. I'm not totally stupid, you know. Turn right, not left."

"It's a one-way street, Kelso, in case you didn't notice."

"So you're going left? Instead of down a block?"

"What difference does it make, as long as we get where we're going. Jesus. You're really on edge. Look, Carla's in the clear now. She was at that party with Deal. She's out of it. You can stop worrying about'er."

"I'm not worrying about her," Kelso snapped. They drove in silence for a while, then he muttered, "Sorry."

"It's okay," Smith said. "I'd feel the same way if it was *my* old flame."

My old flame, Kelso thought miserably. And, as if to remind him, to prevent him from forgetting, he glanced out the window and saw a tree decorated with blue lights.

TWELVE

No one answered their knock at the Huffs' house. They couldn't even see a light on inside, so they left and drove to the Bushnell place, a rather imposing two-story stone thing with dark green shutters, a green front door, green roof, and ivy climbing the walls. It reminded Kelso of an old university building similar to the ones in which he'd taken classes in psychology or math, and brought back a flood of bitterly unwelcome memories of his days with Carla.

The late afternoon sky was depressingly drab, hard dry snow continued falling from it, and a cold wind had come up. A huge red-ribboned wreath on the front door failed to lift his spirits. After Smith pressed the bell button a couple of times, the door opened and Elizabeth Bushnell peered out at them.

"Yes? Oh. It's you. Well, what is it?"

During the time that he and Carla had dated at college, Kelso had once been invited to her parents' house for a weekend before Christmas, and it came to him that her mother, Mrs. Bushnell, had given him just about this same look of mixed irritation and impatience, making him feel as distinctly unwelcome then as now. Well, the hell with it; he wasn't some college kid anymore, he was Sergeant George A. Kelso, Detective Section, Clairmont City Police Department, and he was investigating a homicide, and if she didn't like it she could shove it.

"Sergeant Kelso and Detective Smith," he said, to emphasize the situation and impress it on her mind. She'd better cooperate; he was in no mood to play games. "Mind if we come in and ask you a few more questions about the case?"

"I thought we'd finished with all that last night."

"We're just getting started, ma'am."

She looked doubtful. She was tall, maybe an inch taller than Kelso, which would put her at something close to five eleven. Of course, she was wearing heels; without them, they'd see eye to eye. He grimaced. He and Carla's mother would never see eye to eye.

"I suppose you may as well come in, if it's necessary."

"Thanks."

He and Smith followed her inside, and she led them into a rather starkly furnished room: a marble fireplace with no fire, three wing chairs around a low polished wooden table, a wooden-legged couch on the other side of the table, leaded glass windows along one wall overlooking the snow-covered front lawn. There were no curtains or drapes, nothing on the walls except faded wallpaper. The hardwood floor was bare except for a small Oriental carpet that just covered the area taken up by the chairs, couch, and table.

There wasn't a Christmas ornament or decoration in the room.

"Curious," Kelso murmured.

Elizabeth Bushnell gave him a sharp glance. "What is?"

"Ma'am? Oh, nothing."

"Well, have a seat. May I take your coats?"

"No, thanks, we won't be here that long." Kelso unzipped his parka. Smith took off his sheepskin coat and dropped it onto the floor at the side of the chair he sank into. Kelso took one of the other chairs, and Mrs. Bushnell sat down on the very edge of the middle of the sofa, leaning slightly forward with her knees together and her hands on the cushion to either side, as though she expected that at any moment she might jump up and fly away.

She was a hard-looking woman, even more now than ten years ago. She had that tough, severe look some women get with middle age— black brows heavy and frowning over her black eyes, black thick hair framing a lean chiseled face with rather high cheekbones, a long straight nose, deep lines on either side of lips set in a hard grimace, as though she were sucking on a mint that just happened to taste like manure. All her clothing was black: a turtleneck pullover sweater, wool slacks, high-heeled leather boots. On her left ring finger were a gold band and a huge glittering diamond; on the right ring finger she wore a gold ring set with a brilliant black gem, quite large, matching her earrings. There was something haughty and almost sensuous about the way she held her head up high, emphasizing the slope of her forehead and the pale slenderness of her neck.

Kelso thought about the letters found in Ott's possession, apparently written from Mrs. Bushnell to him, revealing a sexual relationship, and he found himself wondering why she'd been physically attracted to him and how she'd been in bed.

"Well?" she asked, glaring.

And, just at that instant, Smith's portable radio buzzed.

Smith sighed and spoke into it. "Detective Smith."

"Karl? This is the dispatcher—"

"Hold it," he muttered, and stood up. He actually yawned before saying, "Mrs. Bushnell, would you have a telephone I could use?"

"Go back out in the hall," she said. "About halfway down it there's a phone on a stand."

"Thanks." Smith gave her a vague little smile and left the room. There was no door to close; they could hear his footsteps receding down the corridor and, eventually, his voice speaking in a low mumble, but not the actual words.

"Mrs. Bushnell," Kelso said, "this is going to sound a little indelicate, but Paul Ott was murdered, and I can't afford to be too, uh, really diplomatic—"

"Just spit it out for God's sake. I'm a grown woman."

He shrugged. "What was your relationship with him, ma'am?"

On the polished wooden table was a small black box, a black lighter, and a glass ashtray that was perfectly clean. Mrs. Bushnell opened the lid of the box, took out a cigarette, lit it, and let the smoke come out of her mouth in a slowly drifting cloud.

"I believe I've already made it clear that I despised Paul."

"Yes, ma'am. But it turns out he had some letters from you, and we, uh, found them."

"Oh?"

Kelso took a deep breath and let it out. "Apparently they're love letters. From you to him."

She just stared at him for a while, smoking slowly, her eyes as black and empty as holes. Finally she said in a low flat voice, "They aren't love letters."

"Well—"

"Have you read them?"

"No, ma'am. Not yet."

"When you read them, George, you'll realize they aren't about love." She tapped cigarette ash into the spotless tray. "They're about sex. There's a difference, you know."

He wondered if he was out of his depth. "I suppose there often is. But, then, you admit . . ."

"I admit I slept with him, if that's what you're asking. It wasn't important to me, not in any real sense. It was something to do. He had a nice body—well, a young body anyway, and he was good in bed. Surprisingly." Her voice held a constant sneering undertone. "Does that shock you, George? That I had sex with my daughter's husband?"

Kelso wasn't shocked, not in the normal way. He'd been a cop too long, seen and heard too many things to be shocked by something like this. On the other hand, it wasn't just anybody; it was Carla's mother, Carla's husband. The Carla he'd been in love with. If he'd married Carla, would Mrs. Bushnell have tried it with him? For some reason he was angry, not at this woman, but at Carla. Mrs. Bushnell merely disgusted him.

"The only thing I don't understand," he said, "is how you could've done this to Carla."

She gave a short hoarse laugh. "Oh hell—Carla *knew* about it."

"Ma'am?"

"I said, she knew about it. I think she caught him saying things to me on the phone once, something like that. We talked about it very frankly. I suppose you're shocked again."

"What was her reaction?" His voice sounded strained.

Mrs. Bushnell shrugged. "Nothing much. As I recall, she called me a rather vulgar name, then said she'd suspected he'd been screwing around, and that was about it. You have to understand that all this has been recent, like within the past couple of months, and she'd already started to think about divorcing him. What the hell, it doesn't matter now. He's dead."

"I'd like to get this straight," Kelso said. "For the past couple of months you and Paul Ott were sleeping together, and Carla knew it."

"Exactly."

He was having trouble seeing anything in it, anything related to the murder. Unless, he thought, Smith's theory was right. What if Mrs. Bushnell had killed Ott to keep the affair quiet, in order to safeguard her husband's chances of being elected to the Senate. Presumably Carla wouldn't have talked.

"Mrs. Bushnell, while you and Paul Ott were together, on these occasions . . . was it often?"

"I don't know. Depends on what you mean by often. Two or three times a week, maybe. I lost count."

"Did he know Carla wanted to divorce him? Did he ever say anything to you about it?"

She laughed low in her throat again. "He never talked to me about Carla. All he did was brag, try to impress me. He couldn't get it through his stupid little head that all I wanted was sex. I didn't give a damn about his aspirations." She stabbed out the cigarette. "He was such a pompous little ass, full of crap about how he was going to make it big, buy things for me. Very self-important. He told me how powerful he was."

"Powerful?"

"Sure. Arnold Huff, for instance. Paul had something big on him, had him right where he wanted him. Had him in some kind of a business bind, stood to make a bundle of money. Didn't he ever stop to think that I've got all the money I need? With my husband, what the hell did I need with Paul Ott?"

"What did he have on Arnold Huff?"

"Who knows? Another of his little fantasies, probably."

"Ma'am, did your husband know about you and Paul?"

"Of course not." She stood up suddenly, towering over him. "You don't intend to tell him, do you?"

"Not if it isn't necessary," Kelso said.

Smith wandered back into the room, but instead of sitting down again, stood near the door. There was a peculiar expression on his thin pale face, and his eyes were like ice.

"I've got some interesting news for you, Mrs. Bushnell," he said.

"Really?"

"Uh huh. One of our detectives talked to a couple who live across the street from your daughter. Ever hear of the Engels? John and Doris Engel?"

She frowned. "No. Never."

"Well, they're directly across the street from the Otts. It turns out they know Carla, and they know who you are. They know your car. You have a Lincoln?"

"Yes."

"Last night about twenty after nine the Engels saw your Lincoln pull up into Carla's driveway. They saw you get out and enter the house. About ten minutes later they saw you come out, get in your car, and drive away again."

For a moment or so it was absolutely quiet in the room. It felt cold. It was stark, with no fire; it reminded Kelso of a hospital. Finally Smith spoke.

"You care to tell us what you were doing at the Ott place last night between nine and nine-thirty, Mrs. Bushnell?"

George Kelso stood up and glanced at the leaded glass windows. It was almost dark outside; he could see the reflection of the room, with himself and Smith and Elizabeth Bushnell standing motionless like statues. He could hear himself breathing.

He turned his head to look directly at the woman, watching her intensely frowning black eyes and grimacing mouth, and waited for her answer.

THIRTEEN

"I'm going to tell you exactly what happened," she said. "And it's the truth. But you won't believe me."

"Really?" Kelso blinked. "Why not?"

"Because you won't, that's all. If I'd thought you might have believed me, I'd have told you from the start."

"Well, tell us now," Smith said.

"I knew Carla was going to that Christmas party, and I knew she was leaving around seven. Russell, my husband, said he was going out for a while to meet a friend of his, something about insurance. So around nine, after he left, I called Paul but got no answer. That made me angry, because I'd already told him I'd give him a call when Russell left."

"In other words," Smith said, "you and Paul Ott had planned to get together last night."

Kelso wondered if Smith had listened outside the door.

Mrs. Bushnell nodded, frowning fiercely. "We'd planned to meet. So when he didn't answer I simply got in my car and drove over there."

"Wait a minute," Kelso said. "If he didn't answer, why'd you think he might be there?"

"I didn't know. Sometimes he'd get into these pouting moods, he was like a damned child at times, and refuse to answer the phone or even go to the door. I figured he was in another of his moods, probably holed up in his den with a drink, trying to shut out the world."

"Even though he'd planned to see you?"

"He wasn't rational, damn it. That's what I'm trying to tell you."

"He wasn't rational," Smith muttered. "Go ahead."

"I will, if you'll both shut up and let me. Now, as I was saying, I drove over there a little past nine. If those snooping busybodies across the street say I got there at nine-twenty, then I did. I wasn't keeping track of time at that point. The first thing I noticed was that the front door wasn't closed completely; it was hanging an inch or two open, in other words. Nothing occurred to me about it, it was just something I noticed. I knocked, and then I went in. In my own mind I was certain Paul was there. I went back to the den. The door was open. I entered, and saw him at his desk. There was blood on his head. He was dead. So I left the house and drove home." She got another cigarette from the black box, lit it, and hissed out a stream of smoke. "That's it, that's all that happened."

Kelso looked at the woman. He hadn't trusted her ten years ago while dating Carla, and he didn't trust her now. It was obvious that she could have killed Ott. He started thinking about means, motive, and opportunity, trying to sort it out.

Motive: she had that. She'd been sleeping with Ott. If something like that got out it could ruin her husband's political career. Suppose she'd grown tired of Ott and told him it was over, and he'd put up a fight. That might explain why she rushed over there when he didn't answer the phone. The whole thing could've been part of an argument. She said she'd gone in, found Ott dead, and left, but the neighbors had indicated she'd been in there about ten minutes. Maybe she'd gone in, they'd argued, Ott had threatened to talk unless she slept with him again, and she'd shot him.

Opportunity: she'd had that. She'd just admitted going over there last night, within the time frame of the murder. She'd admitted actually being in the room with him.

Means: this was the sticking point. Ott had been shot once in the stomach with a .22 which might or might not prove to belong to Fredricks—the ballistics test would tell that. But he'd been shot in the head with a .357, presumably his own. Assuming Mrs. Bushnell had shot him, which gun had she used? Surely not Fredricks' .22? Ott's gun?

All this rushed through his mind like lightning as he stood in the dismal stark room watching Elizabeth Bushnell frown and puff at her cigarette.

"Mrs. Bushnell," he said, with the strange feeling that he was probing in the dark, "I'm sorry to have to ask this, but do you think Paul Ott was more involved in the affair than you were?"

"What . . . I don't get the question."

"I mean, apparently with you it was just sex."

"Exactly."

"Was it more than that to him? Could he have been in love with you or anything?"

Her face relaxed a little and she gave a low chuckle. "I don't think

Paul knew the meaning of the word. I doubt if he even loved Carla, much less me. He was just a horny little bastard, and I seemed to be able to satisfy him more than Carla could."

Kelso thought about Carla trying to satisfy Ott, then violently forced the image from his mind. He looked at Mrs. Bushnell, and compared her to Carla. Could it really have been that Ott had preferred this woman? She was sensuous in her own way, but at least twenty years older than Carla. Not bad for a fifty-year-old woman, though, if you looked at it objectively. She was nicely built, with a heavy bust, small waist, wide hips, long legs. There was something darkly attractive about her hard face, with those burning black eyes and cruel lips.

"Had you ever considered breaking it off?" he asked.

A shrug. "Now and then. After all, it *was* dangerous. If Russell ever found out, or if anyone else ever did . . . well, the consequences could've been a disaster."

Smith cleared his throat loudly. "Then what the hell were you taking such a risk for? Why'd you write those letters? Did you *want* people to find out?"

"Of course not!" Her eyes snapped at him. "Have you ever had an affair? Probably not, to look at you. When you're having an affair you don't think about things like that, or if you do, you ignore them. You don't think anyone's going to find out. You think you've got it under control. I didn't know Paul was keeping the goddamned letters; he said he was burning them. And how did I know he'd get murdered and wind up having the damned things around for the police to find?"

"Ma'am," Kelso said, "when you went into the den last night, can you tell us exactly what you saw?"

"I already did."

"But more specifically. For example, Ott was at his desk. Can you describe his exact position?"

"I'll try. Well, he was sitting in his chair with his head down on the desk, facing away from me. I've already said there was blood on his head."

"Anything else? For example, a gun? A weapon of any kind?"

"Didn't I mention that? Of course there was a gun. It was on the floor, just under his hand."

"Right or left?" Smith asked.

"Right or left what?"

"Hand."

"Oh. It was under his right hand, of course, because . . ."

Elizabeth Bushnell stopped speaking and got a very strange look on her face. Just for a moment her eyes widened, she seemed to be drifting into a kind of dream or trance, turning inward, shutting off the present. Then, like flipping a switch, her eyes narrowed again, the frown returned, she was back with them. If it had meant anything, Kelso didn't know what.

"Because what?" Smith asked.

"In his, well, under his right hand, because that's where I saw it. On the floor under his right hand, which was dangling straight down. My God, I've just realized he probably shot himself."

"Why?" Kelso asked.

"Are you crazy? Isn't it obvious? He's sitting there at his desk, he's having an affair with me, Carla wants to divorce him. He won't answer the damn phone. It's obvious. Before she went to the party last night, she told him she was kicking him out. So not only does he lose his wife, he loses me as well."

"I thought he wasn't romantically involved with you," Smith said, with a little sneer.

"He wasn't. But he sure as hell loved sex with me."

"And so," Kelso said, feeling depressed, "you're suggesting that Ott shot himself because Carla said she was going to divorce him?"

"Well it sure looks like suicide to me," she replied.

"Why would losing Carla have meant losing you as well?" Smith wanted to know.

"It might've seemed that way to him. Paul wasn't especially imaginative. He might've thought that if Carla kicked him out and I was no longer his mother-in-law, I wouldn't be available anymore."

Kelso decided to press on with the rest of it. "Mrs. Bushnell, did you happen to notice blood on his body anywhere besides his head?"

"No, of course not. But I didn't *examine* him."

"Why didn't you call the police?"

"For obvious reasons. There I was in his den, we'd been sleeping together, I had a lot to lose by being involved in the thing. I knew Carla would be coming home eventually, so I figured let her find him and call the police."

"Gee, that was nice of you," Smith told her.

"I wasn't trying to be nice. I was being practical."

"Mrs. Bushnell," Kelso said, "do you own a gun?"

"No. I detest guns."

"What about your husband?"

"I think he keeps one in the house, but I don't know where, and I don't have the slightest idea what it is. A man in his position . . . well, it's okay to protect your home, isn't it?"

"When you were over there last night," Kelso said, "are you sure nobody else was in the house besides Paul Ott?"

"Of course I'm not sure. I didn't search the place. I went straight back to the den, found Paul dead, and left."

"The neighbors say you were inside around ten minutes," Smith said. "Did you stand there for ten minutes looking at his body?"

Mrs. Bushnell bristled. "I've had about enough of this. I've answered your questions and told you the truth. If you'd rather take the word of a couple of busybodies, go ahead. But I'm telling you I went in there, found Paul in the den, saw he was bloody and dead, and went back out to my car and drove away."

"Do you expect your husband home any time soon, ma'am?" Kelso asked, putting away his notebook.

"He's having dinner with some political friends of his. I don't know when he'll be back. What the hell time is it?" She glared at her watch, which was tiny and gold with a black face. Kelso hadn't noticed it before because it had been hidden beneath the sleeve of her sweater. "Christ, it's almost five-thirty. I'm supposed to meet somebody for dinner. I've got to go."

Smith picked his coat up from the floor, put it on, and nodded at her expressionlessly. "Thanks for your time."

"Sure. I'll show you out."

"It's okay," Kelso told her. "We can find it."

"I'll show you out," she repeated, and led them into the hall and to the front door, which she held open.

"Thank you," Kelso said. "Sorry about the inconvenience."

"Forget it. Oh hell. George, can I speak to you a minute, privately?"

Smith shrugged and went on outside. Kelso stood by the door.

"Yes, ma'am?" They were so close, he could smell her perfume. She was frowning intensely, and seemed suddenly nervous.

"Look, about this thing with Paul . . ." Some of the hardness went out of her face, leaving her looking tired and rather frustrated, like someone who has lost a valuable possession and has almost, but not quite, given up hopes of getting it back.

"Ma'am?"

"Do you think it'll have to come out? I mean, publicly?"

Kelso almost felt sorry for her. "I'll see if it can be kept private, Mrs. Bushnell."

She'd gone as far as she could. The hardness returned. "Thanks. Goodnight." She looked away, avoiding his gaze.

"Goodnight," he said, and went out into the yard, where Smith stood puffing a cigarette and snow fell in the gathering darkness.

FOURTEEN

As they were driving away in the LTD Smith said, "Do you mind if we call it a day? This case is driving me nuts."

"It's okay with me. Who was the phone call from?"

"Meyer, of course. He'd sent Broom around to those neighbors, the Engels, and to the rest of the people in the area. Now he's decided the Bushnell broad did it, and we should arrest her instead of Fredricks. How that little idiot ever got to be a detective sergeant is beyond me."

"Have you ever noticed," Kelso said, peering gloomily out at the Christmas lights, "that the ranks in our department don't coincide with the ranks in most other police departments?"

"Why should they? Everything else in our department's screwed up, why shouldn't ranks be, too? Hell, they've put Leill in charge of the Detective Section and made him a frigging lieutenant, and promoted Meyer to detective sergeant. I'm a detective, you're a sergeant . . . I mean, what does it *mean?*"

"Frigging," Kelso said. "What's that?"

"Huh? Oh, it's just an expression I use occasionally. By the way—"

"Are you planning to stop for this light?"

"I can see it, I know it's red." Smith hit the brakes and the LTD skidded into the intersection. He slammed it into reverse, backed until he was even with the corner, and said, "See?"

"By the way, you were saying . . ."

"Oh, yeah. What're you doing about Susan?"

"In what way?"

"Did you stay over there last night?"

He wasn't sure it was any of Smith's business, but they had become friends as well as mere partners, so maybe it was. He shrugged. "Yeah."

"No kidding, how'd it go?"

"What do you want, a blow by blow?"

"Don't get all huffy. I was just curious."

"I feel guilty, if that's what you're getting at. Here I am, supposedly semiofficially or unofficially or some damn way or another quasi-attached and not quite but almost engaged to Susan, and now here's Carla back in my life, and I feel guilty."

"You'd better watch it with Carla, Kelso. That broad's trouble. Sorry, but I mean it. I can understand how she wrapped you around her little finger . . . well, what I mean is . . ."

"I'd rather not talk about it. The light's green now, by the way."

"I can see it. I mean, I *can* drive, after all." Smith gunned the engine and shot through the intersection. The rear end fishtailed slightly on the snow that was building up. "Like to see you do that in your VW."

"I can only drive safely in my VW. Do you want to get a bite somewhere? I'd like to know what you thought about Mrs. Bushnell."

"Hunter's?"

"Sure."

They arrived there just before six and went inside. Hunter's was what Kelso thought of as a plain food restaurant. They sat at a Formica-topped table near plate-glass windows with a view of Main Street, which was starting to resemble a so-called winter wonderland since there wasn't enough Sunday traffic to keep the snow from accumulating. All the buildings across the street were dark except for a corner drugstore, so the only other lights out there were the red, green, blue, and yellow ones the city had strung from lamppost to lamppost. Kelso expected a horse-drawn sleigh to come along at any moment, then wondered if there were sleighs that weren't horse-drawn.

A dozen regulars dotted the place and the atmosphere was vaguely festive; Christmas tunes played softly in the background, somebody had put up lots of fake holly and mistletoe, and fake snow had been sprayed around the edges of the windowpanes. The current musical selection was "It's Beginning to Look a Lot Like Christmas."

"Is that the Lennon Sisters?" Smith asked, lighting a cigarette.

"I think it's the Supremes."

"They never did this song."

A young blond waitress named Florine came over to take their orders, batted her big blue eyes at them, and smiled.

"Hi, honey," she said to Smith; and to Kelso, "Hello, sir."

"I'm not 'sir,' Florine. I'm George."

"I'll have vegetable soup," Smith told her. "And a glass of milk. And a date with you."

"Soup and milk. And you, sir?"

"Meat loaf, mashed potatoes, and hot apple pie. Some coffee."

"You boys working on Sunday?"

"Naw," Smith said. "We just came out to find some women."

"If I see any, I'll let you know." She grinned and went away.

"Mrs. Bushnell could've shot Ott," Kelso said.

"Sure she could've."

"She could've gone in there last night at nine-twenty and shot him in the guts with a .22 she got from somewhere, and then decided to finish him off with his own .357."

"Or," Smith said, "she could've found him already bleeding from the .22 wound and killed him with his .357. But you have to remember a couple of things."

Kelso sighed. "Such as?"

"Such as, Fredricks has a .22 and it's been fired, and he admits to being over there last night."

"He admits to being there with Carla, but we already know Carla wasn't there. She was at the party with Tony Deal."

Smith leered. "You're really stuck on protecting that broad, aren't you?"

"I'm not protecting her. She was at the party. Deal backed her up on it."

"That sleaze? He'd lie to the Pope. And he can't back her up a hundred percent; he wasn't with her every second."

"Okay, okay, so what's your point?"

"Point is, all we've really got is a bunch of people who maybe had a reason to hate Ott, who maybe were at Ott's house last night and maybe weren't, and we're still no further along than we ever were in terms of those two gunshot wounds. I mean, even if ballistics says Fredricks' .22 fired the gut shot, where's that leave us? Fredricks as a possible for deadly assault, or maybe attempted murder, and nobody to hang the actual killing on. Assuming the bastard didn't blow out his own brains, however few they may have been."

Florine brought coffee and milk and they stopped talking, then she went away and Kelso said, "We're going to have to start eliminating some people. I'm tired, I can't think. You know, this affair between Ott and Mrs. Bushnell is driving me crazy. I can't see how it fits into the rest of the picture. Would she sleep with the guy three times a week and write him letters about it, practically inviting a scandal, and then turn right around and murder him just to keep it quiet? It doesn't make sense."

"Her wanting to screw Ott doesn't make sense, if you ask me."

Kelso looked at him. "What about his attraction to her?"

"Well, I wouldn't kick her out of bed, if that's what you mean."

Kelso laughed softly. "You wouldn't kick anybody out of bed."

"I've been known to."

The food came, and they ate for a while without talking. The meat loaf was perfect, the mashed potatoes were real, and the apple pie was freshly baked in a bowl with heavy cream. Kelso stirred two sugars and some cream into his second cup of coffee and leaned back in his chair, found his pipe, filled it and lit it. Outside the windows it was completely dark now, making the interior of Hunter's seem brittle and cold under the fluorescent ceiling lights. "Silent Night" was playing.

"That song always depresses me," Smith said.

"Why?"

"I don't know. It just does."

"We've still got Russell Bushnell to interview. And those people, the Huffs. I suppose we can do it tomorrow."

Smith said, "Well, I'm sure as hell not doing it tonight. Hey, Florine, can I have a cup of tea?"

"I'm beginning to think you were right," Kelso said.

"Oh yeah? About what?"

"I'm beginning to think Fredricks went over there and shot Ott in the stomach with his .22, and then Mrs. Bushnell got there sometime later and killed him with his own .357."

"Did you happen to ask her if she knew about his .357, Kelso?"

"Oh Jesus Christ," Kelso muttered. Then, with a heavy sigh, "I'll do it tomorrow."

"You know, Kelso, we could go back to the simplified version of this thing. Fredricks packs his .22 automatic in his briefcase full of mementos, drives down here from Kokomo on Friday and checks into the Downtowner. He broods, tries to call her, she hangs up on him. Maybe by now he hates her guts. She calls him last night, or maybe he just goes over there on his own, and winds up begging and pleading with her. Too bad, she's married to Ott, he's out in the cold. He thinks, what the hell, I'll get rid of Ott and then I can have her. He finds Ott in the den, pulls out his .22, shoots Ott in the stomach. Suddenly he's terrified. He's just committed a murder. What to do? Make it look like suicide. He gets Ott's .357 Magnum and lets him have it in the head, places the gun on the floor under Ott's hand, and beats it out of there." He sipped his tea, waiting for Kelso's response.

Kelso puffed thoughtfully at his pipe. "I can punch a few holes in that, unfortunately."

"Be my guest."

"Okay. First hole, Fredricks claims he was over there last night between eight and eight-thirty, with Carla. If he was actually there and shot Ott, why'd he tell us he was there, and why'd he lie about the time? He's not exactly stupid. Surely he'd have known Carla would contradict him on it. Second hole, why'd he admit to having the .22 at all? We didn't know it until he told us. Third hole, how'd he know about Ott's .357? It supposedly was in a desk drawer."

Smith drained his tea. "I don't know about the times. Maybe Carla's lying about it, too. As for the .22, we were about to look in his briefcase, we'd have found his gun."

"And Ott's .357?"

"Ott might've had it out, or gotten it out to try to defend himself after he was shot. Hell, I don't know. Let's go home."

They paid and left. During the short drive to Smith's apartment Kelso was silent, mulling over the complications in the case. Nothing really fit. And however he tried to sift the pieces, everything seemed to come back to the two gunshots and the two guns. It was completely dark and snowing lightly. At the apartment he got out and strode toward his VW.

"Want to come in for a drink or some chess?" Smith asked.

"No thanks. Susan's waiting for me."

"Lucky you. Well, see you in the morning, I guess."

"See you."

"Good luck tonight, Kelso."

"Shove it, Smith."

"G'night."

"Goodnight."

He got in, started up the Bug, revved the engine a few times, and drove north, shivering in the cold and trying desperately not to think about Carla.

As soon as Susan Overstreet opened her door and let him in, he could tell by the look on her face that something was not quite right. She hardly ever got really angry or shouted at him, but when irritated a kind of coolness would set in, she would become rather reserved, almost aloof, and watch him closely as though waiting for some sort of reaction which usually he was at a loss to provide. She had that look now, and that attitude.

"You got some messages, George." She took his coat. "Three people called here for you. Are you ready for dinner?"

"Dinner," he said lamely, remembering that he shouldn't have eaten with Smith. "Dinner."

"Did you and Karl eat, after you said you'd be here for dinner?"

"We had a snack. What're the messages?"

He followed her into the kitchen, where he could smell chicken. She looked good, as usual, in tight faded jeans and sneakers, a bulky brick red sweater, little gold earrings.

"One of your favorites," she said, putting plates on the table. "Fried chicken, mashed potatoes, no salad. Hot rolls. And I made a chocolate pie with whipped cream on top."

He hated himself. "I could use a bite."

"A bite, huh?" They sat facing each other. "Meyer called. He wants you to call him back, he wouldn't tell me what it's about. Stanley Broom called and said he found Russell Bushnell and he wants to tell you about it." She gave him her reserved look.

"Yes?"

"That Carla woman called. How'd she know to try here? Did you give her my number?"

His face felt warm. In reality, he had no idea. He definitely had not given Susan's number to Carla. "The department has it. I suppose they might've given it to her, if she was trying to get in touch with me about something important."

"Aren't you going to eat anything at all, George?"

Sighing, he put a drumstick on his plate, a dab of potatoes. There was something green in an oval dish. He regarded it suspiciously. "What's that?"

"Green bean casserole. It's delicious—but you aren't required to have any. Do you want to know what Carla said?"

"I suppose so." If he just didn't feel so damned guilty. And the guilt angered him. Surely there was nothing to feel guilty about, he'd done nothing wrong, he hadn't instigated the kiss in the hallway, he'd acted properly, he was only conducting a murder investigation.

Susan's wide brown eyes, less than warm, gazed steadily at him from across the table. "She would like you to come over to her house sometime this evening. She's got to talk to you in person, and it's important." She watched him, waiting.

He could hear the tap-tap-tap of her toe against the table leg, like a ticking bomb.

"No kidding." He shrugged, forced himself to take a bite of the chicken leg. "Well, I'll give them a call after we eat."

"Is that all you've got to say?"

He knew what she wanted to hear. He was supposed to say that he loved her, that although he'd once been in love with Carla there wasn't anything left now, that Carla meant nothing to him, that she was simply a possible suspect in a probable homicide. That might disarm the ticking bomb. But the words didn't seem to want to come out of his mouth. He swallowed the chicken and said, "It's not what you think, Susan."

Her eyes were big, her eyebrows were raised very high.

"I love you," he blurted, something he never said, something that, for him, was like taking his clothes off in public.

For another few seconds she stared at him, then a faint smile crinkled the corners of her eyes and softened her lips. She shook her head and said, "Poor George. Just shut up and eat."

"Yes, ma'am."

The tapping of her foot ceased.

Somehow he managed to consume the entire piece of chicken, which was quite good, and two or three more dabs of potatoes, which were creamy just the way he liked them. He even ate a small piece of her famous chocolate pie, feeling his stomach bloat against his waistband. Then she poured him a cup of coffee and started out of the kitchen.

"You can use the phone in here. I'll be in the living room." Her tone was still slightly severe, and he thought it best not to disagree. When she'd gone, he got up, went over to the wall phone, got out his notebook, and called Meyer at home.

"It's me," he said. "Susan said you called."

"Kelso. Where the hell are you?"

"At Susan's house. Eating supper."

"Jesus Christ," Meyer snapped. "I've got the lab working overtime and you're socializing."

"I was—"

"Forget it. I've got some information for you. They checked that .22 you and Smith took off of Henry Fredricks. The ammo in its clip is identical to the ejected shell they found on the floor of Ott's den, and when they test fired it and compared the slug with the one they took out of Ott's belly, whatta you suppose they found?"

"They were different?"

"No, you idiot, they were identical. Fredricks' .22 fired the bullet that hit Ott in the guts."

Kelso considered this for a moment, then said, "Were there any prints on the gun?"

"That's my second point. The gun itself had been wiped clean. But whoever wiped it forgot about the clip. Criminals are such stupid bastards, it's unbelievable. Anyway, they took three or four good prints from the clip. Would you like to guess the result?"

Kelso felt a curious churning in his stomach. "No."

"Then I'll tell you. They don't match the ones we took from Carla Ott, or any of her husband's. They're going to run them through the files, but I'm betting they belong to that guy Fredricks."

"Fredricks," Kelso muttered, frowning hard.

"That probably doesn't mean a damn thing, of course. You'd expect to find his prints on his own gun. Whoever shot Ott wiped the outside of it but not the clip. Could've been Fredricks or anybody else."

"They're probably his," Kelso said. "Otherwise, you'd have found two different persons' prints. Of course . . . you don't know yet."

"Brilliant, Kelso." Meyer's voice was full of sarcasm. "But the point is, you can eliminate Carla Ott for now, unless she did it wearing gloves. Are you listening, Kelso?"

"Yes."

Did he feel relieved? He wasn't sure.

"Lieutenant Leill's been talking to the mayor on and off, and to some aide or other in the mayor's office. This case is what's called politically sensitive. Do you understand that?"

Kelso sighed. "I understand."

"Good. Now here's the thing. As you may or may not fully appreciate, Russell Bushnell's politically important around here. Lots of dough's being spent to put him in the Senate next fall. Okay?"

"What's the point?"

"The point is, Kelso, you're to hold off on making an arrest until the prosecuting attorney completes a full investigation on his own and talks to Leill. You're to continue your investigation, but don't make any arrests. You got that?"

"Yes. I've got it." He was very tired.

"Good."

Kelso said, "Even if it's Fredricks?"

"Even if it's Fredricks. This is very explosive. Are you reading me, Kelso?"

"Yes."

"Good. I'll see you in the morning. Try being at work on time for a change." Meyer hung up.

Kelso shut his eyes tightly and tried to think. Then he put off thinking, opened his eyes, and pressed the numbers for Stanley Broom.

"Hello?" A familiar pleasant voice. Kelso visualized the almost perpetual smile that went with it, in the plump good-natured face.

"Hi, this is Kelso. I'm at Susan's, she said you needed to talk to me." It was an effort for him to sound polite.

"Hi, George. How's it going?"

"So so."

"Well, I managed to locate Russell Bushnell late this afternoon, and talked to him for a while. I'm sorry to bother you, I thought you might be interested."

"Sure."

"Bushnell was with his wife last night, at their home, until about nine, then he left and met a man named Lawrence Vandenberg, an insurance agent with an office on Fourth Street. He says it was partly to discuss insurance and partly just to have a drink with a friend."

"I see."

"So in other words," Broom said cheerfully, "he has an alibi until 9 P.M., and then again shortly afterward. I didn't talk to him for very long, I thought you might want to follow up on him yourself. But he does have an alibi."

"Thanks," Kelso managed to say, gritting his teeth. "I'll check with him tomorrow. Was there, uh, anything else?"

"Just one other thing. I suppose you know about the tape of that old movie, *Topper Returns*, in Ott's VCR? Well, I checked all the television and cable stations in the area, and it wasn't being shown anywhere in the Clairmont City viewing area last night. So I went back through all the listings for two months, and drew the same blank."

"Yes." Surely the man was leading up to something.

"But," Broom said, sounding enthusiastic, "three months ago, on a Tuesday night in September, it was shown here locally on channel four, at 9 P.M. So Ott could've taped it then. They're checking it now, for commercials and things like that."

"Hmm."

"So now we know he taped it, and was watching it last night."

"Thanks," Kelso said.

"George? You sound sort of down. Are you all right?"

"Just tired."

"Well, I'll let you go. Have a nice evening."

"You too."

He hung up. The inevitable had arrived. The chills returned and his stomach jumped. Angrily he punched the number, wondering if Susan was within hearing distance. The phone was answered on the first ring; Carla must have been waiting over it.

"Yes?"

"This is George."

"Can you come over here right away?"

He cringed. It was going to be very difficult. "I'm not sure how soon, Carla. It might be a while. I'm sort of . . . tied up."

"Who's Susan Overstreet?" she asked, point-blank.

And he snapped, "It's none of your damned business."

Her voice was softer. "I'm sorry. But I've got to talk to you. When can you get here?"

"I don't know. I'll make it as soon as I can, but I can't promise when it'll be."

There was a long pause; he could hear her breathing. Then she said, "Well, I'll be here. Okay?"

"Okay."

"Please hurry." She hung up.

Kelso replaced the receiver with a bang and turned to see Susan standing in the hall doorway gazing at him with grave eyes, frowning slightly.

"I think you should go right away, George." There was little warmth in her voice. "It's your job."

"I don't . . ." Words failed him.

She stepped into the kitchen and put a hand on his arm. "I'll still be here when you get back."

"Okay."

He put on his parka and went out.

FIFTEEN

All the way to Carla's house, down Amsterdam Avenue and then east on Washington to Lincoln Avenue, all Kelso could think of were the fingerprints on the magazine of the .22 automatic that had been used to shoot her husband in the stomach. Despite Meyer's reasoning, Kelso knew that no one was ruled out. Even if the prints turned out to belong to Fredricks, anyone—including Carla—could've used the gun and wiped the outside of it clean. On the other hand, it was starting to look more and more like Fredricks. So why did he have this terrible burning in his guts?

He wondered what she wanted with him.

When he pulled the Volkswagen up in the driveway of 1704 Lincoln Avenue the porch light was on and it had quit snowing. Shuddering, he got out and went up the walk. Carla opened the front door just as he was reaching for the bell.

"Hi, George."

He stood woodenly, like a toy soldier, staring at her. In the front window the blue lights glowed on the Christmas tree.

"Hello," he said.

"Would you like to go for a walk?" He noticed that she was wearing a coat and gloves. "Remember how we used to walk around the campus at night, at Christmas, and it was always so magical, with snow on the ground and those woods so pretty with the little river running through them?" Without waiting for his reply, she stepped outside, pulled the door closed and locked it, then turned to smile at him. Her gray-green eyes seemed very bright. She looked beautiful.

"Where'd you want to walk?" he asked helplessly.

"Oh, maybe just around the neighborhood. We could look at the Christmas lights, some of the homes near here are knockouts. Come on, it'll be fun." She slipped her arm through his and led him down to the sidewalk, which was covered with an inch or so of very dry snow. "It'll be like old times," she said softly.

Kelso fell into step alongside her. The air was cold on his face and he shoved his hands into his pockets. She held tightly to his right arm.

"Poor George. No gloves?"

"Lost 'em."

"You need to buy another pair."

"I know."

It was like a fairyland; the snow was on the evergreens that proliferated along here, and on the lawns. On either side, large houses loomed darkly, many of them displaying light arrangements ranging from pretty to spectacular. He was acutely aware of her body next to his as they walked.

"Are you cold?" she asked.

"I'm okay. Why?"

"I can feel you trembling."

"Sorry."

"George, do you remember that dinner we went to in the Union Building, the first year we dated?"

"The Madrigal Dinner."

"Right. And afterward, we walked into the woods and there was snow all over the place, and we sat on a green bench in the dark and . . . do you remember?"

"Sort of." Actually, he did remember. His pulse quickened.

"It was the first time you told me you loved me."

She stopped walking suddenly and turned to face him. They were in the middle of a block, in the blackness between streetlights, but he could see her face in the light that was reflected from the snow. Her eyes were very wide, and it seemed to him that they held tears.

She whispered, "George?"

He was aware that his legs were shaking, his knees banging together. He tried to control it but wasn't successful.

"What?"

Her arms went around his neck, pulling him toward her, and she kissed him. Her lips were warm, soft, and slightly parted. Kelso put his arms around her waist and hugged her to him, letting himself go. All the anger and frustration he'd felt about her came surging out of him, all the repressed memories and hopes and dreams, all the stuff about the blue Christmas tree and the family with two children and a big dog, all the love and promises and magic, and he kissed her, pressing himself against her. She buried her face in his neck and whispered in his ear, clinging to him.

"George?"

"What?"

"Stop shaking."

"I can't."

"George?"

"What?"

"I still love you."

"Carla—"

"I still love you, George. I never stopped loving you. Oh God, George, I'm so sorry. For everything. I didn't know what I wanted." She was crying now, sobbing, he felt her slender body racked with it, she held him tighter. "I love you so much, George."

And shaking, freezing, knowing it was wrong, yet believing it then and there in spite of everything, he said gently, "I love you, Carla. Don't cry. It's all right. I love you."

"I'm sorry. I'm so sorry."

"It's all right. I love you."

He pushed her away from him, carefully, and kissed her cheeks, tasting her tears. "I've got a handkerchief." He got it out, dabbed at her face and eyes with it.

"Here, I'll do it." She laughed a little, sniffing but no longer crying. "I'm sorry, I feel so damned stupid. Here." She handed him back his handkerchief, put her hands on his upper arms and gripped tightly, looking closely into his eyes. "What am I going to do, George? I love you, and I don't know what to do."

"What about your husband?"

"He's dead."

"That's not what I meant."

She sighed. "I know. What I mean is, there isn't anything to do about him. I didn't love him, not in the past several years. I don't know if I ever did. He came along, I was confused, I married him without really thinking about it. Can you understand that?"

"There was a guy before him," Kelso said softly.

"Hank?" She gave a little laugh. "Poor Hank. He was my rebound. You know what a rebound is, don't you, George? We'd just broken up, you and I, and I was on the rebound, I'd have dated any creep who asked me out. The creep happened to be Hank, and he fell head over heels in love with me. No, not love—infatuation. I was like a high school prom queen to him, he adored me, but he didn't really love me."

"How'd you feel about him?"

"He was nice in a way. Gentle. Tame. Reliable. But kind of dull. I guess I gave him the wrong impression."

Kelso peered into her eyes. "I saw the picture you gave him, and what you wrote on it."

"I'm not going to lie to you, George. Sure I *told* him I loved him. He practically demanded it. I was still in love with you, and I wanted to love somebody. Hank was the nearest thing around. It didn't mean anything."

"He thought it did."

"I know. I'm always hurting people." She shook her head. Her eyes were filling with tears again. "George, you believe me, don't you? I'll die if you don't. I do love you. Tell me you believe me."

"I believe you," he said.

"George . . ." She put her arms around him and hugged him again. Now it was she who was shaking. She whispered, "Just hold me, George . . ."

He held her. After a while she pulled back slightly, looked at him, then kissed him again, hard, passionately, sending her tongue into his mouth, in and out. For Kelso the rest of the universe ceased to exist; he and Carla were isolated in space and time on this snow-covered sidewalk on this street on this night, and it could have been ten years before, on a sidewalk on the campus, on a magical night, with no place to go and nothing to do but love each other.

Then she stopped and whispered, "We'd better go back. I'll make you some hot chocolate. Do you still like it?"

"Sure."

They walked back to her house arm-in-arm. Inside, they took off their coats and he followed her into the kitchen, where the lights were so bright compared to the outside darkness that he felt blinded and kept squinting at everything. It was hard to get his breath, he could still taste her kisses on his lips, and he wanted to hold her to him again but had to be content to watch her moving around the kitchen, making hot chocolate. She was wearing corduroy jeans and a beige sweater and she looked like a million dollars.

He was miserable. His entire existence had exploded in his face— Susan Overstreet, the investigation, ten years of forgetting about Carla. Unexpected forces were jerking him in five directions at once, and he could feel his emotions boiling in a pot totally separate from his intellect. For the first time in his life, he had absolutely no idea what he was going to do next.

She brought two mugs of hot chocolate to the table and they sat down next to each other and she took his hand, squeezing it firmly and gazing into his eyes.

"George?"

"Yeah?"

"That wasn't just for show. I really do still love you."

"I know."

"Do you want to know why I broke up with you?"

"If you'd like to tell me."

"I was terrified. I wasn't ready for marriage, or I didn't think I was, and you seemed so certain about it. I wanted time."

He said, "Maybe you should've just asked for time."

"And then it was too late. But it's not too late now, is it? I mean, we're together again. It could still work out. Right?"

"Why don't we just take it easy and see what happens, Carla? I don't think either of us is in a position to make any promises just now."

"I don't care. I just know I love you. Is that so wrong?" She let go of his hand. "I'm sorry, I need a cigarette. Would you like one?"

"No, thanks."

While she lit up, he leaned back in his chair and tried to get a grip on himself, tried to bring himself back into the present. It was like trying to walk when the floor's disappeared, or one of those weird dreams in which his feet moved but he didn't go anywhere.

"Can I talk to you about something, Carla?"

"Of course. Anything." Her gaze was steady, wide-eyed.

"I'd like to talk to you about Henry Fredricks," he said.

In the silence that followed, he could hear his heart beating.

SIXTEEN

"Let's go to the living room," she said. "It'll be more comfortable in there."

With a resigned sigh, Kelso followed her down the hall and into the front room. Something seemed to have changed in her attitude; she sat down on the edge of a chair, watching him with a slight frown, puffing at her cigarette. In the grate a log shifted and made sparks fly. He glanced at the blue lights on the Christmas tree, then turned toward her.

"My partner and I talked to Fredricks." He paused. He was having trouble getting started, finding the right words.

"Yes?"

"He gave us a statement about last night. He says you telephoned him at his hotel room about ten till eight—"

"That's not true!"

"Just a minute, Carla. Just let me get it all out before you say anything, okay?"

She shrugged. "Go ahead. Be my guest."

"All right. Fredricks says you called him about ten till eight and invited him over here, to your house. He agreed, and you gave him instructions on getting here. He drove here from the Downtowner and met you here around eight-fifteen or so. He says you told you were sorry about everything. You kissed him, and said you were thinking of divorcing your husband because, among other things, you'd decided you wanted a family and he wasn't cooperating. Fredricks says you then took him upstairs to your bedroom and told him you wanted to make love to him, to show him how you still felt. He went into a bathroom to undress but changed his mind, decided he couldn't go through with it, and came out to find you on the bed in your underwear. When he said he couldn't do it, you went into a rage, threw his briefcase at him and ordered him out of the house. He went. That was around eight-thirty. He returned to his hotel and that was that."

She just stared at him, but her lips were compressed and a flush had spread over her face. Her greenish gray eyes actually looked darker. He remembered that look from ten years ago—she was fuming.

He'd been pacing back and forth as he spoke; he quit pacing and stood in one place, looking down at her. "Okay. That's it."

"He's lying—"

"Look—"

"Don't interrupt, George. I heard you out, now you listen to me. I don't understand how in the hell you can take the word of a person like Henry Fredricks over my word, after all we've meant to each other. Hank isn't rational, George. My God, don't you see what he's doing? I dated the man, on the rebound from you, like I said before, and then I broke up with him. He didn't mean a thing to me, but he was head over heels in love, like an adolescent boy. So he gets this weird idea he'll find me again, he writes me and calls me, he actually gets in his stupid car and drives down here and checks into a hotel. Is that rational, George? Is that what a normal sane person does? And when I still refuse to have anything to do with him, he can't stand it, he makes up this absurd story to get me into some kind of trouble." She stood up and put her fists on her hips, bringing her eyes level with Kelso's. "The man's a lunatic, and you believe him?"

"Are you through?"

"For the moment."

"Well, I didn't say I believed him, Carla. You've got to understand that I'm a cop, I'm investigating a homicide, I've got to ask you these questions officially no matter what I think personally about you. I've been given two flatly contradictory versions of last night, and officially I've got to ask questions, check it all out."

"Okay, so officially you've checked it out. And what conclusion have you come to?"

She was still mad, her eyes were flashing, her feet were wide apart. She was beautiful and angry and forceful.

"I haven't come to any conclusion yet. That's later. Right now I'm just trying to sort everything out the best way I know how. I'm just doing my damned job."

She softened a little at that, shook her head, smiled faintly, and sat down again. Kelso backed to the sofa and sank onto it. His mind was racing, he didn't know what was what.

"I'll try to make it easy for you, George. I'm being very patient, okay? I left here about seven last night and went to that law office party. I spent most of the evening with Tony Deal or other people in his firm, and then I left again around ten and came back here and found Paul dead in the den, and I called the police. Between seven and ten I was at that party, I wasn't here. If Hank says he came here, then he came alone. If he was here, I don't know who let him in, unless it was Paul."

"Did you know Fredricks had a gun?" Kelso asked.

"What?"

"I think you said that he was never armed and didn't like guns, something like that. But he had a gun. It was in his briefcase."

Carla gazed at him for a dozen heartbeats. She lit another cigarette before speaking again in a low voice. "I'll confess to one tiny lie, George. Just one. I knew Hank kept a gun. At least, when we were dating he always had one. He was paranoid, afraid of his own shadow, always worried that somebody was going to attack him or rob him or whatever. He even showed it to me once, on a date. It was in his glove compartment. I didn't mention it to you because to me Hank's a harmless idiot, not a killer. I was afraid of getting him into trouble."

"What kind of gun did he have?"

"When we were dating? That was nine years ago, and I wouldn't know a gun just by looking at one."

"What about now," Kelso said. "Did you know he brought a gun down here with him from Kokomo?"

"Not really. But I'm not surprised. It fits with his personality."

Kelso hesitated. He was debating whether to tell her about the .22 or not. What the hell—he might as well get her reaction to it.

"As a matter of fact," he said, "he had a .22 automatic in his briefcase when my partner and I questioned him at his hotel, and he actually let us have it."

She didn't say anything, so he kept going.

"The lab looked at it. They'd already found an ejected .22 shell in the den. It was the same type of ammunition as the bullets in Fredricks' gun. And they did a ballistics test, and it turns out the bullet they took from your husband's stomach was fired from Fredricks' gun."

Very quietly, Carla said, "Are you trying to tell me that Hank murdered my husband?"

"No. All I'm saying is that either he, or someone else, used his gun to shoot your husband in the stomach. As far as the murder's concerned, that was separate, with your husband's own revolver, that .357 they found on the floor at his fingertips."

"And you think Hank did that?"

"I don't think anything. I really don't know."

She stabbed out her cigarette and stood up. "Then why're you telling me all this?"

"Because I'm trying to be as honest with you as I can, Carla. Because you mean something to me."

She sat down again. "Well, I'm being honest with you too, George. I told you the truth. Hank's lying."

"Did you happen to call him up from the party?"

"Why the hell would I? Of course not. I have absolutely nothing to say to that man."

"Well." Kelso got up and sighed heavily. "I suppose I should be getting back."

Carla stood, too, and stepped close to him. "George? Who's Susan Overstreet?"

His pulse throbbed. "Just a friend of mine."

"No kidding. Just a friend. And you're staying with her?"

"Somebody tell you that?"

"The guy I spoke to at the number you gave me. The detective section number."

"Her aunt's out of town. We're sort of . . . friends . . ."

"Friends." She went into the hall and he followed her to the front door. She gave him his coat. "I do love you, George." It sounded less convincing than it had before.

"Me too," he said. Even less convincing. His ears burned. He was beginning to feel used. Manipulated. Or was it his imagination?

"Thanks for coming over, George," she said, and kissed him lightly on his lips, very quickly and briefly, not with any of the passion of the earlier kisses. Her expression was bland. "Will you let me know how the investigation goes?"

"I'll keep in touch."

"Goodnight, George."

"G'night."

He went outside and the front door shut softly. The porch light went out. He shivered, zipped up his parka, and hurried down to his yellow VW Beetle parked at the curb. He got in it and drove back to the northwest corner of town, to Susan's house, feeling angry and guilty and depressed.

They sat next to each other on the sofa, facing the fire, and he told her everything that had happened at Carla's house except for the kisses and the part about "I love you." After all, he reasoned, if they had been strictly fake, then there was no reason to get Susan all riled up about it, and if they'd been in any sense legitimate then he'd be a damned fool to bring them up. Maybe when he was sure which they'd been he'd tell her.

"There are three possibilities," he said, at the end. "Number one, Carla's telling the truth and Fredricks is a liar, which means he might have gone over there and shot her husband with that .22 of his. Maybe he's cunning and devious, and handed over the gun to Smith and me on a silver platter just so we'd decide he couldn't possibly have done it. Number two, he's telling the truth, Carla's lying, it all happened just like he said. But if that's the case, then Tony Deal and all those other people at the party have to be lying, too. An entire law firm of liars. Number three, they're both lying, they're both in on it, or at the very least she knows he shot her husband and is covering up for him by pretending he wasn't there."

"I like number three," Susan said. "It fits. Carla's obviously a bitch, and Fredricks wants her bad enough to drive down here from Kokomo and find her. His old flame. She's already decided to get rid of her husband, but this way it'll be permanent; he's probably got loads of insurance or something, money she'd never get in a divorce settlement. She calls Fredricks up at the party, sneaks out, meets him at her house, together they go in and maybe offer Paul Ott an ultimatum. Something like, either he agrees to a divorce with a big cash settlement for Carla, or else."

"Or else what?" Kelso asked.

"I don't know. Maybe they just shot him. Anyway, I think they're in it together."

"You said something interesting," Kelso told her. "She sneaks out of the party. I wonder if she could've. Without being seen, I mean."

"I suppose anything's possible. By the way, is there anything still between you and this Carla person? I'm just asking because, if there is, I want you to know it's okay by me. I'm a big girl. You can have all the damn girlfriends you want. Do you still like her?"

"You don't mean that," he said.

When she didn't reply, he peered at her in the dimness—all the lights were out except for the ones on the Christmas tree and, of course, the fireplace—and saw that her eyes were wet with tears.

"Susan . . ."

He kissed her, and she clung to him—the second time it had happened, and the second woman, in one night. By the time he'd walked her up the stairs to the bedroom she'd stopped crying, but she was still holding on tight. He took her to bed, and at some point thought,

"Carla, I don't love you anymore," but it didn't make him feel much better. When he woke up again the next morning he still hated himself, but it was daylight and snowing and time to get up and go downtown to the office, so he sighed and said to hell with it and got dressed.

Susan fixed him a couple of pancakes and they left together in the VW. He dropped her off at the hospital, promised to pick her up again after five, and drove on through the snow to the Municipal Building, gritting his teeth and feeling guilty as hell.

SEVENTEEN

There were other conference rooms, but 06-D was the one generally used by the members of the Detective Section, and they were using it now. It was ten minutes after eight on the morning of Monday, December twenty-first, and to Kelso it felt very cold in the room as he sat more or less huddled in his corduroy suit coat, puffing at his pipe and sipping terrible tasting coffee from a plastic cup. His stomach was upset, he was mad at himself, and he had a headache.

Karl Smith sat to his left, leaning back casually and looking totally bored, his eyelids lowered fully halfway over his icy blue eyes, smoking a Kent and drinking black coffee. To Kelso's right sat Stanley Broom, fresh and bright and pink as usual, smiling shyly as he played with the inevitable new pencil, bouncing it on its eraser. Broom's smile was practically angelic at times, and this made it all the more mystifying to Kelso, who knew—as did everyone else in the section—that Broom's wife was an obese whining nag who generally made the plump young detective's life miserable.

The smile was, however, merely irritating to Detective Sergeant Meyer, who sat hunched over like a small dark bird opposite Kelso; he scowled briefly at Broom's pencil, then spoke.

"We've got some problems here. The first one's this. The mayor's been putting heat on the chief of police about this Ott murder. There's all kinds of political crap going along with it, because of Carla Ott's old man, this Bushnell character. We're being pressured to make an arrest, but we're not supposed to touch Carla, the precious goddamned daughter."

Smith looked up. "That's interesting. What do we do if it turns out she did it?"

"I don't know," Meyer snapped. "The next problem is, the two guns in the case. I still can't figure it out. Was Ott shot by two people, or one person? I'm expecting to hear some more from the coroner's office this morning, and from the crime lab. But whoever fired the gut shot did it with the .22 automatic this creep Fredricks was carrying with him, and they wiped the damned gun clean afterward. As for the

.357 Magnum, Ott's prints were all over it, along with some glove imprints. In my opinion somebody wearing gloves shot him in the head with that gun. But there wasn't any glove imprint on the .22. So what the hell's it mean?"

"Two different people," Stanley Broom murmured.

Meyer glared. "The third problem is this. That pervert burgled another house last night, up in the Sherwood Heights subdivision. Bunch of rich doctors, lawyers, real estate assholes, you know the type, live up there. Lots of heat's coming down about that, too, and the lieutenant's not happy at all, if you know what I mean."

"We don't know what you mean," Smith said.

"Shove it, Smith. So the point is, Lieutenant Leill's put me and Broom full-time on this burglary thing until we can make an arrest. Which means you, Kelso, and Smith, will be full-time on the Ott murder from now on. No weekends off, no evenings off, no nothing. You'll work around the clock until you make an arrest. A *good* arrest."

"Do we get to eat and go to the bathroom?" Smith asked, with a faint sneer. "And sleep once in a while?"

Meyer ignored it, which for Meyer was something. "Kelso, according to my notes you've still got to interrogate a couple called Arnold and Anne Huff, and, uh, have you talked to the Bushnells yet?"

"Briefly to Mrs. Bushnell," Kelso said. "Broom spoke to Russell—"

"Oh yeah." Meyer scowled at his notebook. "Bushnell stated he was with his wife till 9 P.M. on Saturday night, the night of the murder, then he went out and met a friend of his, an insurance man named Lawrence Vandenberg. Correct?" He glared over at Broom.

Broom smiled politely and nodded. "Correct."

"Who the hell's this Vandenberg creep? Anybody talk to him yet?" Nobody replied.

"Right. Well, Kelso, you and Smith can handle that. Now." He banged his notebook shut, leaned back, hunched his narrow shoulders, and scowled. "The way I've got this damned Ott thing, Carla wanted kids and Ott didn't. Carla wanted a divorce. She's got this old flame, this Fredricks character, who came down here from Kalamazoo—"

"Kokomo," Smith corrected.

"Whatever. From Kokomo, just to see Carla after nine years. She wouldn't see him. Smart broad. She goes to a party thrown by some damned law office. Old man Baxter's firm. I know him, sort of. What a jerk. So she's there from seven to ten. During that time, somebody goes into Ott's den and puts a .22 in his guts, and that person, or some other person, puts a .357 in Ott's brains. Okay, Ott's dead. Who did it?" Meyer paused to crack his knuckles, all of them all at once, then continued, scowling hard. "Carla's got an alibi. Some lawyer creep named Tony Deal was with her at the party, or she was with the other people from the firm. She's out of it. Some neighbors saw her old lady, Elizabeth Bushnell, drive up to Ott's house and go in after nine and leave again ten minutes later."

"She admits it," Kelso put in.

"She admits it. Okay, Kelso, see if she was wearing gloves. If she was, she might've left a glove imprint on the .357. She's a possibility. There were letters; she and Ott were having some kind of an affair. Her husband, Russell Bushnell, wants to be a senator. So Liz goes in there and rearranges Ott's brains so he can't tell anybody about their affair, so Bushnell doesn't lose the election before he runs."

"And then," Smith said, "she leaves the letters lying around for us to find."

"Murderers don't always think rationally," Meyer muttered. "Anyway, she's a possibility. Fredricks is another possibility. He couldn't get Carla for himself, he thinks it's her husband Ott who's in his way, he works himself into a rage, take his .22, goes over there, plugs Ott in his stomach. Then he realizes Ott's not dead, or he finds the .357, or Ott's able to get the .357 out to try and defend himself. However it happened, Fredricks wound up with the .357 and blew out Ott's brains, to finish the job. Then he wipes the .22 clean but forgets about the clip."

"If Fredricks bothered to wipe the .22," Kelso said, "why didn't he wipe the .357? And what about the glove imprint?"

"He maybe didn't have time," Meyer said. "He simply beat it the hell out of there. When he got back to his hotel room, there was plenty of time then to wipe the .22. Maybe he was wearing gloves."

"If he was," Broom said softly, "then why bother to wipe his .22? In fact, since it was his own gun, why wipe it at all?"

"That's for Kelso and Smith to find out," Meyer snapped. He glared at Broom. "You and I've got to find a pervert."

"Was it the same M.O.?" Smith asked. "Did he strip some cute little housewife and tie her up and take her picture?"

"Jesus," Meyer said. "You're as bad as the burglar, Smith. Of course he did, but it's none of your business, is it?" He glared. "Okay, you and Kelso get the Ott case. Forget about the nude pictures. And by the way, Kelso, remember what I said."

"About what?"

"This is politically sensitive. Don't make an arrest without checking with me or Leill first. But *move* on this thing. When you're ready to make an arrest, tell one of us at once."

"What about the prints on the .22 clip?" Kelso asked.

"Nothing yet."

Smith looked annoyed. "Why don't we just go get Fredricks and arrest him and take his fingerprints, and compare'em with the ones on his gun clip? That'd settle it once and for all."

"Because," Meyer snapped, "Lieutenant Leill hasn't told me to arrest anybody yet. Yeah I know it's nuts. Look, the damn gun's registered to him, his prints are on file with the state police, we'll have an answer on it in a few hours. Just go out there and find out who the hell killed Ott."

Kelso and Smith walked out into the hall. Kelso's head pounded. If Carla's guilty, don't arrest her. If it's Fredricks, don't arrest him. But make an arrest. Or get ready to make one. It was crazy. Politicians, he thought. Smith had said something.

"What?"

"I *said*, are you all right? You look weird."

"I feel weird. Let's get something to eat and plan the day."

They put on their coats and went outside, where snow fell straight down in large puffy flakes and Fourth Street with all its decorations looked like a scene from something by Dickens.

"The Pancake House?" Kelso suggested, squinting against the pounding in his head and eyes.

"Didn't Susan make you any breakfast?"

Kelso shrugged. "A couple of pancakes, but they didn't seem to stay with me long."

"You threw them up?"

"Don't try to be cute, it's not cheering me up."

"The hell with you then."

Kelso nodded. "That's better."

They walked the four blocks to the restaurant and went in. It was warm and cozy, with a sizable crowd. Kelso ate French toast and crisp bacon and Smith had a cheese Danish. Snow fell past the windows and the music system treated them to Christmas music, including a jazz rendition of "Deck the Halls," which depressed Kelso by reminding him of a Christmas concert he'd taken Carla to when they'd dated. He couldn't tell Smith any of it, though he wanted to tell someone. He couldn't tell Susan, for obvious reasons, so he had to keep it bottled up inside him, with the pressure building. Presumably, he thought, it would eventually explode, probably with disastrous consequences.

When they had eaten, they walked back to the Municipal Building, got Smith's huge LTD from the police parking lot, and drove toward the residence of Arnold and Anne Huff.

The Huffs lived in a neat one-story brick at 2103 Waverly Drive, in the northwest sector of the city, not too far from St. Luke's Episcopal Church where Kelso and Smith had once investigated a severed hand found lying on a grave. It was in the general direction of Susan Overstreet's house, making it seem to Kelso that there was no way for him to escape. The two women—Susan and Carla—whirled around in his brain like a perpetual cyclone, a tornado that kept touching down on raw nerves, dislodging synapses until, in the end, he would be destroyed.

Someone in the Huff household had been busy; the driveway and the sidewalk and porch had been cleared of snow, though it was building up again. In the front yard a snowman looked at them with black button eyes and sported a rather new felt hat, red scarf, and cotton gloves at the ends of tree-branch arms.

"I wonder if they have kids," Smith mused.

"Why?"

"I can't imagine an adult doing that."

"The snowman?"

"Grownups don't do that kind of thing, do they? Unless they've got kids?"

"Susan does. She made one last week."

"Susan is weird."

They went up onto the porch and used a heavy brass knocker. After a couple of minutes the front door was opened by a rather short, thin woman who looked out at them with dark heavy-lidded eyes that for some reason reminded Kelso of a dog he'd had once. They were large and bright and seemed to dominate her small-featured face. She was attractive, not beautiful, with short dark hair, high cheekbones, and a mouth made up with dark red lipstick. She was very small all over, but at the same time there was something sensual about her. She was wearing a dark green wool sweater over a blouse, and green corduroy slacks. On her feet were penny loafers, which had recently come back in style.

"Yes?"

"Morning, ma'am," Kelso said. He took out his leather ID folder and held it up for her to see. "I'm Sergeant Kelso and this is Detective Smith. Police officers. Could we talk to you for a few minutes, if it's not too inconvenient?"

She looked completely at a loss, as though he'd announced them to be aliens from the planet Mars come to ask for a cup of engine oil.

"Well I . . . I *guess* so . . ." She stepped back, letting them in. "May I ask what it's about?"

She seated them in a warm, comfortable living room which evidently had just been cleaned, since there wasn't a speck of dust anywhere, not a book or magazine in view, nothing but the furniture. The carpet was spotless. Any spider wanting to live here would be out of luck. A five-foot fake tree in one corner was decorated with a few miniature lights in all the colors, a few plain red, blue, and green balls, and not much else. There were six or seven wrapped presents beneath it, all very neat.

"It's about the murder of Paul Ott," Kelso said kindly.

"I see." She sat opposite them, perched on the very edge of an armchair, knees primly together and elbows resting on them, gazing wide-eyed at Kelso. She looked concerned now, the way people look when discussing the death of a relative with someone who might have been close. "What is it you wanted to ask me? I'm afraid I don't know much about it."

"Is your husband at home, ma'am?"

"Arnie? No, he's at his bank. Clairmont National." She paused. "If it's important, I could call him . . ."

"Not that important," Kelso said. The room was sterile, even with the tree. He noticed there was no fireplace. One of his relatives had had a house like this, an aunt whose name he'd forgotten; she'd devoted virtually every waking hour to cleaning, sweeping, dusting, straightening. As a boy he'd gone there and been offered milk and cookies, only to have his aunt follow around after him picking up the crumbs as fast as they fell from his mouth. Compulsive personality, Susan would call it. Was Anne Huff compulsive? "Did you know Paul Ott very well, Mrs. Huff?"

She blinked. "The Otts were—are—friends of ours. Were, I guess. We saw Carla and Paul, you know, from time to time. We played euchre, went to movies or restaurants, that kind of thing." She paused. "I guess it's like with most couples. If you and your wife are

the same, then you know what I mean. Carla and I talked a lot, and
Arnie and Paul talked, but not the other way around. You know?"

"Yes, ma'am."

"So I sort of knew Paul, but not really well." She looked apologetic.
"I don't guess that helps much."

"It's fine," Kelso told her. Next to him on the couch Smith sat back
casually, with his long legs crossed at the ankles, actually stifling a
yawn. At one point he took out a cigarette, looked around, didn't see
an ashtray, and put it back in the pack. Anne Huff, who'd obviously
seen him do it, said nothing. "Well," Kelso said, "do you have any
idea who might've wanted to kill him? Who any of his enemies were,
anybody who hated him, that kind of thing?"

Anne Huff blinked again. "I'm sorry. I'm really not going to be
much help. To us, to Arnie and me, the Otts are, or were, just a
normal couple. I mean, they had their problems like anyone else, but
nothing unusual. I really don't know why anyone would've wanted to
. . . to kill him."

"I'm going to have to ask you some routine questions, Mrs. Huff,
but they're just routine, okay?" She nodded, still looking slightly
bewildered. "Would you mind telling us where you were and what
you were doing on Saturday night, two nights ago, from, say, seven
o'clock on?"

"Yes, that's easy. We were here, both of us. Just the two of us, I
mean. I was watching television, and Arnie was reading." She paused.
"Arnie reads a lot. Bank stuff. He brings his work home with him."

"All evening?"

"Yes. No—wait. I have to take part of that back."

"Yes, ma'am?"

"Arnie wasn't here the whole time. I mean, he left at some point to
go downtown to his office in the bank building, some sort of project
he was working on that had a deadline."

"On Saturday night?" It was Smith, speaking for the first time and
sounding harshly skeptical.

"He often did that," Anne explained, turning her gaze on him.
"He'd spend the whole day thinking about a problem, then suddenly
jump up and say he'd figured it out, he had to rush right down to his
office, and do this or that with the computer. You know how bankers
are."

"No," Smith said. "I don't, really."

"Well, that's how Arnie is."

"What time Saturday night did your husband leave?" Kelso asked.

"I'm really not sure. I'd guess it was around nine. In the middle of my movie. Yes, around nine, there were lots of commercials; I think I made a sandwich."

"Going back to this other thing, Mrs. Huff, are you on friendly terms with Carla's parents, the Bushnells?"

Something flickered in her dark eyes. "Well . . . I know them, if that's what you mean. I mean, I've met them and spoken to them. Liz more than Russell."

"First-name basis, huh?" Smith asked, smirking.

She frowned for the first time, and her voice hardened slightly. "I call most people by their first names. Don't you?"

"Kelso calls me Smith and I call him Kelso," Smith said.

She didn't seem to know how to deal with that, and looked at Kelso again, as if asking for help.

"Mrs. Huff," Kelso said, "did either of them, Elizabeth or Russell Bushnell, ever talk to you about Paul Ott or express their feelings about him one way or the other?"

He'd expected to draw a blank, but she straightened a little and replied, "As a matter of fact, it's funny you should ask. You know—is this confidential?—I was talking to Liz one day, maybe a couple of weeks ago, and she told me that she, well . . ."

Kelso smiled encouragingly. "Yes, ma'am?"

"Well, that she despised Paul Ott. That's the actual word she used. Despised."

"Enough to kill him?" Smith asked.

Her dark eyes went to him and hardened. It occurred to Kelso that Anne Huff was a tough little woman, despite the puppy-dog eyes. There was a hint of cold steel under the softness. He wondered if all women weren't that way.

"I really wouldn't know," she said calmly. "I mean, I don't know how much you have to despise someone before you . . . kill them."

"What about the Otts themselves," Kelso asked. He thought there might be something here, but Anne Huff seemed reluctant. Maybe he could switch back and forth and get something. Catch her off guard. "Did they get along very well?"

"Except for her pregnancy." Anne shut her mouth quickly and actually put a hand to it. It might've been an act, or maybe not. "I think I'm revealing a confidence."

"This is a murder investigation," Smith said gruffly. "We're *asking* for confidences."

"Yes, I suppose that's right." She looked at Kelso again, her dark eyes wide once more. She shrugged her small shoulders. "Well, it's out of the bag now anyway, as they say. The truth is, Carla really wanted to have a baby, but Paul just wouldn't hear it; he was emphatic about it, he didn't want a kid. A brat, as he called them."

"Did they argue about that a lot?" Kelso asked.

Another shrug. "Not in my presence, but Carla told me that they'd had a few yelling and screaming contests in the past couple of weeks over it."

Kelso decided to switch back the other way again. "Mrs. Huff, I realize this is personal, but did Carla ever say anything to you about the possibility that Paul might be seeing another woman?"

Something definitely flickered in those dark eyes this time. He saw it, and knew that it was there, something solid and substantial. Pay dirt. Come on, he thought, tell me. You know, so tell me.

"Mrs. Huff?"

"I have a feeling you already know this," she said quietly, "or you wouldn't have asked me. The answer is yes. Carla thought he was seeing somebody, but . . ." She paused, and Kelso let her wrestle with it for a while. It was quiet in the room. Not a sound. He heard his stomach rumble, digesting the French toast. Finally she set her little red lips stubbornly, frowned, and said, "Paul was sleeping with Carla's mother. Liz. Is that what you wanted to hear?"

"It's not a question of what we wanted to hear, ma'am." His head still hurt, but not quite as much. He felt that he was on to something. He had to keep pushing. "Was Elizabeth Bushnell in love with Paul?"

"Definitely not. She despised him. It was just that she found him, well, physically satisfying. If you know what I mean."

Smith chuckled.

"Do you know that they actually slept together?"

She nodded. "Liz told me. And Carla told me, too. Yes, Carla knew it. She didn't really care. Look, if you want to know the God's honest truth, this thing about getting pregnant was making her crazy. She was darned close to filing for divorce. So if Paul was screw . . . sleeping with her mother, then . . ." She shrugged.

Kelso had a sudden idea. "Was Carla interested in anyone else?" Shot in the dark, he thought. But he'd had a feeling.

Anne Huff gave him a strange look, as if he'd just told her something about herself that no one could possibly have known.

"This is bizarre," she said softly. "How could you . . ."

"Ma'am?"

"You're not going to believe this, Sergeant. But about a week ago I was downtown Christmas shopping, and I saw Carla and a man named Tony Deal looking at jewelry. And after they left I went over to see what they'd been looking at, just out of curiosity. And you know what it was?" She paused. "Wedding rings."

EIGHTEEN

"Wedding rings," Kelso murmured, and gazed at Anne Huff. She was as plain and neat as her living room, she seemed very open; yet, Kelso had the sudden feeling that she was holding something back. He had no idea why. "Carla had thought about divorce. Do you think she was planning to marry Tony Deal?"

"I don't know, really." Anne shook her head. There was nothing in her dark eyes to give anything away. "I just don't know." A brief pause. "But I wouldn't be surprised. She's talked about him, how nice he is to work for, how smart he is. She's got a thing for lawyers. Well, they were definitely looking at wedding rings."

"Are you right-handed?" Kelso asked suddenly.

She blinked. "Excuse me? Right-handed? Yes, I am . . . but why? What does it matter?"

"Just curious, ma'am. What about your husband?"

"Arnie? Yes, he is, too. Both of us are."

Kelso was thinking about the murder, and a thought was slowly beginning to form. A nebulous thought, like the beginnings of a new solar system. He wasn't even certain where it would lead, but he wanted to hang on to it. Taking out his notebook and pen, he jotted down a few words. "Gun. Right side. Suicide or not." When he put them away he caught Karl Smith giving him a strange look.

"Well," Anne Huff said, glancing at her watch, "was there anything else?"

"Just a couple of things, ma'am." Kelso got out his notebook again and flipped through several pages. "When I was talking to Carla, she mentioned that her husband seemed to keep things from her a lot, but that you and your husband didn't have that problem." He glanced up at her. "Would you say that's a fair assessment?"

She seemed slightly flustered. "Well, I suppose so. I mean, Arnie and I don't keep secrets from each other, for what it's worth. But I don't really see . . ."

"And also, ma'am, about Paul Ott. Apparently he'd gotten around to promising Mrs. Bushnell some presents, he seemed to think he was about to come into some money. Would you know about that?"

"No. Neither of them ever said anything about it to us. About Paul coming into money or anything."

"And," Kelso persisted, "do you know if Paul Ott ever threatened your husband in any way?"

He'd struck pay dirt. He could see it in her eyes. Suddenly she was wary, frightened, intense. Something was there. Tell me, he thought. Tell me. You can tell me.

"Why would Paul have threatened Arnie? I think you're making it up, Sergeant."

"I have it from a pretty reliable source," Kelso said calmly, "that Ott had been making some kind of demand on your husband."

"Demand?" Her voice had gone up several notches. She stood up, frowning hard, dark eyes snapping. "What kind of demand?"

"I was hoping you could tell us."

"Well, I can't. I don't have the slightest idea what you're talking about, and that's a fact."

"I see. Well, sorry to have troubled you." He put away his notebook and stood up. Smith got up, too, towering over the small woman.

"I'll show you out," she said. "Look, I didn't mean to sound so mad, it's just that I've been upset by this whole thing. It's not every day somebody you know gets murdered."

"We understand," Kelso told her. "Thanks for your help."

Outside, it had stopped snowing for the moment, but the sky was low and gray and a cold wind was blowing the fallen snow all over the place. They climbed into the LTD.

"You lost me in there," Smith said. "Did you know what you were doing, or was that just a lot of crap?"

"Some of each. Elizabeth Bushnell said something about Ott having something on Arnold Huff. I think Anne Huff knows about it, but she's not going to spill it."

"Yeah," Smith agreed, "she comes across as a pretty tough little broad. You want to go find her husband down at that bank?"

"I suppose we'd better."

Smith aimed the big car downtown. "What was all that about being right-handed?"

"I'm not sure. Let me think about it some more."

They drove through the white-covered neighborhoods while Kelso chewed at the stem of his pipe and thought about it. Left hands and right hands. He remembered back ten years. Dating Carla. She was left-handed, because she'd always made a point of contrasting it with Kelso's own right-handedness. And then she'd laugh and say, "Opposites attract." But the question was . . .

"We've got to find out whether Ott was left or right-handed," he said, as the residential neighborhood gave way to the business district.

"Why?"

"It's what I've been thinking about. Look, suppose Ott was left-handed. Then we can rule out suicide. Probably."

"Oh, you mean . . ." Smith swerved to avoid a young woman in a business suit who had wandered out across a traffic light. He rolled down his window and yelled out at her, "Bitch," then accelerated again. "You mean, if he was a lefty, he'd have used his left hand to shoot himself, in the left side of his head, and dropped the .357 under his left hand. But the shot was on the right, and the gun was under his right hand."

Kelso nodded. "Exactly."

"So what if it turns out Ott was right-handed?"

"I don't know. Carla was, and is, left-handed, by the way."

"So what?"

"I don't know. Here's another thing. Suppose Ott's left-handed but the killer didn't know it. The killer, being right-handed, shot Ott in the right side of his head and left the gun under his right hand."

"So all we have to do," Smith said, "is prove Ott's a lefty, and then find somebody who hated his guts who is right-handed but didn't know Ott wasn't."

"Yes. It's simple," Kelso said.

The Clairmont National Bank was downtown on Third Street, on the first floor of a large old five-story brick structure called the Oldham Building but which everyone loosely referred to as "the bank building." Kelso and Smith were shown into a private office, very small and drab, with a desk and chair, two visitors' chairs, and no window. The nameplate on the desk said "Mr. Huff" but the office was empty. A tall young girl with long dark hair and an aloof manner asked them to wait.

"It won't be a minute," she said, as if bored. Her heels clacked away.

It wasn't a minute, it was ten minutes. A rather short heavyset man entered the office and glanced at them with dark nervous eyes. His jet black hair was combed straight back. He wore black horn-rimmed glasses, a plain gray suit, white shirt, gray tie, black shoes. Kelso thought the man was probably about fifty pounds overweight. Everything about him was nerves. He sat down behind the desk, leaned forward slightly, clasped his thick-fingered hands together on his desktop, and peered at them through his glasses. There seemed to be a twitch in the corner of his left eye.

"You gentlemen are from the police?" Even his voice sounded agitated, rather high and unsteady.

"Sergeant Kelso. This is my partner, Detective Smith. We'd like to ask you a few questions about Paul Ott."

Huff had left open his door; now he got up, hurried over, closed it, and returned to his desk to lean forward and clasp his hands again. He was pale. It might mean something, or not. Kelso was keenly aware of the various ways in which people reacted to any contact with the police. Some citizens were badly frightened by the experience, whether they had anything to hide or not. Possibly Arnold Huff fit into this category. Possibly he was a murderer. They would see.

"What would you like to know?" Huff asked, his eye twitching away.

"Do you own a gun, Mr. Huff?"

Kelso wasn't sure why he'd suddenly decided to use the direct approach. The man was already afraid; perhaps that was it. Somewhere he'd read that the Russians had a theory, that you pushed until you found a soft spot, then you pushed harder. Maybe that's what he was doing.

"A gun?"

"Yes, sir."

"No. I have no use for them. I hate them. They only cause trouble."

"Mr. Huff, would you mind telling us where you were between seven and ten on Saturday night?"

"Seven and ten? Saturday night?" Huff licked his lips. "I was at home with my wife. And then, I don't know when, around nine I suppose, I left and came down here to my office. You can check. See, if you come in after normal bank hours you've got to sign in and out with the security guard. You can check."

"We'll check," Kelso said. "Do you know a man named Tony Deal?"

"Sure. That is, yes, I know him. To talk to him. Why?" His dark eyes behind the glass lenses darted from Smith to Kelso, back and forth.

"Do you happen to know what Carla Ott's relationship with Mr. Deal was? Were they friends, for instance?"

"She liked him. I know that. I'm not sure."

"Did he like her?"

"How would I know? I'm sorry. I'm not sure."

"I heard," Smith said, getting in on the act, "he and Carla were thinking about getting married, after she divorced Paul Ott."

Huff's eyes widened. "Divorced . . . who told you that?"

"Is it true?" Smith asked.

"I don't know. My wife mentioned it a couple of times. These are confidences. I don't know that I should be discussing confidences with you. With the police."

"It's all official," Smith told him. "It's murder, after all."

"What's more important," Kelso asked quietly, "some confidences, or finding out who killed Carla's husband?"

"I know. I know." He unclasped his hands. They appeared to tremble, so he clasped them again. His eye twitched. "I heard something about it. Evidently Carla and Paul weren't getting along very well. I wasn't aware, am not aware, that Carla had spoken to Tony Deal about marriage, but I can tell you that Deal had spoken about it. To me."

Kelso was interested. "What do you mean?"

"I mean, Deal's been telling me for weeks that he'd love to figure a way to get Carla away from her husband. For various reasons. Can I level with you gentlemen?"

"We wish you would," Smith said.

"All right. Here's the thing. Deal told me that not only was Carla a great, uh, lover, or some such word." He cleared his throat loudly and blinked a couple of times. "But also, she had good connections. See, I don't know if you know it or not, but Deal is low man in the law firm he's in. I mean, he's practically a leg man. A runner. He doesn't make much money. He wants to hang out his shingle, go it alone, but do you know how much money that takes? A lot, I can tell you. More than he's got. And so Deal's told me several times that with Carla as his wife, he'd have two things. One, he'd have some money, presumably from her parents, the Bushnells. Two, he'd have connections."

"Connections," Kelso said softly.

"Last week," Huff said nervously, "Deal had lunch with me. And he said, 'Arnie, it's a lot easier to be a local lawyer if you've got a wife with all the right connections.' That's what he said."

"How'd you get along with Paul Ott?" Smith asked.

Huff jerked his glance toward Smith, his eyes popping wide behind the glasses. They slid down on his nose, and he pushed them back up with a chubby finger. "Paul Ott?"

"Yeah." Smith nodded, his blue eyes coldly piercing. "You know Paul Ott—Carla's husband, thin little guy with a couple of bullets in him?"

"I . . . what was the question?"

Smith sighed and repeated loudly, "How'd you get along with him?"

"He was okay. I mean, my wife and I socialized with the Otts off and on. Cards, dinner, that kind of thing. He was okay."

"Recently," Smith said, "has he or did he threaten you about anything?"

"Threaten me? Of course not." The eye twitch sped up.

"Did you owe him money?"

"No."

"Did he have something on you? Was he blackmailing you?"

"I haven't done anything!" He almost shouted it.

Obviously, Kelso knew, Huff was hiding something. He was desperate and terrified. Whatever it was, his wife knew about it. That's what Kelso had seen in her eyes—guilty knowledge. This overweight little banker was into something, probably something illegal, at least something immoral, and Paul Ott had found out about it and had been blackmailing Huff.

And *that* was a motive for murder.

An overweight little banker. He'd left his house on the night of the murder to come down here. They would check with the security guard's records to see if Huff had signed in and out, and at what times. He'd said it was around 9 P.M. Maybe he'd left his house, gone over to the Otts' house, shot Ott, and then come down to the bank. Getting rid of a blackmailer.

"You ever been in any kind of trouble, Mr. Huff?" Smith asked. "Any trouble with the police?"

"Never." He was licking his lips often. The left eye, with the twitch, was practically closed. "I don't get into trouble."

"Did you go straight here when you left your house Saturday night?" Kelso asked.

"Yes. I told you. Straight here. Checked in with the security guard. Checked out. Went straight home."

"What time did you leave the bank that night?"

"About ten-thirty."

"You ever read girlie magazines?" Smith asked casually. "You like pictures of naked girls?"

Huff's face reddened. "I would suggest that you gentlemen leave now, unless you have something official to ask me." His voice was high.

"Paul Ott must've had something on you," Kelso said, almost kindly. "Someone told us. Someone reliable."

"They're lying! It's a lie! Who was it? I'll sue!"

Kelso stood up. "Mr. Huff, I'm sorry if we upset you. But it's all routine. These things get said by people, and we have to check it out. It's our job."

Huff stared wild-eyed without speaking. Actually it was one-eyed; his twitching eye was squinted into a slit.

"We'll get back to you if we need anything else," Kelso said, and glanced at Smith. "Ready?"

Smith got up and they left Huff's office. A check with the security records for Saturday night revealed two things: one, that banks do not especially like showing such things to the police; two, that Arnold Huff had checked in and signed the security form at 9:34 P.M. and signed out again at 10:40 P.M. on the night of the murder, Saturday, December nineteenth.

Outside on the street Kelso put a dollar into a Salvation Army pot and asked, "What do you think?"

"I think you're cheap," Smith replied. "Only a buck?"

"I didn't notice you putting anything in there."

"I did, earlier."

"Well, I meant about Arnold Huff."

"I think Huff's lying out his ass. I think he's into something bad, and Ott found out and was blackmailing him, and Huff went over there and blew Ott's brains out. No? Why are you shaking your head?"

"It doesn't explain the two guns and the two gunshots."

"Fredricks went over there and shot Ott with the .22," Smith said. "So he could have Carla for himself. Then Huff went over there and found Ott bleeding, and got Ott's .357 and let him have it in his head. How's that?"

"Maybe," Kelso said. "Here's the Pancake House. Let's eat lunch."

"It's not time for lunch."

"Let's have a coffee break."

They went inside and sat down. Kelso said, "Arnold Huff really is into something, or was, and I'm sure Ott knew it and was gouging him. We've got to find out what Huff was doing."

"Maybe he's the perverted burglar, breaking in and taking nude pictures of those housewives."

"He's a banker," Kelso said. "Maybe he's embezzling money from his bank."

"I think he killed Ott," Smith said.

NINETEEN

The atmosphere in the Pancake House was rather festive, with Christmas music blaring from the sound system and colored lights strung here and there. They were playing "Good King Wenceslas," and Kelso found the whole thing somewhat depressing, considering his mood. Looking at Smith, he felt reckless.

"Could I talk to you about something?"

Smith took a bite of a fruit Danish and nodded. "Sure."

"You were right about Carla. It's hard for me to be objective at this point. There's something I should tell you."

"You don't have to tell me a damn thing, Kelso."

"I know I don't. But I feel like it."

"Well, then, tell me."

"Carla made a pass at me, I guess that's what you'd call it. When I was over there last night we went for a walk in the snow and she kissed me."

Smith nodded again and said reasonably, "I suspected something like that would happen. Those big eyes of hers. What else?"

Kelso hesitated. He wanted to get it all out, wanted to trust Karl Smith. He trusted him implicitly as his partner, in any police work, but rarely had he ever confided anything really personal to the man. Smith himself was a private person and normally kept his feelings to himself. But he had to talk to somebody, wanted to talk.

"She told me she still loved me."

Amazingly, Smith didn't sneer or even laugh. All he said was, "And you told her the same?"

"Yeah. As a matter of fact I did. I feel terrible."

"Guilty?"

"That, too. I don't even know how I feel about her. Hell, I thought I was in love with Susan, and now Carla comes along. I keep reliving the past, when we dated, and thinking about how great it used to be."

"She was married until Ott was shot," Smith observed. "And there's this Fredricks guy. You want my personal opinion, Kelso?"

"I'd like to hear it."

"Then I'll tell you. But you won't like it. I've known broads like Carla. They come on hot and cold, hot and cold. You never know where you frigging stand with them. One day they're all over you, hanging on you, can't get enough of you, it's all 'I love you' and 'I can't live without you,' and then the next day it's the arctic, they don't have time for you, they're not interested, they're busy. They're selfish bitches, spoiled, and all they really want is to be admired and worshipped by as many people as possible. You ever watch that TV show, 'Taxi,' used to be on a few years ago?"

"Yeah, I watched it."

"There was an episode with the Louie character, that little dispatcher guy. He'd met some broad and she was falling all over him, telling him she loved him, and he was living with her and doting on her. Anything she asked for, he gave her. So in this episode she wanted blueberries, fresh blueberries, even though it was the middle of winter in New York and they were out of season. But Louie walked all over Manhattan in the cold and snow, trying to find some fresh goddamned blueberries for her, and he couldn't find any. Well, she wound up telling him that there was one way she'd love him forever, and that was if he'd go away and never come back, never see her again, never call her. The longer he stayed away, the more she'd love him. You get the point, Kelso?"

Kelso nodded somberly. "I get it."

"My opinion is, Carla's exactly that kind of broad. She'll send you all over creation looking for fruit out of season, and promise to love you if you stay away or do some other impossible damned thing. She'll make you give and give till you don't have anything left, and then she'll smile and walk away. Is that what you want?"

"Obviously not."

"Is Susan like that?"

"No."

Smith grinned. "What else would you like to know?"

Kelso looked out the window. A salt truck was moving slowly along First Street as the snow continued to fall. Shoppers carrying packages were bent into the wind.

"I wish I had your objectivity," Kelso said.

"It comes from long years of practice."

"Have you ever been in love, Smith?"

Smith's pale blue eyes went cold. "Once. But I'm not going to talk about it. Let's talk about the case. We've got to solve it one way or the other, you know."

"I've been thinking about it," Kelso told him, finishing a piece of toast and lighting his pipe. "It's got to be either Fredricks or Mrs. Bushnell."

"What about Anne Huff?"

"What about her?"

"Suppose she knew Ott was blackmailing her husband," Smith said. "Huff himself's unwilling to do anything but stew in his own juice, but Anne Huff's not about to let it continue. She doesn't have an alibi after Huff left that night for the bank. She goes over to the Ott house, finds him home alone, and shoots him."

"With Fredricks' .22? How'd she get it?"

"Not with the .22. Fredricks had already been there and done that one himself. She goes in, finds Ott bleeding from a stomach wound, realizes he's still alive and might stay that way, gets his .357 out of the desk drawer and kills him. Wearing gloves, of course. Maybe we can find her gloves and see if they match the weave pattern the lab found on the .357."

Kelso sighed. His pipe went out. "It could've happened that way, I suppose. There're too damn many possibilities in this case, too many people who could've done it. It's driving me nuts."

"I know." Smith lit a Kent. "What we've got to do is start eliminating suspects once and for all. Let's talk to that lawyer, Deal, and the other people in his law firm, and get some more corroboration of Carla's presence at that party Saturday night, so we can cross her off the list permanently."

"That's a start. And we should talk to Russell Bushnell and find that insurance agent he supposedly saw Saturday night, and cross them off the list too."

"Good," Smith said. "We might even be able to cross off Mrs. Bushnell in the process. I tell you, it's going to turn out to be Fredricks. It's just logical. He came down here, wanted Carla back, the poor fool, shot her husband, and all this other bullshit that's happened is just circumstance."

Kelso nodded. "You know, another thing I've been thinking about. Those neighbors across the street, the old couple who saw Mrs. Bushnell drive up after 9 P.M. and leave again?"

"Yeah?"

"I wonder if they saw Fredricks drive up?"

"Probably not, or they'd have said so."

"Let's ask them anyway," Kelso said.

Kelso went to the pay phone, flipped through his notebook, found the name and number for John and Doris Engel, and made the call. Doris Engel was at home, but with that his luck ran out. She clearly remembered that evening, and stated emphatically that she'd only happened to be looking out of her window when Elizabeth Bushnell's car had arrived. Prior to that time, she'd been watching television with her husband. If anyone had driven up earlier, she wouldn't know about it. Kelso thanked her and hung up.

"She was watching TV," he told Smith, back at the booth. "Let's get out of here."

"You leave the tip," Smith said. "I don't have any change."

"Thanks a lot."

Outside it was colder, and heavy thick clouds were moving in, making the sky dark and threatening. The snow seemed to be coming down harder. As they were unlocking the doors of Smith's LTD, Kelso's radio buzzed.

"Call Meyer at the office," the dispatcher told him.

"I'll be back in a minute," Kelso said, and went inside the restaurant to the pay phone again and called the detective section number. Meyer answered.

"It's me," Kelso said.

"I've got some information for you, Kelso. That Fredricks creep came in and gave a statement, in case you're interested."

"I already have the gist of it. He didn't admit to anything, did he?"

"Are you kidding? Anyway, he's gone back to his hotel room. I told him not to leave without telling us. Dr. Paul called. They couldn't find any traces of gunshot residue on Ott's hands."

"Did they check both the left and the right?" Kelso asked.

"No, Kelso, they're all a bunch of damned fools and they only checked the right. Jesus Christ, of course they checked both hands."

"Meyer, do you happen to know if anybody knows whether Ott was left-handed or right-handed?"

After a very long pause, Meyer said, "Is this some kind of joke, Kelso?"

"Not at all. If he was left-handed, then it probably wasn't suicide, because the gunshot and the gun were on his right."

Meyer muttered something Kelso didn't catch, and then said irritably, "I'll try to find out. Are you guys close to making an arrest yet?"

"No."

"Well remember what I said. Don't, till you check first."

"I'll remember. Goodbye, then."

"Right," Meyer said, and hung up.

Kelso depressed the button, got a dial tone, checked the number, and called the law firm of Baxter, Eisenberg, Ubik, and Baxter. He was told by a pleasant-sounding lady that Tony Deal was in, and could see Kelso and Smith right away.

He went back out to the car and got in. "That was Meyer. Fredricks gave his statement but didn't confess. The GSR test on Ott's hands was negative, so probably he didn't shoot himself. And Tony Deal's waiting for us at that law firm."

"Have you ever noticed," Smith asked, pulling away from the curb in front of an oncoming station wagon, "how we seem to spend a hell of a lot of time talking to lawyers?"

"I really hadn't given it much thought."

"I hate lawyers."

They drove off through the blowing snow.

TWENTY

The law firm of Baxter, Eisenberg, Ubik, and Baxter occupied offices in the ground floor of a large brick building three blocks from the mall on Fourth Street, smack in the middle of Clairmont City's business district. It had its own parking lot off the street, where a sign on the side of the building threatened to have towed any cars not belonging to the firm.

"Does that include visitors?" Smith asked.

"Probably," Kelso said.

Inside was a large lobby, sporting a tall live tree dead center, decorated to the hilt and surrounded by gaily wrapped packages. There were holly wreaths here and there along the walls, and a large old-fashioned Father Christmas on the desk of a young blond receptionist whose expression indicated that either she had indigestion or she'd bite off the head of anyone who dared speak to her without permission. Kelso cleared his throat and dared to speak.

"Excuse me, miss, I'm Sergeant Kelso and this is my partner Detective Smith."

She gave him a pained look, picked up her telephone receiver, pressed a button, and said sullenly, "Tony? They're here." Then she replaced the receiver, glanced up at Kelso, and in the same sullen tone said, "You can go on back. Last door down the hall on the left." After which she frowned at a sheet of paper she seemed to have been reading.

"Thank you," Kelso murmured.

Smith stared at the receptionist for a few seconds, then said cheerfully, "Want to go out with me sometime?"

"What?"

"Oh well, forget it." He leered at her and followed Kelso into the hallway.

The last door on the left was open, and they entered a tiny windowless office with a desk, shelves crammed with books, and Tony Deal. He was standing behind the desk watching them with his black squinting eyes, a long black cigar jutting from his lips, looking big and strong and aggressive.

"How you guys doing?"

"We're doing fine," Smith said. "What about you?"

"Better and better. Shut the door, will ya?" Kelso shut it. "You know, you guys were talking to me the other day about money. I've got a little secret to let you in on."

"Gee, tell us," Smith said.

"Take a gander at these." Deal opened a desk drawer and took out a cardboard box, removed the lid, and shoved it at them. Kelso took it and he and Smith look inside. The box contained good-quality letter-head stationery and a set of business cards, printed with Tony Deal's name, attorney-at-law, at an address nearby. "Whatta you think?"

Kelso handed it back to him. "Very impressive."

"Striking out on your own, huh?" Smith asked. "Did you come into some money?"

Deal reddened slightly, put the lid back on the box, and returned it to its drawer. "I've managed to put a little back, and some investments paid off."

"That's a high rent building," Smith said. "Lots of high-priced lawyers in there."

"That's right." Deal puffed at the cigar, which smelled horrible. "So what's it about? You make an arrest in the Ott case yet?"

"Not yet." Smith eyed him cooly. "When you were at that party Saturday night with Carla—"

"I wasn't *with* her. I told you, she showed up without her husband, and I more or less escorted her around for the evening."

"Whatever. You said before that you were with her the whole time, or else within easy view of her. Is that still pretty much your story?"

"It's not my story. It's the truth. The only time I lost sight of her was when she went off to the ladies' room, which was a lot, because her stomach was upset all night. Did I tell you that before?"

"No," Smith said, rather abruptly.

"Must've slipped my mind. Anyhow, her tummy was upset; she kept going off to the can. I think she went up and lay down for a while, at some point."

"But she didn't leave?"

"Of course not. Not till around ten. As I've already said."

"Did you go up and lie down with her?" Smith asked casually.

Deal's black eyes glowered. "I'll pretend I didn't hear that."

"It was a serious question, Mr. Deal. We're investigating a homicide, and it was a serious question."

"Then I'll give you a serious answer. No, I did not. Okay?"

"I understand," Smith said, "that you and Carla have been looking at wedding rings?"

Tony Deal's face went dark red again. "Who in hell told you that?"

"A little bird."

"Well it's a damn lie."

"Just asking." Smith looked at Kelso. "You have any questions for Mr. Deal?"

"Are any of the others here?" Kelso asked. "You know, people who were at the party Saturday night?"

"Sure. How'd you like to talk to old man Baxter?"

"Lead the way," Smith said.

Tony Deal put his cigar in an ashtray and took them out into the hall and along to a door nearer the front. He knocked and a deep gruff voice called out, "Come in!" Deal opened the door and showed them inside.

It was a quite different office from Deal's—very large, paneled on two sides, bookshelves on the other two sides, a thick dark carpet on the floor. On one paneled wall hung black and white photographs of severe-looking men who were, Kelso decided, former Supreme Court justices. There were no holiday decorations. There was a huge wooden desk piled with books, yellow legal pads, and a brass lamp with a green shade. Behind the desk, in a high-backed leather chair, sat a sixtyish man, white hair, watery blue eyes, thick white mustache, a rather reddish complexion, a pronounced scowl. He reminded Kelso of a grim old judge.

"Mr. Baxter?" Tony Deal's whole demeanor had changed. Now he was obsequious, almost nervous. "Sir, these are Sergeant Kelso and Detective Smith, from the city police, sir. They'd like a word with you, if you've got a few minutes."

"All right, Tony," the old man said, and Deal, practically bowing, backed into the hall and closed the door. "John Baxter," he said, standing and extending a thin red hand. "What can I do for you gentlemen?"

Kelso and Smith shook his hand. Behind them was a low sofa and an armchair, both in black leather, but the detectives remained standing.

"Are you familiar with the Ott murder?" Kelso asked politely.

Baxter frowned. "Yes. Terrible thing. Is that what this is about? I don't see how I can . . . oh yes, his wife is one of my secretaries, I believe. Carla."

"Yes, sir," Kelso said. "Apparently she was at your office Christmas party Saturday night."

Baxter nodded gravely. "Yes. That's correct."

"Did you actually see her there, Mr. Baxter?"

"I know exactly why you're asking that, of course." He paused, then answered, "I saw her there shortly after seven, and several other times throughout the evening. She spent quite some time going to the ladies' room and told me her stomach was upset."

"Do you know whether she went up to lie down at some point?"

"No. I wouldn't know about that."

"Do you know when she left?"

"At some point, after 10 P.M. or so, I became aware of the fact that she was no longer there, but I can't tell you a precise time. I didn't actually observe her leaving."

"I see. Well, thanks for your time, Mr. Baxter." Kelso turned toward the door.

"Excuse me," Baxter said. "I suppose this is none of my business, in a way, but she's an employee of mine. Can you tell me if you think she had anything to do with her husband's death?"

"At this point," Kelso told him, "it doesn't look like it."

The old man's features softened somewhat. "Thank goodness. I'd hate to lose her. She's the best legal secretary I've got."

"Yes, sir. Well, thanks again."

"Merry Christmas to you boys."

"Same to you, sir."

They left the office and came face to face with Carla Ott. She was standing in the middle of the hall, smiling rather smugly, her greenish gray eyes wide, her auburn hair fresh and shining, wearing a light gray skirted suit, a white blouse, green and white floppy bow tie, gray heels, gold earrings, gold watch. She looked great. Kelso's stomach jumped and his pulse raced.

"Hello, George." She didn't even glance at Smith, just kept her gaze fastened on Kelso, smirking. "Looking for me?"

"Actually," he said, feeling awkward, "we were talking to Tony Deal and, uh, Mr. Baxter."

"I see. Are you doing anything for lunch?"

"Huh? Well, Smith and I . . ."

"I've got some errands to run at lunch," Smith said rather abruptly.

"Look, Kelso, I'm going to find a telephone. Meet you back at the car, okay?" With a frown, he hurried off toward the front.

"Let's meet somewhere," she said. "I'd like to talk to you."

"I don't know. There's this case, and—"

"Your partner's got errands to run. Aren't you going to eat something? Listen, it's eleven o'clock. How about noon? Do you still like plain food? We could meet at Wyatt's, it's just around the corner."

"I know where it is," he said, his face burning. He wiped his palms on his coat, trying to do it unobtrusively.

"Great. Wyatt's at noon, then. Don't be late." With a big smile, she hurried away, disappearing behind one of the hall doors. A little whiff of her perfume, Chanel No. 5, lingered in the air.

TWENTY-ONE

Kelso sat shivering in the passenger seat of Smith's LTD in the law firm's parking lot, watching snow accumulate on the parked cars. It was melting and sliding down the warm windshield of the LTD. Shoving his bare hands into the pockets of his parka, he frowned; he had the feeling that he was staring at one of those jumble puzzles, an ordinary word whose letters had been rearranged to form a nonsense word. The answer was right in front of him, but he was unable to restore the letters to their proper order. Something she had said, way back there at the start of things, and something about gloves. He was too emotionally involved, could not back up to the right distance.

Smith opened the driver's-side door and climbed in, slammed the door, and started the engine. "I called Russell Bushnell's law office," he said, "and they couldn't tell me where he is. So I tried his home and got his wife. Did you ever remember to ask her if she knew about Ott's gun?"

"I don't think so," Kelso replied. "What difference does it make?"

"Don't sound so depressed. It's just an ordinary murder case; we're trying to rule out suspects. I asked her. She didn't know about it. So she says." He pulled the car into the street and drove slowly. "However, I did get ahold of someone. That insurance guy, Vandenberg, is in his office and will see us. It's just down the street."

"The whole problem in this case," Kelso muttered, "is the two gunshots. If there was just some way we could separate out the two gunshots, allocate them to two different people, we might get somewhere. Even if Fredricks used his .22, who used the .357?"

"We'll find out."

The insurance office had no off-street lot and Smith drove around for ten minutes until he found an empty parking space on a side street a block away. They got out and trudged along the snow and slush that was rapidly building up on the sidewalk, kept messy and slippery by the pedestrian traffic. The noon rush had begun, and in addition the extra crowds of shoppers made it almost impossible to walk in a straight line. They found the office and went in.

Lawrence Vandenberg was somewhere in his mid-fifties, rotund, balding, blue-gray eyes behind steel-framed glasses. He sat at a gray metal desk and smiled innocently at them, nodding pleasantly at Kelso's identification folder.

"I expected a visit from the police at some time or another," he said in a rather high-pitched voice. "It's terrible about Carla's husband. Just terrible."

Kelso and Smith sat down in a couple of upholstered armchairs facing the desk. It was extremely hot in the office. A large potted plant stood in one corner; in another, a four-foot plastic Christmas tree had been decorated with twinkling red lights and a few ornaments. Behind Vandenberg was a window, through which Kelso could see snow falling heavily into what looked like an alley.

"So how can I help you?" the insurance man asked.

"Just some routine questions," Kelso said. He didn't even have his notebook out. The feeling persisted that this was irrelevant, that he already had all the answers, that all that remained was to plug the correct facts into the right holes. "Would you mind telling us where you were and what you did on Saturday night, from around 7 P.M. until, say, ten-thirty?"

"I'd be glad to." The high-pitched voice was whining, grating. "My wife and I ate dinner at home, and I spent the early part of the evening with her. Let's see. Oh yes, I went out, I believe it was a little before nine, and met Russell Bushnell at a bar we go to. Have you ever been to the Lucky Roundup, out near the reservoir? It's one of those Western places, you know. The waitresses wear cowgirl outfits and there's a Western band. No? Well, anyway, we met there a little past nine and had a few drinks, and then sometime after eleven we left and I went home." He blinked and smiled. "Does that help?"

Not a damned bit, Kelso thought. He said, "Neither of you left during that time, sir? I mean, you were both there, together, the entire time?"

"Sure. Oh, a minute or two now and then to go to the gents, but other than that . . ." He waved a plump hand. With his round pink cheeks and wide eyes, he looked as wholesome and innocent as a little boy. He goes to church and sings in the choir, Kelso thought.

"I understand," Kelso said, "that Mr. Bushnell was your client." It was leading nowhere; he simply wanted to ask all the questions and then get out of this stifling office.

Vandenberg nodded and smiled. "Yes, that's right. And still is. And, of course, so was Paul Ott . . ."

"Paul Ott." Was there something here, after all? Kelso tried to concentrate. "Ott had an insurance policy with you?"

"Oh yes. Quite a sizable one, too. With his wife as the sole beneficiary, as you probably already know." He beamed.

"So Carla's coming into a lot of money," Smith said.

"Well, it was a hundred thousand dollar policy," Vandenberg said.

Kelso asked, "Mr. Vandenberg, do you know how Russell Bushnell got along with Carla's husband?"

For the first time, Vandenberg seemed ill at ease. His bland smile wavered, the innocent eyes looked a little worried. "I don't know as it's really my place to say it . . ."

"We're investigating a murder," Smith said gruffly.

"Of course you are. Of course you are." Vandenberg seemed to weigh pros and cons, and blinked rapidly several times. "Well, I can tell you that Russell didn't much care for his son-in-law. He, uh, pretty much disliked him. But if you're thinking that he might have murdered him, I'd like to say that, in my opinion, you're way off the track. With all due respect."

Kelso nodded. "Off the track, how?"

"Well, I've known Russell for several years. He's my client, of course, but I believe we're good friends as well. I respect and admire him. My honest feeling is that Russell Bushnell's about as upstanding a citizen and as good a man as you'll find in this town. He'd never do anything to hurt anyone." Vandenberg paused, his eyes widened, he spread his plump hands wide. "Much less *murder* someone."

"A character reference," Smith said wryly.

Vandenberg took it literally and said, "Yes. Definitely. A character reference." Then the smile returned full force. "But as to his daughter, well, that's another story. Russell loves his daughter. The point being, that he'd never ever do anything to make Carla unhappy, so he can't have done anything to her husband. Do you see? Why, he'd probably die for Carla."

They mumbled a few more routine questions and got the expected routine replies: Vandenberg couldn't think of anyone who might have wanted to murder Paul Ott; Vandenberg owned neither a .22 nor a .357 nor, for that matter, any other kind of firearm; he knew nothing about any serious marital problems between Carla and Ott; he'd never heard of Henry Fredricks. Kelso thanked him and went back out to the street with Smith, and they jostled and shoved their way back to the LTD through the surging mass of shoppers. The air was thick and white with snow.

"Are we having a blizzard?" Smith asked.

"We skipped Christmas," Kelso said. "It's January." His radio buzzed just as he was opening the car door, and the dispatcher asked him to call Stanley Broom at the office.

"I'll wait in the car," Smith told him. "Where it's nice and warm. There's a phone booth in that drugstore. Across the street. Through the cold and snow."

Kelso was too depressed to think of an appropriate response. He crossed the street, getting his shoes and pants wet, and used the pay phone in the drugstore to call Broom.

"Hi, George."

"What've you got?"

"You sound upset. Are you all right?"

"I'm fine."

"Well, you know, I've been working on this burglary thing, but I remembered that Paul Ott might've been blackmailing Arnold Huff, so I decided to check Huff. Just on the chance, the outside chance, that Huff had been committing these weird burglaries and stripping and photographing the housewives, and Ott had found it out and was blackmailing him. I mean, stranger things have happened, right?"

"Right," Kelso said, wondering what in hell Broom was getting at.

"So, I went over to the Clairmont National Bank for a talk with Arnold Huff, and wound up talking to some of the bank officers, and guess what?"

"What?"

"A large amount of money is missing from the bank. The auditors say it's embezzlement, and they think it's Huff. They hadn't reported it yet because they wanted to be certain, though you and I both know that banks tend not to prosecute in these cases. Probably he'd just be dismissed."

"Stanley—"

"Yes, I'm getting to the point, George. So I checked Huff's bank account, and wound up checking Ott's account, and here it is. Every week or so, or every few weeks, periodically, there's a substantial withdrawal from Huff's account and, on the very next day, the exact same deposit to Ott's."

"Huff was taking out money and giving it to Ott," Kelso said.

"Yes. Exactly."

"Blackmail."

"Exactly. And, obviously, a motive for murder. Don't you agree?"

Kelso sighed. Yes, it seemed to fit. Except that he'd have sworn Arnold Huff didn't have the personality of a murderer. Except that Huff had no connection with Carla's old boyfriend, Henry Fredricks, and probably hadn't known about Ott's .357 in the desk drawer in the den. Nevertheless . . .

"George? Are you there?"

"Yes," he said wearily. "I'm here."

"So anyway, I'm still on the burglary case, but Meyer wants you and Smith to locate Arnold Huff and bring him in for questioning. Suspicion of murder. Oh, and he's not at the bank."

"I see. Okay, thanks Stanley."

"I hope you feel better, George."

"Thanks." They said goodbye and hung up, and Kelso left the drugstore. He trudged back across the street, almost blinded by the snow, his feet soaked, and got inside the LTD, where Smith sat warm and dry listening to "God Rest Ye Merry, Gentlemen" on the radio.

"You shouldn't be outside in this weather," Smith told him. "Especially without your boots and mittens. You'll catch your death."

"Shut up," Kelso said. "Arnold Huff's been embezzling from his bank. Broom found withdrawals from Huff's account matching deposits to Ott's. It looks like Ott was in fact blackmailing Huff over the embezzlement. We're to find Huff and take him into custody on suspicion of murder."

"I told you so," Smith said.

TWENTY-TWO

"Keep something in mind," Smith said, pulling into the street. "Huff signed into the bank Saturday night about nine twenty-five and out again at ten-thirty or something on that order. He easily could've gone over to Ott's place first, say around nine, and shot Ott."

"I know," Kelso said.

"Carla's alibi held. Lucky for you. That makes Fredricks a liar. So Fredricks obviously went there and used his .22 on Ott and left again. Then Huff arrived and killed Ott with the .357." He swerved to avoid two women crossing in the middle of the block, cursed them, and added, "It all fits. It's over, Kelso. We can arrest Fredricks and Huff, and it's over."

"Then why do I have the feeling it's not?"

Smith chuckled. "Because you're weird."

"Huff's not at his office. We'll have to try his house. It's 2103 Waverly Drive. Turn up the heat, will you?"

It took them twenty-five minutes longer than normal to drive up to the northwest corner of town to the neat one-story brick house, thanks to the rapidly deteriorating condition of the streets and the traffic, which seemed to consist primarily of terrified people apparently just in from Florida. Everyone was driving as though they'd never seen snow in their lives. Smith yelled and swore and used his horn a lot, while Kelso leaned back in the seat with his eyes closed and tried to think.

He thought about Fredricks, who had come here from Kokomo to see his old flame, with a .22 automatic in his briefcase. That automatic had been used to shoot Paul Ott in the stomach. He thought about Paul Ott, who apparently had been blackmailing Arnold Huff and who had been shot dead with his own .357 Magnum, kept loaded in the desk drawer in his den. He thought about Carla's mother, Elizabeth Bushnell, who had despised Ott but had been sleeping with him. The jumbled word still refused to revert to anything meaningful. Something still was missing.

What was it?

It was going on twelve-thirty, Monday afternoon, the twenty-first of December. The snow kept coming. Smith pulled up into the driveway of the Huff place and they got out. In the front yard the snowman stared bleakly at them with its black button eyes, bravely weathering the storm in its felt hat, red scarf, and gloves. They plodded up to the porch and Kelso used the brass knocker.

Anne Huff let them in, looking worried, her dark eyes and small features tense, running a thin hand through her short dark hair. "Have you seen him? I called the bank, but they said he left suddenly, over an hour ago."

"He's not here?" Kelso asked.

They stood in the spotless living room with the forlorn fake tree, everything as sterile as before. It felt colder, though; or maybe it was because Kelso was nervous and his feet were freezing.

And something occurred to Kelso.

"Mrs. Huff, did you build that snowman?"

She stared. "What?"

"Did you build it? The one in your yard?"

"What the hell kind of a question is that? Of course I did. Well, Carla and I did. Together. She came over on Sunday and we . . . what *difference* does it make? Have you seen Arnold?"

"The hat and gloves and scarf," he said. "They're yours?"

"Who *cares?* Yes, I suppose so. No, only the hat and scarf. Carla had the gloves in her trunk, an old pair. What about *Arnold?*"

Smith said, rather gruffly, "I notice you've got a two-car garage, Mrs. Huff. I take it he's not in the house. Did you bother checking the garage, to see if his car's there?"

She whirled on him. "Why would it be? Christ, if he left for work . . . wait, I was in the shower at one point, you can't hear . . ." A very peculiar look came into her dark eyes. "You don't think . . ."

"I don't think a damn thing. Until we look. We know about the blackmail scheme, by the way. And if he panicked . . ."

"Jesus Christ." She turned and trotted out of the room. "It's this way."

Kelso had listened to all of this woodenly, as if in a daze. It wasn't what he'd expected. Then he hurried after them. A door from the kitchen led down two steps into the garage, which was cold and dark. Anne Huff switched on a light. They saw two cars, side by side. Someone was slumped over the wheel in the farther car.

Smith muttered something and ran over to the car, peered in the driver's window, and straightened.

"Keep her away, Kelso," he warned. But she'd already gotten to the car, standing in front of it and staring in through the windshield in the glare of the naked overhead bulb.

She screamed.

Huff's head rested against the steering wheel, at a slight angle. There was a bullet hole in his forehead, just over his nose, from which blood had trickled. Kelso came up to the car and looked in the passenger window. Huff's right hand lay on the seat at his side, still gripping a small nickel-plated revolver. Next to it was a white business envelope.

Anne Huff was still screaming.

"For God's sake, Kelso, get her inside, can't you?"

"Please, Mrs. Huff." Kelso gently took the woman by her shoulders, feeling how petite she was, and led her out of the garage, back into the neat sterile living room. He sat her down on the sofa, sat beside her, and held her awkwardly with one arm around her shaking shoulders while she cried.

Kelso looked at his watch. He was thinking several things at once. Paul Ott sitting at his desk with a hole in his head and a gun at his fingertips. Arnold Huff sitting in his car with a hole in his head and a gun in his hand. A small sobbing woman with a motive for murder. A woman waiting for him in a restaurant.

"Excuse me," he said, let go of Anne, and went out into the hall where he'd noticed a telephone on a stand. There was a directory. He found the number for Wyatt's and called.

"Hello?" It was hard to hear over the noise of talk and laughter and "Jingle Bells."

"Yes?"

"This is Sergeant George Kelso, city police. Can you page Carla Ott for me? It's important."

There was some delay before she came on the line. "George? Where *are* you?"

"I'm sorry. There's been an emergency. Do you want to wait there for me? It'll be a while. If you have to get back—"

"I'll be here. I get an afternoon off for shopping."

"I'll get there as soon as I can. Goodbye."

In the stark living room Anne had stopped crying. Smith came in, scowling. "I called it in," he said. "They're on the way." He glanced down at the woman. "Is she all right?"

"I don't know."

Anne Huff nodded, her eyes red, tears streaking her cheeks.

Uniformed officers arrived quickly, then Detective Sergeant Meyer, who glared at everybody and snapped orders. The lab crew came, finally, and Dr. Paul from the coroner's office. Time seemed to drag by. Kelso kept looking at his watch. After a while he sat down next to Anne Huff again and asked her a few questions, gently and patiently, hiding his anger.

"It's my fault," she said. She cried again, stopped again. "It'll all come out now, I suppose. Poor Arnie. He was taking money from his bank. Oh God."

"I know," Kelso said.

"That Paul Ott. That terrible horrible little man. He found out, I don't understand how. Arnie thinks he somehow got into the bank's computers. It doesn't matter. He found out, and Arnie was paying him. It was terrible. He thought he was going to jail. He was so depressed. I could've stopped it, by going to the police. And now . . ."

"I'm sorry," Kelso told her. And meant it.

Smith motioned to him from the hall and Kelso joined him there. "What is it?"

"He's only been dead about an hour. He must've come back here from his office, then sat out there and shot himself, presumably while she was in the shower." He shrugged, his eyes like ice. "His prints are all over the envelope and the sheet of paper inside. It's a suicide note. It says he was embezzling from the bank, and Ott knew it. It says he was in a bind, he couldn't pay it back, he was paying Ott. It says he couldn't go on."

"They never think they can go on," Kelso said.

"Yeah. Well, it's pretty cut and dried. His prints are on the gun, too. It's a .38 Colt. You want to see the note?"

Kelso shook his head. "Not now. I've got to get out of here. She's waiting for me downtown."

Smith stared. "Who is?"

"Carla."

"God, Kelso, don't you ever learn?"

"Come on, drive me down there." His tone was now as angry as he felt. "I've been a damn fool."

Outside, the snow had let up a little. As they started down the walk to the LTD, Kelso trudged out through the three or four inches of snow in the yard and looked back at Smith.

"Get an evidence box, will you?"

"What? Are you nuts?"

"Just do it."

Something in his voice made Smith open the trunk.

Kelso went over to the snowman and pulled one of the gloves off of its tree-limb arm, holding it by one edge. He put his nose up to the opening and sniffed, then repeated the procedure with the other glove. He took them over to Smith, who stood holding the box, scowling.

"Now listen," Kelso said. "Drop me at Wyatt's, then take these to the lab and have them checked for gunshot residue and also for blood. Tell'em to check the insides, too. Give me a buzz on the radio as soon as you hear anything. Tell'em it's urgent, top priority."

"I think you've finally lost it, Kelso. All this pressure has finally gotten to you. Two women, the Ott murder, two guns. You've finally cracked."

Smith drove them downtown. It didn't take as long this time, since the snow had let up and the road crews had had a chance to plow the main streets. Traffic was lighter. Kelso got out in front of Wyatt's Cafeteria.

"Let me know as soon as you've got something."

Smith shrugged. "What the hell. I don't have anything better to do than hang around the lab all afternoon."

Kelso went inside, skipped the serving line, and found Carla in a booth, sipping coffee and smoking a cigarette. He slid in opposite her.

"Where *were* you?"

"I'm sorry. It was an emergency. It's Arnold Huff."

She looked at him. "Arnold?"

"He shot himself this morning."

"Oh my God."

He thought he detected a curious absence of real emotion in her response; but after all, she hadn't been especially close to him. Close to Anne, maybe. Or, possibly Carla had never really been close to anyone.

"Do you know why?" she asked, her greenish eyes grave.

"I'd rather not say right now, until the investigation's complete. But there are a few things I'd like to ask you about."

"About us, George?"

"No. Not about us. About your husband."

Her expression hardened. "I thought we were through with all that."

"We've found some new evidence, Carla. To tell you the truth, I think you've been lying to me. I'm sorry, but I think you were at your house that night. I think you sneaked out of the party and met Fredricks there."

It was Kelso's big play, his wild card. It wasn't just a shot in the dark; it was based on guesses, hints, clues, pieces of the puzzle that didn't seem to fit any other way. The gamble was in telling her point-blank, to see how she'd respond. He waited, frowning hard.

"I never lied to you, George." Now she looked hurt. "I love you. I don't lie to people I love."

So the gamble had failed. He'd lost.

"I talked to some of the people who were at that party," he said, pushing it straight through to the end. "There are periods of time when you're, well, unaccounted for."

It was after 1 P.M. The lunch crowd was dissipating, it was growing quiet in the cafeteria, with its elegant antique pieces and chandeliers and red drapes and red tablecloths. From somewhere came the clink of a spoon against a coffee cup, and a child laughed. The Muzak was treating them to "Winter Wonderland."

"Unaccounted for," she said. "You make it sound as though I'd missed roll call or something."

"No one saw you for a long period of time, Carla."

"All right, George. If you must know, I was sick. My stomach was upset. I went upstairs to one of the guest rooms and lay down for a while. Quite a while. I can't prove it, of course. Except . . ." A kind of cunning gleamed now in her greenish gray eyes. A new confidence made her smile faintly. "Except, well, there was a TV set in the room. That's sort of an alibi, I suppose. I mean, I was watching a program; you could check to see when it was on."

"You were watching a TV program?"

"Yes. My stomach was upset, and I lay on the bed in a guest room and watched television. It must've been for forty-five minutes at least. Maybe close to an hour. I remember, it was an old movie."

Kelso gazed at her across the table and thought, don't do this to me, Carla. I really did love you. Don't do this to me.

And then he asked, "What movie, Carla?"

Frowning as if in concentration, she brightened suddenly, smiled, reached out to take his hand, and replied, "Yes, I remember. It was called *Topper Returns.*"

Gently, but firmly, Kelso pulled away his hand.

TWENTY-THREE

All the pain came back.

Kelso sat there in the booth of Wyatt's Cafeteria, forty miles and ten years removed from the time he had been so madly in love with her on that college campus, and felt it rush over him like molten lava. It wrenched his guts and made his face go hot, and his hands shook. Somehow, he found his voice.

"I'm going to tell you something, Carla."

"George—"

"Shut up!"

She stared, surprised; he'd never said that to her before, had never been so angry. Her eyes widened.

"Just listen to me," he said. "I was in love with you. I don't know whether you can comprehend that or not, but I was. I honestly believed you were in love with me. And you lied to me. Finally, you broke up with me. I remember when you walked away from me that night in your dorm. I had a birthday present for you, a bottle of Chanel No. 5. I went out and walked around in the rain without an umbrella. I couldn't believe it was over. But it was. And ever since I ran into you the other day, you've done nothing but lie to me all over again. You lied to me when you kissed me, and you lied to me when you held me and said you still loved me. And you've been lying to me about Saturday night." He paused, out of breath. Sighed heavily. "And now you're lying to me again."

"George?"

"Your husband had a videotape in his VCR. He'd been watching it that night, after you left for the party. It was *Topper Returns*. It wasn't being shown on television in this city, on any channel, pay or otherwise. It hasn't been televised since sometime back in September. There's only one place you could've seen that movie Saturday night, and that's in your husband's den. Not in any other room. Not on any other TV set. Not at that party."

"I'm telling you—"

"Do you want to force me to go over to Mr. Baxter's house and see if he's got the same movie on a tape, and see if there's a VCR in a guest room, and see if that movie was on a tape in the VCR? You know damned well it wasn't."

Something went out of her. She slumped slightly forward, hunching her shoulders, and the expression on her pretty face went sullen, like a spoiled little girl denied candy. When she lit another cigarette her fingers trembled.

"All right. I'll tell you the truth."

He waited, furious.

She spoke very quietly. "I went to the party at seven, just as I said. Around eight, I went up to one of the guest rooms and called Hank at his hotel. I was worried about him, he was very upset with me, and I thought I should try talking to him. I guess I was feeling a little guilty about it." She shrugged. "So I called him, and he insisted on seeing me right away. He said it was urgent. I told him I was at a party, but he said he didn't care, he had to talk to me. So I left the Baxters' house and drove over to my house."

"Was Paul there?"

"I peeked into his den. He was in there, watching that movie. It was one of his favorites, he'd taped it back in September when they showed it on one of the local stations. He didn't see me, and I didn't say anything. Then Hank came, and I took him upstairs so we could talk privately. I just didn't want Paul to know he was there. And then . . ."

He glared at her. "Well?"

"George, he grabbed me. It was quite sudden. He tried to rip my clothes off. I was terrified—not of him, but that Paul might hear and come up and, well, *do* something. He was so jealous. So I locked myself in the bathroom and told Hank to leave, to get out of my house. I waited in there for a few minutes. I thought I heard a loud noise, then another. I decided one of them was the front door slamming, so I came out. He was gone."

"What'd you do then?"

"I left the house and went back to the party."

"Without checking on Paul?"

Her face reddened slightly. "Why should I have done that? I had no idea . . ."

"You didn't even go back to the den?"

"I went near enough to hear the movie still playing, that was all. I assumed he was still watching it."

"So Fredricks left and you left. And when you found out your husband had been shot and that Fredricks had brought a gun with him, did you form any particular conclusion?"

"I don't like this anymore. You're being cruel, intentionally cruel." She paused. Her voice had gone high and sharp. "Obviously I thought that Hank could have gone in there and shot Paul before leaving the house."

"And why in hell didn't you tell me any of this before? Why'd you have to lie to me?"

"Because I still love him. Is that what you want to hear?" She stood up, glaring at him, and practically shouted it. "Because I still love him, goddammit." She grabbed up her purse and coat. "I've got to get back."

And she was gone.

Just like ten years ago in the dorm, Kelso thought. And for a long time he sat there, numb, staring at nothing.

Gradually his mind began to clear. Gradually the scrambled words took shape, growing clearer like a ship coming in out of the fog, a detail here, a detail there, until the whole thing was suddenly visible in sharp detail. And he thought: of course. He remembered Carla's house on the night of the murder, and the telephone call she'd made to the police. The .22 in Ott's stomach, the .357 on the floor beneath his dangling hand, Ott's fingerprints and the weave pattern of a glove on the .357. The story Fredricks had told about that night, and the one Carla had just given him. Elizabeth Bushnell's physical affair with Ott, who had been blackmailing Arnold Huff, who was now dead.

Kelso could read the word.

He got out of the booth and found a phone, checked his notebook, and called Room 726 at the Downtowner Hotel.

"Mr. Fredricks?"

"Yes?"

"This is Sergeant Kelso, city police. Are you planning to be there a little while longer?"

"Well, I was asked not to leave . . ."

"Yes. Fine. Look, I'd like to come over and talk to you. Would you mind sticking around the hotel for a while? It may be an hour or so."

"I guess so."

"Thanks. I'll see you sometime this afternoon, then."

He hung up, checked another number, called it, and a secretary put him through.

"Russell Bushnell speaking."

"Hi, Mr. Bushnell. This is Sergeant Kelso, city police. I wonder if I could see you for a while today."

Bushnell's voice was low, firm, pleasant. "Well, I'm a bit busy, Sergeant. Is it something that could wait?"

"I'm afraid not, sir."

"Hmm. Well, as it happens I was just on the way out to grab a late lunch. If you'd care to join me—"

"That'd be fine, sir."

"Do you know Bender's?"

"The steak place out west on Second Street?"

"Exactly. It turns into Nashville Road when you cross the river, and Bender's is on the left, sort of back in the woods. Can you meet me there in, say, half an hour?"

"I'll be there, Mr. Bushnell."

He hung up, zipped his parka, and went outside. It was snowing harder again. He would have to walk the four blocks along Fifth Street to the Municipal Building's police parking lot to get his VW, and his shoes and socks were already soaked. Should've remembered to put a dry pair of socks in the car, he thought, then hunched his shoulders and made his way down the sidewalk, dodging shoppers laden with packages. For the first time since the case had begun he felt a rising sense of excitement, the feeling of closing in on a quarry. He was under orders not to make an arrest without clearing it first with Meyer or Lieutenant Leill, but he could close the net, trap the killer, and be ready.

It was one-thirty when he reached the little yellow VW Beetle, and 2 P.M. by the time he drove it across the river bridge and spotted Bender's Steak House considerably off the road on his left. He followed a curving drive into the parking lot, got out, and went inside.

It was very rustic and dark, with bare rough boards on the floor and rough beams on the ceiling. Like every other place in town it had been fitted out for the season, with holly wreaths, miniature lights, and even a small live tree in the lobby. An amiable young woman in a short black skirt and gold low-cut blouse welcomed him.

"I'm George Kelso, ma'am. I'm supposed to meet Russell Bushnell here."

"Yes, sir. He's at his table. Right this way, sir."

He followed her into a maze of narrow corridors running between rows of booths. She stopped at one, handed him a huge menu, wished him a pleasant lunch, and hurried away, the click of her high heels on the boards reminding him of Carla walking away from him ten years ago in her dorm. His stomach jumped.

"Sergeant Kelso?"

The man in the booth was big. Not especially fat, but big. Muscular. Well fed. His shoulders were broad and massive, his chest was wide and heavy, he filled out his expensive well-cut business suit the way a fullback fills out his football uniform but he didn't need pads. He had a big-featured face, jutting jaw, impressive nose, hard steel gray eyes with just a hint of green. He was handsome and rugged. In his mid-fifties, Kelso guessed, with auburn hair graying at the sides, thick dark eyebrows. There was an air of supreme confidence about him, an air of toughness. He might have been a general, or the president of a huge corporation, or a senator. Running for the Senate, Kelso recalled. He felt slightly intimidated.

"Yes, sir," he said. "I'm George Kelso. Do you remember me?"

"Russell Bushnell. Have a seat, Sergeant." His voice was low, smooth, relaxed, with the force of natural authority. He would give orders easily, and they would be carried out. There was a glass of red wine in front of him, and he puffed at a pipe that looked dwarfed in the huge hand that held it. His eyes twinkled. "So what was so urgent? Go on, sit down."

Kelso sat. "Yes, sir. Well, I wanted to talk to you about your son-in-law's death. I'm really sorry—"

"No need to be sorry, Sergeant. I realize you're doing a job. We've all got jobs to do. Don't worry about my feelings. I feel badly about it for my daughter's sake, but not especially for his. We weren't close. What would you like to know?"

Kelso relaxed a little. Bushnell seemed very normal and natural for an important lawyer and politician. "Well, sir, I'd like to ask you a few questions. It's just routine. I know you've already spoken to some other police officers, but I'm more or less handling the investigation, and there're a few things I'd like to clear up for myself."

"Clear away, Sergeant," Bushnell said.

A waiter came, a too-cheerful young man in dark trousers and white open-necked shirt. Everything was "Merry Christmas" and "How are ya?" and "The veal's really super today." They ordered steaks and the waiter went away. Kelso waited until he'd been given a cup of coffee, then drew in a deep breath and spoke.

"Sir, I understand that you and your wife were at home on Saturday night, and you went out at some point to have a drink with Mr. Vandenberg, your insurance agent."

Bushnell nodded. "Yes, that's right. We had a couple of drinks and chatted. Larry's a nice guy; I've known him for some time."

"I understand, sir, that your son-in-law had taken out a rather large insurance policy, with your daughter as the beneficiary. A hundred thousand dollars is the amount I believe Mr. Vandenberg mentioned."

The steel gray eyes were a bit less twinkly. "Yes, that's correct, Sergeant."

"I'm sorry to have to intrude like this, Mr. Bushnell, but we've found out that, well, Carla and Paul Ott weren't getting along very well. It seems she wanted children, and Paul wasn't interested. Had she mentioned to you that she intended to divorce him, sir?"

Even the smile was gone now. The features on the wide heavy face were as hard as stone. "I'm very close to my daughter, Sergeant. I don't believe there's anything we haven't shared with each other. Yes, I knew she was considering leaving him."

"And did you know, sir, that she'd been thinking about marrying a man named Tony Deal?"

Bushnell frowned and set down his wine glass. He took out a silver pipe tool and began scraping the bowl of his pipe.

"She'd mentioned it once or twice as a possibility. I'll tell you, Sergeant. Your business is homicide and mine's law, and I don't want to tell you your job—but I'm not sure how this all fits into the scope of Paul's murder."

I'm not going to let this man intimidate me, Kelso thought. And he said, "Well, sir, all these little facts run around here and there like ants, and some of them mean something and some don't, and it's my job to sort them all out to see which is which. So I have to ask the questions."

Bushnell shrugged. "Whatever you say. What else?"

"This is a little harder, sir. Did you have any idea that Paul Ott might've been seeing another woman?"

Politicians and lawyers, Kelso thought. They were trained to be careful about their reactions, or they learned it from experience. They were like actors. He tried to read something in the big man's expression, but all he saw was a hard frowning face with no emotion, no response.

"No, Sergeant. I had no idea." He paused, pocketed his pipe and the silver tool, and asked almost casually, "And, was he?"

"Sir?"

"Was Paul Ott seeing another woman?"

Kelso thought about Ott and Mrs. Bushnell and felt his face going hot. Thankfully it was extremely dim in the place. He almost spilled his coffee trying to take a sip. "Well, we heard rumors to that effect." He shrugged. "It's probably nothing."

"I see."

"Sir, there are a few more routine questions. I'm not accusing you of anything, I just have to ask."

Bushnell nodded and the smile returned, but not the twinkle in his eyes. "Go on and ask, Sergeant." His voice was tight.

"Do you know of anyone who might've wanted to kill Paul Ott?"

"Not really. I assume you've talked to this old boyfriend of hers. The one she dated after she broke up with you, back in college."

"Yes, sir. Henry Fredricks."

"Right. Well, I suppose he might've had a reason to want Paul out of the way. On the other hand, my assessment of Fredricks isn't consistent with a killer. I just can't see him shooting someone in cold blood." He shrugged. "Other than that, I can't think of anyone."

"Do you still own a gun, sir? When Carla and I were dating, I think she mentioned several times that you liked shooting guns."

Bushnell seemed to hesitate before replying. "To tell you the truth, I've got a shotgun that I never use, and also a revolver that I use to do target practice with. You know—tin cans, paper targets, that kind of thing. Trees."

"What caliber?"

"Colt .38."

The steaks arrived. The cheerful waiter made sure everything was all right, and left. For a while they ate in silence. Kelso had virtually no appetite and merely picked at his New York strip. Bushnell, on the other hand, ate with gusto and consumed every bite of his twelve-ounce fillet along with all the mushrooms, bacon, and French bread. They had more drinks, wine for Bushnell and coffee for Kelso, who longed for some of the wine but doggedly reminded himself that he was, after all, on duty.

Finally Kelso said, "Sir, you do remember me, don't you?"

Bushnell glanced up in surprise. "Certainly I do. What kind of a question is that?"

"Well, when I first came in, it was almost as if you were introducing yourself to me. And you keep calling me 'Sergeant.' When Carla and I were dating and I met you, you called me George."

Bushnell nodded. "It's been ten years. George. I'd almost forgotten what you looked like. I only saw you a couple of times, remember.

And also, I thought you might want to keep this on a strictly business footing, strictly policeman and suspect, so I was asking if you were 'Sergeant Kelso' as opposed to just 'George.' If you'd prefer . . ."

"What makes you think you're a suspect, sir?"

"Well . . ." He spread his massive hands wide. "Isn't that what all this is about? All these questions? I'm no fool; I see where it's leading. You think I shot Paul Ott, although I'm at a loss to understand what you think my motive was."

"Sir, I never said I thought you did it."

"Then what's this about?"

The moment of truth. Kelso's hands were wet; he wiped them on his corduroy trousers. Tried to catch his breath. Set his jaw. And said, "Sir, I believe your daughter killed him."

TWENTY-FOUR

The happy waiter picked that moment to return. Bushnell took out his wallet. "Here you are." Handing the guy some bills. "This ought to cover it, and some for you."

"Well, thanks, Mr. Bushnell. Was everything all right? Can I get you anything else?"

"No, we're through." He glanced at Kelso. "Unless . . ."

"Nothing for me. But I can pay for mine." Kelso reached for his billfold.

"Forget it, George. This is on me. Come on, I want to show you something, and ask you a question."

Kelso followed Bushnell out to the lobby. They put on their coats and went outside. Bushnell had leather gloves and a felt hat; Kelso's hands and head were bare. Outside, it was snowing in earnest, big wet flakes descending like rain, putting down a fresh white layer on everything.

"This way," Bushnell said, walking away from the parking lot and toward the rear of the steak house.

Kelso followed. The restaurant sat off the road surrounded by woods that extended back into the countryside. They were on the very edge of town. There might have been a path, but it was only indicated by an opening between the trees. Five inches of snow on the ground, probably; Kelso's feet sank into it up to his shins, rewetting his trouser legs. The snow beat at his face and hair, wetting it, so that he blinked often. Everything was stark black and white, nothing but the black of the leafless oaks, maples, and poplars and the endless white of the snow. Here and there weeds or shrubs poked up above the surface of it. A random evergreen provided the only color, dark green and covered with snow. It was cold.

They reached a small clearing in the middle of the woods and Bushnell stopped. Part of an old stone fence could be seen, crumbling. The black trees towered around them in the curtain formed by the falling snow. Bushnell stood looking at him, his gray eyes shadowed by the brim of his hat, his gloved hands at his sides. Kelso huddled with his bare hands in the pockets of his parka, feeling snow trickle down his neck and scalp. His nose started to run and he sniffed.

"Know what this place is?" Bushnell asked.

In the soft silence of the snowy clearing his voice was loud.

"No, sir," Kelso replied, shivering.

"This was one of Carla's favorite places when she was a little girl. Sometimes we'd come here together, especially in the summer or in the fall, and have long talks together. Father-daughter talks." He smiled. "It was very nice."

"Yes, sir."

"Why do you think she killed her husband, George?"

He took out a Kleenex, blew his nose, put his hands back in his pockets. He took them out again and pulled the hood of the parka over his head. "It's just a theory," he said.

"Tell me."

"Carla didn't want to be married to Paul Ott anymore, sir. She wanted children, she was desperate for them, and he didn't want any. She'd met this guy at her office, Tony Deal, and they were seen recently looking at wedding rings. I think she wanted to marry Deal. But Deal's got a rather low-paying job in a law firm, and he wants to go out on his own. With enough money, he could do it. Carla gets a hundred thousand dollars in insurance money because of Paul's death. That's more than enough to set up Tony Deal in his own law office, provide for their children, buy them a new house. I think that's what she decided to do, sir. He may even have helped her, with her alibi. I think she left the party she attended Saturday night after arranging to meet her old boyfriend, Fredricks, there, at her house. She knew he always carried a gun with him. In fact, he had a .22 caliber pistol in his briefcase that night. I think she got him to go to the bathroom, got the .22 out of his briefcase, went down to the den, and shot her husband in the stomach with Fredricks' .22."

He paused. Snow had gotten into his eyebrows and was melting down into his eyes, making it difficult for him to see the expression on Bushnell's face. Bushnell stood there like a stone statue, snow on his felt hat and the shoulders of his overcoat, motionless. It was so quiet he fancied he could hear the soft plop of the fat wet snowflakes hitting the surface at his feet.

"Go on," Bushnell said.

"I believe she then ran back up to the bedroom, wiped the .22, and replaced it in Fredricks' briefcase. When he came out of the bathroom she ordered him to leave, and he did. We've got a lot of this from Fredricks himself."

"An entirely reliable source," Bushnell said dryly.

"I believe Carla then went back down to the den and found Paul Ott bleeding from the gunshot in his stomach. She realized he might not die, at least not right away. She'd implicated Fredricks in the shooting, but she still wanted Ott dead. So she got his .357 Magnum from the desk drawer he always kept it in, something she well knew, and shot him in the head with it. This time she wore gloves. She put the gun on the floor under his hand to make it look like suicide."

"Suicide? Why would he have killed himself?"

"Because of the stomach wound, sir."

"I see. Anything else?"

"I think that's about it, sir."

Bushnell took a step forward. "Tell me, George. What makes you think she'd have committed a murder just to gain some money and a husband? And possibly a child? I know Carla. She's my daughter. She may have wanted to divorce Paul, may have wanted a child, may even have entertained thoughts of marrying Tony Deal. But she's not a cold-blooded reptile. Something more would've been required to provide her with enough hatred to do something like that. I *know* her."

Kelso wiped at his face, trying to see through the falling snow. It was everywhere, thick and wet and filling the air. There was an impossible amount of it.

"Sir, there is something else. I didn't want to have to tell you . . ."

"Don't spare my feelings now, George. Not after you've already accused my daughter of murder."

"Well, sir . . ." Did he have the nerve? He had to have. It was required. He gritted his teeth. "Sir, Carla's husband, Paul Ott, was sleeping with your wife."

The words seemed to hang in the air, trapped in the thickness of the snow. Bushnell took another step closer.

"You have any proof of that?" His tone was hard now, and dangerous.

"Letters to him from your wife, sir. I'm sorry." He paused. "And she's admitted it."

Something moved nearby. They both looked. A small brownish rabbit had come into the clearing. Seeing them, it froze, sitting motionless, ears alert, watching. Russell Bushnell reached under one side of his coat and brought out a heavy-looking nickel-plated revolver and aimed it at the rabbit. All was quiet.

Kelso could hear his heart beating.

"I don't approve of shooting defenseless animals, sir," was all he could think of to say.

Two things then happened simultaneously. Kelso lunged forward at the rabbit, waving his arms wildly and yelling, "Run, rabbit!" And Russell Bushnell pointed the revolver out to his side, away from the animal, and fired. The shot was deafening. The creature bounded away into the snowy woods and disappeared.

Bushnell looked around at Kelso, smiling faintly. "I don't kill living things, George. I told you, I only shoot at targets. However, there's an exception to that."

"Yes, sir?"

"I'm going to tell you what happened on Saturday. If you're willing to listen with an open mind. I'm going to tell you what *really* happened."

"I'm listening," George Kelso said.

In the silent thickness of the ever-falling snow, Bushnell spoke, his voice low and intense and hard.

"When I left home that night to meet Larry Vandenberg, I decided to stop by Carla's house first and have a talk with Paul. I wanted to talk to him about Carla. I knew they were having problems, and I thought possibly I could help. I knocked, but nobody answered the door. Then I noticed it was standing ajar. I went inside, thinking that Paul was there and hadn't heard me because of the TV set or something. I went back to his den, and I'll never forget what I found in there as long as I live." He paused. He had brought up the revolver and was aiming it at Kelso.

Kelso took his hands out of his pockets. His parka was zipped up, there was no way for him to reach his revolver without unzipping it, or pulling it up over his hip. He blinked wet snow and tried to keep his eyes on Bushnell's gun.

"Paul Ott was sitting at his desk," Bushnell said. "He was holding his stomach with both hands and moaning. Carla was standing there looking down at him. She looked terrified. My only thought was that she'd shot him. I didn't stop to wonder how or why, I just thought she had. She doesn't own a gun, but anybody can get one these days.

"Paul started whining. He was in great pain and kept asking someone to put him out of his misery. I assumed Carla still had whatever she'd used to shoot him in the stomach, and I told her to finish it. Don't let him suffer, I told her. Finish it.

"But she couldn't. Or wouldn't. She just stood there, staring at him with her mouth open. I knew about Ott's gun; she'd told me about it. She pointed to the desk and I found it in a drawer. I tried to give it to her, but still she refused. Suddenly I realized that if the police came, she'd be charged with Paul's murder. I wasn't rational. All I thought was, I can't let them take my daughter. No matter what she did, I can't let her be taken by the police.

"So, George, I risked my whole career, my very life, for my daughter. I took that gun of Ott's and I shot him in the head. Naturally I was wearing gloves at the time. I put the gun on the floor under his hand and told Carla to leave, to get away from there. She did. Then I left, too. It wasn't until later that I realized that Henry Fredricks had probably shot Ott, and not Carla."

He paused again, hefting the silvery revolver in his hand, still pointing it at Kelso.

"Well," he said, "now you've got your murderers. Fredricks for the shot in Ott's stomach, and me for the actual fatal shot. You can arrest me now, George. If you care to try."

The barrel of the revolver did not waver.

"What about the gloves you wore that night?" Kelso asked.

"I burned them."

"And you did it just to save Carla?"

"If you want the whole truth, I knew he'd been having sex with my wife, and I did it partly for that. But mostly I did it for Carla. And, of course, to put the poor bastard out of his pain."

"Did you happen to notice what was on Ott's television set at the time?"

"I didn't notice."

"And," Kelso said, trembling violently, "do you now plan to kill me, too?"

"If necessary," Bushnell replied. "Subject to the following conditions. You promise to leave my daughter alone. You promise to figure a way to pin this entire thing on Henry Fredricks. You get back to the steak house and drive away from there, and forget any of this ever happened."

"And if I don't promise, Mr. Bushnell?"

"Then I drop you right here. I tell people there was a hunting accident. You and I had decided to have a few laughs and shoot a few rabbits. Unfortunately, you got in my way just as I turned suddenly to fire, and I hit you instead of the rabbit."

"Nobody's going to buy that, sir."

"Bull. Everybody's going to buy it. Don't forget, George, I'm a very important person in this city. I'm getting ready to run for the U. S. Senate. My word is gold. It'll be my word against nobody's. You're just some sergeant on the police force. A cop. They'll believe me, all right."

The snow fell steadily, heavily, blurring the image of the big man with the gun. Kelso shook, cold and angry.

"What's to stop me from promising you now," Kelso said, "and then arresting Carla as soon as I get back to town?"

"Because I've still got this gun. And if you so much as look at her, I'll find you and blow your brains out. I'll think up a cover story, depending on the circumstances. But I'll do it."

"I'm not promising a damn thing," Kelso said, and turned away. He began walking out of the clearing, into the woods, in the direction they'd come. Hopefully back toward the road; all footprints had long since been covered.

"Two more steps and you're dead, Kelso," the man shouted.

Bushnell wouldn't shoot that rabbit, Kelso thought. Surely he wasn't a killer. Surely he hadn't shot anybody and wasn't going to start now.

"Come back, Kelso!"

But he kept walking, lifting his feet clear of the several inches of snow and then plunging them down into it again, his pants soaked to the knees, hands and feet freezing, straining to see through the heavy wet flakes that batted at his face and mouth and eyes, hearing the big man's harsh voice behind him.

"You're dead, Kelso! Do you hear me? *Dead!*"

Kelso was tensed for the shot, but it never came. He kept walking. He'd known, really, that Bushnell wouldn't shoot. He'd wanted to talk to the man to confirm the stories about Carla's insurance money and her desire to marry Tony Deal. And what he had confirmed was the insurance man's assertion that Bushnell would probably die for his daughter. At least lie for her, at least confess to a murder he hadn't committed.

Eventually Kelso reached the restaurant, gained the parking lot, found his VW, knocked the thick accumulation of snow from its windows, got in and drove away, the wipers clack-clacking like the receding footsteps of a girl he'd once loved.

TWENTY-FIVE

It was difficult driving back downtown. All the streets that earlier had been plowed were now covered again by the incessant snowfall. Fortunately, the little yellow Bug negotiated the buildup better than some cars. Shortly after three, Kelso pulled into a parking garage adjacent to the Downtowner Hotel, entered the lobby, blew his nose several times, and used a pay phone.

"Hello, Smith? This is Kelso."

"Hi. I was just about to call you."

"What about the gloves?"

"Oh. Was I supposed to do something with them?"

"Look, I'm not in the mood for—"

"It was just a joke. Don't get all hostile. The right-hand glove tested positive for gunshot residue. They also found some blood on it, and they're checking that now. Did you know the insides of those things smell like perfume?"

"Chanel No. 5," Kelso said.

"You're kidding. How do you know that?"

"I'm clairvoyant."

"Bullshit you are. Another thing. The state police report came back on the fingerprints on the magazine of Fredricks' .22. They're his."

"Have we been given permission to arrest anyone yet?" Kelso asked.

"Meyer's in Lieutenant Leill's office right now, with the chief of police and some hotshot from the mayor's office. They're probably debating it. With any luck, they should decide in a few weeks. Where are you, by the way?"

"In the lobby of the Downtowner. Listen, I'm going to go up and have a talk with Fredricks."

"You'd better not arrest him yet."

"Give me a buzz if you hear anything," Kelso told him, and hung up.

Then he rode the elevator up to the seventh floor and knocked at the door of 726. Fredricks opened it.

"Can I come in for a few minutes?"

"Oh. Sergeant Kelso. Yes, come in." Fredricks stepped back. He looked pale and tired. His light brown hair was mussed, as if he'd been lying down, and there were dark circles under his amber eyes. He sat down on the end of the bed, which was unmade, and touched a finger to his mustache. His dress slacks were wrinkled, so was his white shirt. Cigarette butts were piled high in the ashtray on the bedside stand and smoke hung in the room in a palpable cloud. Kelso went over and sat down in one of the armchairs, then stood again, unzipped his parka and removed it, and put it in the chair.

"What was it you wanted to see me about?" Fredricks asked.

Next to the ashtray on the stand was the framed photograph of Carla, with the handwritten inscription across the lower portion: "Hank, All my love forever, Carla." Fredricks' eyes went to the picture, so did Kelso's; then they both looked away.

"I've got some information to give you," Kelso said. He sighed, and added, "About Carla."

"Yes?"

"It was hard for me to figure it out at first," Kelso said. He began to pace. "But then things started occurring to me, and I remembered some stuff. For instance, you said you started getting undressed in her bathroom that night and you heard noises. One of the noises was the sound of a car backfiring. I don't think that's what you heard."

"I don't understand."

"I think you heard a gunshot, from down in the den. Carla knew you were usually armed. You'd left your briefcase on the bed, with your .22 inside. While you were in the bathroom trying to decide what to do, whether to make love to her or not, she got the .22, went down to the den, and shot her husband in the stomach."

Fredricks sat on the end of the queen-sized bed and stared.

"Another thing that I missed the first time around," Kelso said, walking to the windows and back again, "was what she said when she called the police. She said she walked just far enough into the den to see that Paul Ott had been shot and there was blood on his head, but when she called the police she didn't report a shooting or an injury or even a suicide. She reported a murder."

"A murder," Fredricks murmured.

"Yes. It didn't hit me at the time. How'd she know it was a murder? It could've been anything. Unless she already knew it was a murder." He glanced at Fredricks. "But the worst part of it is, she tried to pin the whole thing on everybody else. Mostly on you."

"On me . . ."

"She called you from an office party that night and asked you over to her house. It was all planned. She wanted to get rid of her husband and marry Tony Deal, a local lawyer. They needed money. Ott had a large insurance policy with Carla as the beneficiary. She was setting you up for it from the start. All kinds of pieces fit into the total puzzle. I don't know if you care . . ."

"I do."

"Well, her husband was sleeping with her mother. I think that's the other reason she decided to kill him. It must've driven her crazy, wanting desperately to have a baby, having Paul refuse to cooperate, then finding out he was actually going to bed with not only another woman, but her own mother."

Fredricks shook his head and grimaced.

"There're a lot of other things. There's no need to go into each and every detail now. She even tried to blame her mother for the murder at one point. She lied about knowing you always had a gun with you, then later admitted it. She wiped her prints from your gun and used gloves to shoot Ott in the head, after you'd left the house, with his own gun. We found the gloves on a snowman in a neighbor's yard. Anyway, she kept lying, all the way. Finally she told me some godawful story about how she met you that night at her house and you tried to attack her, and implied that you went down and shot Ott while she hid in the bathroom. She made the mistake of knowing about an old movie he'd taped and was looking at that night on his VCR. All this probably sounds very confusing to you. I haven't exactly told it in a logical order."

"I get the main idea," Fredricks muttered.

Kelso stopped pacing and tried to collect his thoughts. His mind had been racing faster than his tongue. He took a deep breath and let it out. "The upshot of it all is this. While you were in the bathroom that night, she shot her husband in the stomach with your .22, then wiped it off and returned it to your briefcase. You heard the shot and thought it was a car backfiring. She stripped to her underwear and waited for you to come out, then ordered you to leave. After that, she put on gloves and went back to the den and finished him off with a shot to the head with his own gun. She left in a hurry, left the front door ajar, then returned after ten and pretended to find the body. And the rest of the time since then she's tried to set you up for the shooting. At least for the shot in Ott's stomach, maybe even the whole thing."

Fredricks sat on the end of the bed and stared at the floor, head down in a position of utter defeat.

"I'm sorry," Kelso told him softly. "As a matter of fact, she tried to use me, too." He paused. "You can go home now."

When after a long time Fredricks still had said nothing, Kelso went to the door and opened it. He glanced at the slumped figure for a moment, then shook his head and went out into the corridor. He closed the door and rode the elevator down to the lobby.

He used the pay phone again.

"Smith? Any more news?"

"Naw. Those assholes are still in Leill's office. Wait, here's something else from the lab." A rustle of paper. "The fabric pattern on Ott's .357 matches the weave of those gloves you took off the snowman. Supposedly Carla's gloves."

"They're hers," Kelso said.

"Oh, and here's one more thing. Paul Ott's blood type is AB positive."

"So?"

"So's the blood on her gloves."

"I'll see you later," Kelso said, and hung up.

He had just seen Henry Fredricks walking rapidly across the hotel lobby to the exit, not stopping at the desk, and in his left hand he was gripping the brown leather briefcase.

Kelso went after him.

The exit Fredricks used took them along a short tunnel to the enclosed parking garage. As Kelso was climbing into his VW he saw Fredricks going past him, headed out, in a blue Ford. At the exit gates Fredricks paid a man in the booth, then shot out into South Central Avenue, heading north. Kelso pulled up to the booth, showed his ID folder, shouted, "Police emergency," and accelerated. The gate was still up. He heard the man shout, "Hey!"

The blue Ford was easy to follow, mainly because it couldn't go very fast in all the snow. The streets were horrible and there were minor accidents at intersections here and there. Kelso kept back several car lengths. He didn't think Fredricks would be expecting someone to follow him, but it wouldn't hurt to be cautious.

He wasn't even certain in his own mind exactly why he was following the man; it was based more on instinct than anything else. But, after all, Fredricks had just learned that his old flame had been using him, trying to frame him for the murder of her husband, and now he was heading in the direction of her house.

It was still snowing heavily. Kelso's wipers clacked back and forth, smearing the wet snow around. It all seemed to be blowing directly toward him, making it extremely difficult to see. Sometimes there was no indication of a street at all, just a broad white expanse between rows of buildings and, always ahead, the vaguely seen blue Ford.

He thought about how ironic it was. He'd fallen in love with Carla and planned to marry her. Then she'd gotten rid of him, and Fredricks had fallen in love with her. After that, it had been Paul Ott. Now Ott was dead, and they were proceeding backward in time, Fredricks up ahead followed by Kelso, a time tunnel in the snow.

And then, for some reason, he started reliving that ten-year-old past again, moving along the white ghostly streets in the tiny car, with reality blurred outside his fogging windows, and he was back on campus in a snowstorm, walking with Carla in the woods along a small stream that had frozen over. Everything was black and white except for the few people who had ventured out. They had stopped on the banks of the stream to embrace.

The churning started again in his stomach. It had been so perfect. He couldn't understand what had happened. He felt bitter.

"Carla," he muttered.

It seemed to take years. They reached the Ott house on Lincoln Avenue. Through the falling snow Kelso could discern the blue-lit tree in the front window. A car was backing out of the driveway into the street, and he thought he caught a glimpse of auburn hair. His stomach flip-flopped. The car drove off, and the blue Ford went after it.

Kelso followed, his hands gripping the wheel.

TWENTY-SIX

So now it was the three of them, three little specks in history on a chain linking the past to the present, Carla and Kelso and Fredricks. And one of them a murderer. She led them west to the state road, then turned south. He thought he knew where she was going. It was like a dream, or a Bergman film—stark, desolate, nothing but the white of the snow on the ground, the snow falling in the air, the low clouds, and the black lines of trees, shrubs, and telephone poles. At times he lost sight completely of Carla's car, and just followed the blue Ford driven by Fredricks.

He wondered what was going through the man's mind now. He must be devastated. Did he seriously intend trying to get her back after all? Or was it something else?

It seemed to take forever. The road ran north and south and in some places had drifted to one lane. Finally he saw Carla turning right onto Nashville Road, followed by Fredricks. He made the turn in his Volkswagen and kept going, knowing now he'd been right but not certain why. They reached Bender's; he saw them turn off into its parking lot. But instead of going inside, Carla got out and immediately struck out on foot into the woods. He saw Fredricks get out and hurry after her. By the time he'd parked the Beetle and stepped out into the snow they were both out of sight.

He followed, head down, not bothering with the hood of his parka, plunging his soaked shoes into the half foot of wet snow. It was difficult to go very fast in this. A sense of urgency turned it into one of his nightmares, in which he had to run but could not.

This was the way he and Russell Bushnell had come earlier in the day. His heart was pounding with the exertion and he sweated despite the cold. Snow got into his eyes and nose and mouth, wet and feathery and frigid. He could see nothing but the terrible whiteness all around him and the black of tree trunks and twisted limbs. He had hurried across the university campus in just such a way as this, numerous times, in the dead of winter, trudging through the snow to Carla's dormitory, desperate to get there as quickly as possible and see her again after the two-week absence of a Christmas vacation or a semester break, knowing she'd be there waiting for him, smiling with those gray-green eyes, arms outstretched to hug him, lips parted for a kiss. He heard her whispered words, "I love you." Grimacing, he pushed on through the snow.

Suddenly he was in the clearing, and two things happened almost simultaneously.

The snow stopped, as though someone had pulled a switch in the heavens. The big wet flakes thinned, a few small ones spiraled downward as if lost, and it had quit, leaving the air clear and fresh and cold and sharpening the view of endless white on the ground and on the trees.

And he saw them, Carla and Fredricks, standing five feet apart, facing each other in the middle of the clearing. She wore a long quilted coat and a kind of furry hat, and there was snow in her auburn hair. Fredricks wore an overcoat.

In his right hand he held a gun. So he'd had a backup.

Their profiles were toward him, Carla's right and Fredricks' left. He was staring at her, scowling furiously, his lips pulled back tightly to show his teeth. She looked small and helpless. He wanted to go over and put his arms around her and kiss her. He wanted to hold her to him tightly and tell her he loved her. He stood there in the cold, with his hands and feet freezing and his nose running and his head starting to pound, and thought about all the things she'd said to him and all the things she'd done. He thought about the promises and the love and the plans and the Christmas tree with the blue lights. He thought how she'd stood in the rain and told him she'd never leave him, never, and how she'd stood in the lobby of her dorm with her eyes and voice as cold as ice and told him she was through with him and there was nothing he could do about it, and how afterward he'd walked all over campus in the rain carrying her birthday present, that bottle of Chanel No. 5. He thought about Louie the taxi dispatcher walking all over New York City searching for blueberries out of season for a spoiled selfish bitch who didn't deserve them and was only using him.

He looked at Fredricks holding the gun.

They were talking.

"I wasn't lying to you, Hank," she said, her voice high and brittle in the silence of the clearing. "I'm not lying to you now. I love you."

"You tried to set me up," he said. He was shouting, as if over a wind, but there was no wind. "You tried to make them think I shot Paul."

"No I didn't. Give me a chance to explain, Hank."

Kelso took a step toward them, and they noticed him for the first time. Already he was unzipping his parka, reaching for the .38 Detective Special at his hip, pulling it from his holster.

"George . . ." She turned her head to stare at him. "What're you . . ."

"Drop the gun, Fredricks," Kelso said. He stood with his feet apart, holding the .38 in his right hand, bracing it with his left palm under the butt. Aiming at Fredricks. "Just drop it. It's all over now, there's no need for that."

Fredricks kept his gun pointed at Carla and glanced sideways at Kelso. He sneered. "Did she love you as much as me, Kelso?"

"Don't throw your life away over her," Kelso said. "She's not worth it."

"I don't care!" Fredricks looked directly at Carla again, raising his gun slightly.

Carla's eyes were on Kelso, wide and frightened. "I told you, George. I told you he's nuts. He's paranoid. First he killed my husband, and now he's trying to kill *me.*"

"You're dead, Carla."

"Shut up, Fredricks," Kelso snapped. He was beyond patience. It had gone too far. It had to end. "Drop that gun *now!* Carla, he already knows you did it. He already knows you used his gun to shoot Ott in the stomach, and how you went back and used Ott's gun to finish him. Fredricks, drop that gun!"

"I'll drop it," Fredricks said. He lowered the weapon, another small black automatic. "Carla? I really did love you."

"That's good," Kelso told him. "Now just let it go. Drop it in the snow."

"I really did," Fredricks said. "But not anymore." He raised the gun and fired.

The shot thundered around the woods. Carla screamed and fell backward into the snow. Kelso saw bright red blood near her mouth. For an instant he did not react. Fredricks took two or three steps forward and aimed the gun down at her fallen body.

"Not anymore, you goddamned lying bitch," he said.

Just as he fired again, Kelso squeezed the trigger. The .38 jumped in his hands; the noise made his ears ring. Fredricks twitched like a puppet jerked on strings and went down in a heap. He rolled over onto his back, then lay still.

Kelso plodded through the snow and knelt down beside him. The

.38 slug had taken him in the left lower part of his chest and blood was soaking his overcoat. It looked bad. Kelso crawled over to Carla and her eyelids fluttered. She gazed up at him and spoke in a high little girl's voice.

"George?"

"I'm here, Carla."

"Am I going to die?"

"I don't know." His voice came out low and gruff. He was very tired, and had started to shake uncontrollably.

"George?"

"Yes?"

"I really did love you . . ."

"Okay."

She closed her eyes and lay still.

It started to snow again. The flakes came down and landed gently on her face, touching her nose and cheeks and eyelids like frozen kisses.

TWENTY-SEVEN

Kelso used his radio and within thirty minutes the clearing was descended upon by various levels of police officialdom. Dr. Paul forced Kelso to return to the parking lot and sit in a warm car sipping hot coffee, so that he discovered many of the results after the fact.

Henry Fredricks did not die. Kelso's .38 had caught him at an angle, tearing away flesh and destroying a couple of ribs; he was listed in serious but stable condition.

Carla Ott, on the other hand, did die. Fredricks' first shot had grazed her face near her mouth, but the second one had entered her chest and severed her aorta. She had been pronounced dead on arrival at St. Augustine's Hospital.

Homicide charges were filed against Henry Fredricks.

Kelso was ordered to make a full report of the case against Carla Ott for the murder of her husband, Paul Ott; but he was informed that he would be permitted to file it the next day, essentially on the recommendation of Dr. Paul that he go home and go to bed.

Lieutenant Leill had been given permission by the mayor's office to have Carla Ott arrested approximately fifteen minutes before she was shot by Fredricks in the clearing. Leill had communicated this permission to Detective Sergeant Meyer, who had been trying to locate Kelso and was about to call him on his radio just as Kelso was calling to report the shootings.

Kelso drove his Volkswagen back through the snow to Susan Overstreet's house, telephoned the hospital to ask her to find a ride home with someone else or take the bus, made a pot of coffee, took off his wet shoes and socks, and lay down on the couch under a blanket. He thought he might get up in a few minutes, take a hot shower, eat something, and take some aspirin, but he promptly went to sleep.

He woke up again a few hours later when Susan shook his shoulder and asked repeatedly, "George? Are you awake? Are you all right? What *happened?*"

She fixed him a hot meal of vegetable stew, and he told her most of it while they ate.

"So," she said when he'd finished, "it was Carla all along."

"Yes. I've got a sneaking suspicion Tony Deal was in it with her, but I don't know if we'll ever be able to prove it. But she lured Fredricks over there, used his .22 on Ott, kicked him out, then went back to the den and used her husband's .357 to kill him."

Susan nodded. "But why'd she shoot him twice?"

"I think she was actually trying to kill him the first time, with the .22, but she blew it. And with Fredricks still up there and no way to know when he'd come out, she didn't want to take the chance on finishing it then. Maybe she didn't even realize she hadn't killed him the first time until she went back to the den and found him still alive, after Fredricks had gone."

"That's terrible."

"Yeah. Funny thing. If Ott hadn't been watching his tape of that old movie, and if Carla hadn't lied about it, and if she hadn't called the police to report a murder instead of a shooting or a suicide, and if I hadn't found her gloves on that snowman she and Anne Huff built . . ."

"You don't look well, George." Susan got up and pulled him from his chair. "I'm putting you to bed. Did you take any aspirin or anything? You don't take care of yourself. By the way, I bought you a present." She led him to the living room, where the Christmas-tree lights were on and a fire blazed on the hearth, and handed him a red package with a green bow. "I was going to wait till Friday, but you need this now."

"What is it?" he grumbled. "Medicine?"

He opened it. It was a new pair of leather gloves with soft pile lining, to replace the ones he'd lost.

"Merry Christmas, George." She kissed him.

"Thanks." He felt sheepish, and guilty. "Susan . . . would you mind leaving me alone for just a minute?"

Her brown eyes widened slightly. She frowned, but said, "No, I guess not. I'll go up and find the aspirin." With a questioning glance, she went upstairs.

Kelso sighed and got out his billfold. From under the ID card section he pulled a small folded piece of notepaper, opened it, and peered at it in the flickering light from the fireplace. It was written in the same neat blue writing he'd seen on Fredricks' photograph of Carla, and it said:

Dear George,

I'm writing this while waiting for you in the lobby of my dorm. I know I said some terrible things to you last night, and I'm sorry. I want you to put this in your wallet and promise to keep it there always, and never lose it or throw it away.

I do love you, no matter what you think, and I will always love you, forever. Anytime you doubt this or feel uncertain about it, just take out this piece of paper and read what I've written to the man I love more than life itself. When we are married we will read it together.

All my love forever, CARLA

Kelso refolded the paper and held it over the flames. It caught and burned. When he could no longer hold it, he let go, watching it curl into ashes. He had to blink several times.

He heard Susan's footsteps on the stairs and stood up straight just as she entered the room carrying a glass of water and two aspirin tablets.

"Here, George. Take these, and then you're going to bed. George?" She moved closer to him. "Are your eyes watering?"

"Smoke gets in your eyes," he told her.

"What?"

"Nothing. Susan?"

"What?"

He took a deep breath. He could never say it, but it was time now. Time . . .

"I love you."

He took the aspirin, and they went upstairs.